CHASING BULLETS

Suzanne Cass

S C

STORM CLOUD
PRESS

Chasing Bullets

Storm Cloud Press, Perth Australia

Copyright © 2017 by Suzanne Cass

All rights reserved.

To my two sons, who light up my life.

CHAPTER ONE

Would you lay down your life for someone you love?

Tara Hunter closed her eyes. The answer should be a resounding yes. Shouldn't it?

But it wasn't that easy. Life was never that easy.

Tara opened her eyes and picked up her towel, then turned to stare back out into the ocean. The number of surfers heading out towards The Pass were growing and she was glad she'd got onto the water early this morning, just as the hint of sunrise was turning the edges of the horizon a paler shade of indigo.

Now the sun was rising properly and clouds the colour of rose petals decorated the sky. The pink and grey hues reflected in the wet sand at the edge of the beach and the silhouettes of the rocky headlands stood out like sentinels of the sea. It was beautiful, and Tara's heart swelled at the sight.

It was ironic, really. The tiny flat she'd rented when she lived in LA had been right on the beach. And her daily run always incorporated the boardwalk next to the long stretch of Manhattan Beach. But she'd never stopped to appreciate the seascape, not like she did here in Byron Bay. She'd been much too involved in pounding the pavement, keeping her body fit enough to get her through the daily rigours of being an LA cop. Back then she'd been so young and ambitious, only looking for the next way to improve her marksmanship score in the shooting range, or refining her hand-to-hand combat skills. All so she could advance her standing in the police force. That was more than five years ago. God, it felt like a lifetime. Sometimes she wondered why she hadn't just hopped on the first plane to LA after the trouble in Sydney. But something made her stay in Australia. She'd never been able to pinpoint exactly what.

Perhaps she should think about heading home to LA. Before this little part of Australia became so wedged in her heart she started calling it home instead. There was nothing really keeping her here. Except …

An image of David Cooper drifted across her mind.

Why had he done it? Why had he gone and ruined everything? She loved working with Coop, they made an excellent team.

Not wanting to dwell on the issues of why she'd left Sydney, Tara returned her thoughts back to the beach. Soaking in the visage for a few more precious minutes, she finally turned to gather up her belongings and head towards the carpark. If she didn't get her butt moving she'd be late for work. Settling the surfboard in the back of her beat-up old convertible Jeep, she flung the rest of her stuff in the front seat next to her. Pumping the accelerator a few times, Tara was surprised when the car roared into life at the first turn of the key. It rarely started first go, and she took it as a good omen for the rest of her day.

The drive to her house on the outskirts of town took exactly seven minutes, enough time to get her head back into the day as she planned what equipment she'd need to take with her, and the best route to their destination. Her group today wanted to go rock climbing. They were all very experienced, so she'd decided to take them to Mt Doughboy. She needed to remember to phone the landowner to let him know they'd be there, as the crag was located on private property. All the ropes, carabiners, safety helmets, harnesses and everything else they'd need were already sorted into two large backpacks at work. She'd just have to dump them into the van when she got there. Vlad would be her partner in crime today, but she wondered if he'd even remember to turn up to work. His new girlfriend was taking up all his energy, changing his normally steady personality into someone who was now overly sentimental and impulsive. Tara gave a cynical laugh. It was interesting to watch how love changed people, turned them inside-out and upside-down.

Slowing down, she turned into the rough dirt driveway to her cottage. Long, leafy fronds brushed past the car on either side as she drove up the slight incline. It was past time her garden had a good trim, she just couldn't seem to find the half-day or so it'd take to do it. And she did have to admit, she kind of liked the way her garden looked like an overgrown jungle at the moment. It made her secluded cottage seem even more peaceful, hidden away from the world behind the large cabbage palms and tree ferns. She'd been very lucky to get this little two-bedroom cottage and she was paying an absolute premium in rent. But she'd fallen in love with the timber cottage as soon as she set eyes on it, with its wide, airy veranda and polished timber floorboards. This house was the balm her soul needed after ... She stopped her train of thought. No point in harping on about the past.

Leaning the surfboard under the cover of the large eves out the back, she pulled the wetsuit the rest of the way off, stepped into the outdoor shower and let the warm water wash the salt from her skin. Hidden from the neighbour's view by strategically placed clumps of bamboo, Tara loved to strip naked in the shower and stand and listen to the sounds of nature around her. The cicadas were already starting to sing; it was going to be hot today. A rustle in the underbrush told her there was a bush turkey scratching around in the leaves nearby, looking for breakfast.

The loud cry of a catbird directly overhead startled her and in that split instant she found herself reaching for her non-existent gun. Turning the taps off with more force than was necessary, Tara wrapped the towel around her body and headed for the bedroom. After two years, the instinct was still there. She'd never really managed to bury it. It made her mad. Mad at herself and mad at the world. But mostly mad at David Cooper.

* * *

'Wow, what a stinker of a day.' Vlad stopped winding the bundle of rope to wipe droplets of sweat from his brow. 'Why do tourists all think it's such a good idea to go rock climbing in the middle of bloody summer?'

'Yeah,' Tara replied. 'But even you have to admit it was a beautiful view from up there. Worth the climb, I'd say.' She kept the rhythm of winding the metres of rope, eager to get finished and grab a cold drink from the fridge. It was early evening, the orange rays of the dying sun poking fingers of light into the warehouse, taking the fiery heat with it, but leaving a cloying humidity that always left her with a fine sheen of perspiration all over her body. She and Vlad were unpacking after their day-tour with eight Dutch tourists, tidying up so they could lock up for the weekend.

'At least the two youngest guys had a blast on that last overhang. But I thought I might have to drag that old woman up by her helmet. What the hell did she think she was doing, attempting something like that climb?'

'Oh, give her a break, Vlad. She was a good climber, just slow and methodical. Both things you're definitely not.' She gave her partner a gentle kick in the backside and he smiled. Vlad was tall, slim and very athletic. All great attributes, which helped to make him a natural climber. Not bad looking either, if she happened to go for the dark-haired, square-cheekbone type; a characteristic of his Slavic bloodline. She and Vlad had been climbing together for nearly two years, working for the extreme tourism company, Alive and Kicking. They got on well, and they often hung out together on the weekends, meeting down at the beach to go surfing, or do a workout at the local gym.

Vlad hunkered down on the concrete floor and she thought about how well he was doing with his new girlfriend, Laura. She was petite and blonde, the exact opposite to Tara. Laura was also a calming presence. She was into Yoga and meditation and was a practicing Buddhist. On the surface Vlad and Laura didn't appear to be a good match. But Laura was able to lay the balm of her calming influence over his hyper-activity and for some reason they just fit together, like a hand in a glove.

'Come for a beer at the pub tonight?'

'Where are you going?'

'The Rails. Laura's going to meet me there later on. She's having dinner with a girlfriend first.'

Tara only hesitated for a second before she said, 'Sure, why not.' It would've been nice to go home and shower off all the sweat and grime, but there'd be no one special at The Rails to even care what she looked like. It wouldn't hurt to go for a few ice-cold beers to wash the dust out of her throat. 'I think I can hear one of those Railway Pub special burgers calling my name, right now,' she said.

Vlad glanced up and gave her one of his toothy smiles. 'You read my mind. Come on, let's finish packing this away so we can lock up.' She picked up two of the heavy ropes, all wound and knotted together neatly, ready for their next use, and took four long-legged strides over to the rope chest to dump them inside. Now she'd started thinking about food, her stomach was making some very un-lady like rumbling noises. A day climbing out in the hot sun certainly kept her fit and trim and allowed her to eat just about whatever she wanted.

It only took them ten more minutes to pack away the rest of the climbing gear and another ten minutes to drive down through the hinterland and into the township of Byron Bay.

The Rails was heaving with bodies when they walked in through the open glass-fronted doors. Mostly locals, but the odd tourist stood out amongst the crowd in their conservative shirts and pale beige shorts. Byron was renowned for its alternative lifestyle. It attracted all numbers of hippies and surfers, as well as lots of back-packers. Local standard dress generally consisted of the brightest hues possible, all in natural fibres and long flowing swathes. There were also plenty of dreadlocks, tattoos and body piercings. Tara had found it all rather fascinating when she'd first arrived, but now she never lifted an eyebrow at the riotous inhabitants.

She and Vlad both squeezed their way to the bar to order drinks and a meal and as luck would have it, turned around just in time to pounce on a table being vacated by a group of young, giggling girls.

'Bloody backpackers are taking over the place,' grumbled Vlad.

'Yep,' she agreed. 'They're supposed to be good for tourism, but I couldn't tell you the last time we had a backpacker come through the doors at Alive and Kicking.'

'Hmm.' Vlad couldn't speak. He was already downing half a pint in one gulp. 'Ahh, now that's liquid gold.' Using the back of his hand to wipe away the froth from his upper lip, Vlad sat back in the chair to survey the room. 'Quite a crowd in here tonight, hey?'

Tara didn't raise her gaze, she was still enjoying the cold beer as it slid down her throat. It was funny, she'd never been a beer drinker until she'd moved to Australia. Now she could see why people living in such a hot, humid climate loved the beverage so much.

'Even a couple of new faces.' At last she raised her eyes to meet his. Why was Vlad going on about the crowd in the pub tonight? 'See anyone that takes your fancy, Tara?'

'What?'

'Well, you know, I was just thinking, it's about time you hooked up with someone. Even if it were only for one night. It's not good for you. To be on your own all the time.'

What the hell had gotten into Vlad? He normally wouldn't care a fig whether she was seeing someone or not. Then it twigged. Laura had been talking to him. Whether she was seriously concerned for Tara's welfare, or whether it was out of a more selfish need to get Tara off the market so Vlad wasn't tempted, she didn't know.

'I'm quite happy the way I am, thanks, Vlad. And anyway, how do you know I'm not seeing someone and just haven't told you?'

His eyes widened with surprise for a split second before a smug look settled on his brow.

'Don't be stupid, Tara. You know you wouldn't get away with that, not in this town. Everyone knows everybody else's business here.'

Opening her mouth to spit a retort back at him, she was interrupted by a large plate landing on the table in front of her. Their food had arrived. Dropping the subject in favour of tucking into the overflowing plate, laden with a burger as tall as her pint glass, she manoeuvred her food around, looking for the best way to fit the huge thing into her mouth. Sauce dribbled down her chin as she took the first, delicious bite.

'You always did eat like a horse. Though, God knows where you put it all.' The voice came from behind her. She froze, mid-chew. Her stomach cramped painfully. That voice was familiar. She'd know it anywhere. That deep, rich timbre, with the light-teasing note.

An image of tousled blonde hair and eyes the colour of crushed blue flowers flashed across her mind. And if she could ever find the courage to turn around and look at him, she knew he'd have that wide, cheeky grin on his face, daring her. Mocking her.

David Cooper.

* * *

He shouldn't have come to Byron Bay. Coop's hands tightened around the beer glass, his knuckles going white with tension. Why the hell had he agreed to come on this mission? He'd heard the rumours; knew there was a possibility Tara might be in Byron. Why was he doing this to himself? He should've let bygones be bygones.

There she was, sitting directly beneath him. Should he take it as a bad sign she was refusing to turn around and meet his gaze? This was so much harder than he'd imagined. And he *had* imagined meeting Tara Hunter many, many times over the past few years. Confronting her. Demanding an answer. Why had she run away from Sydney? He'd still been in hospital, goddamnit. Recovering from a bullet wound he'd received protecting *her*. It'd been instinctive, throwing himself on top of her. He'd not stopped to think about it for even an instant. Because that's what you did when you loved someone, wasn't it? Protect them with everything you had?

For months that question had been all he could think about. After she left.

Tara had left him a note. A very short, very unsatisfactory note. It said, *Please forgive me, Coop. I cant' do this. I'm not brave like you. I can't live with the guilt of knowing you might have died because of me. We were a great team. I'll miss you.*

His gut clenched tight at the recollection of her words. The emotional wounds Tara inflicted had more than matched the physical ones of the bullet when it entered his side. They left him shattered, and it'd taken him a long time to become well enough to finally leave hospital.

Now here she was in the flesh, right in front of him.

He'd watched her come in through the door, with the big man in tow. Shock at seeing her rooted him to the ground for endless minutes as he scrutinized them while they ordered their food and found a table. The other guys from his team hadn't noticed how quiet he'd become. They continued their noisy banter around him. Slowly, Coop slipped away from the group and circled through the boisterous pub crowd, always keeping her in sight. Was the man her boyfriend, her husband, a lover?

Well, he wasn't the type to sit back and wait for answers. But now standing above her, he was starting to regret saying the first thing that'd come to mind. Then he saw her give a rueful shake of her head and ever so slowly, turn around to face him. Putting on the most devil-may-care grin he could muster, he willed his heart to stop beating so fast.

* * *

Placing the burger back on her plate with exaggerated care, Tara wiped her mouth with a napkin and tried to hide the way her hand trembled.

'Aren't you going to introduce me to your friend?' Vlad stood up and proffered his hand, a look of hesitant surprise lighting up his face. 'Hi, I'm Vlad.'

'David,' he replied. Drawing in a deep breath, she stood up and turned. There he was, in all his six-foot-two glory, dressed in casual jeans and a white T-shirt.

'Hi, Coop.' Her voice came out high and tight. 'What're you doing in Byron?'

'Don't I even get a hug?' Before she could stop him, he pulled her in, enveloping her with his long, strong arms. He smelled as fresh as if he'd just stepped out of the shower.

While she, on the other hand, must smell like the pile of old gym clothes left in the corner of her bedroom for the past week. She tried to remain stiff and resilient, bracing her shoulders forward, keeping her arms at her side. But he just pulled her in harder and her heart-rate skyrocketed as his biceps curled around her shoulders, his solid chest locked against her breasts. Damn her traitorous body. David Cooper still had the same effect on her he'd had two years ago. It wasn't fair.

She was stronger than this. She wouldn't let Coop rattle her. Pushing against him, she freed herself and took two steps away from him.

Catching a glimpse of Vlad's entertained face as she backed away, she shot him an irritated look.

There were a few moments of awkward silence, while both men stared at her, open amusement on their faces.

She tried her question again. 'So what brings you to Byron, Coop?' At least her voice had regained some composure, pity about the rest of her body.

'Work. A couple of the other blokes are here with me.' He indicated towards the bar with a tilt of his chin, and Tara looked over to see a group of men talking quietly. Now she saw them, she noticed their familiar straight-backed stance, reminding her of loosely reigned-in power; predators ready to pounce. She didn't recognise any of them from her time in the Australian Federal Police Force.

'Oh.' She couldn't ask any more of him. If he was here for work, then anything she said might give away him away if he was working undercover. But her mind was immediately abuzz with all kinds of questions. It'd have to be something big to bring a team up here, to this small-town neck of the woods.

'You haven't changed at all.' He cast an appreciative gaze over her tall frame, letting his eyes linger at the top button of her blouse, where a hint of cleavage escaped. She fought the urge to pull her shirt together at the neck, instead leaning a hip against the table nonchalantly, hoping none of her racing thoughts were showing in her expression.

Neither have you.' And that was the truth. He was still tall, long-limbed and lithe, with that eternal three-day growth.

'Mind if I join you?' He pointed at the table and their cooling food.

'Umm ...' What could she say? Her instincts were screaming NO, she couldn't afford to have him this close to her, not even for a few minutes. Not after all the hard work she'd done ridding him from her system over the past few years.

'Sure. Here, you can have my seat. I was just going to head over and say hi to my mate anyway.' Before she could utter a word, Vlad, the traitor, grabbed his plate and gave her a knowing wink. He shook Coop's hand. 'Nice to meet you, mate. Hope to see you around.' Tara watched the back of her faithless partner disappear into the milling crowd.

'Bloody hell,' she muttered under her breath.

'What did you say?' Coop asked as he slid into Vlad's chair.

'Nothing.' Her food now didn't look at all appetising. But she wasn't going to let it show just how much Coop was affecting her, so she picked up the burger and bit into it.

'I mean it, you look great, Hunter.' He was the only one who called her that. 'Nice ear studs by the way, they suit you. Almost a little Goth.' Tara reached up to touch the three studs sitting high on the curve of her ear. She'd gotten them a few weeks after she arrived in Byron. Up here in Byron, she could be whoever, and whatever she pleased.

'And who would've thought you'd end up in Byron Bay, huh?' She squared her shoulders and looked him directly in the eye, trying to determine if he was taking a back-handed swipe at her. Specifically at the way she'd left Sydney without saying goodbye. Guilt squeezed at her stomach. But the guilt quickly turned to righteous anger. She'd done what she had to. To protect him. To protect them both. It'd been for the best. She wasn't going to let him rattle her. The silence stretched, forming an aura of tension around their little table.

Letting go of an audible sigh, he changed tack. 'Tell me what you're up to. Got a good job here?' His voice held a note of curious concern. The hint of reproach she'd heard before replaced with the good-natured Coop she remembered.

Releasing a breath she didn't know she'd been holding, she sent up a silent thank you. It seemed Coop wasn't going to confront her. Not right now anyway. It was obvious he still worked for the AFP, so he must've recovered from his wounds. She noticed when he first sat down he didn't seem to be in any kind of pain. He moved freely, and leaned nonchalantly on the back of the chair, stretching out his left hand side in a normal fashion. But that subject was taboo, it'd bring up too many other questions. Questions she didn't want to answer. Making a conscious effort to keep her gaze away from where the bullet had entered his body, she took another, slow bite of her hamburger, while he hitched an amused eyebrow at her.

'Yup. I'm working as an extreme sports guide. It's fun. And even a little challenging.'

'Still an adrenaline junkie then.' He gave a wide smile, showing a line of perfect white teeth. 'Trust you to find the most dangerous job next to being a cop.' She'd never really thought about it like that before. But now she might have to admit—grudgingly, mind you—he was correct.

Even if she couldn't ask after his well-being, she could at least ask another burning question now they were alone.

'So, are you going to tell me what you're really doing here?'

The smile slid a little from his face.

'That's not a fair question, and you know it.'

'Go on, Coop, you can tell me.' Her smile was flirtatious. 'Go on give us a hint. Just a little clue.' Was he still working for the gun-crime unit back in Sydney? They'd been partnered together to work on something called Operation Talon, which was specifically targeted at gun-trafficking, catching the big-wigs who profited the most from selling illegal guns on the black market. But she purposefully hadn't kept track of him. Had cut off all contact. She didn't recognise any of the men he was with tonight, so perhaps he'd moved to another unit. She and Coop always shared everything when they'd been partners. She'd known just how to manipulate him back then, but would it still work now? 'Pleeeease.'

'Don't think batting those baby browns at me is going to work this time, Hunter. I'm not allowed to talk about it, so drop it, will you.'

So, Coop had changed. He'd become immune to her charms.

'Sorry,' she demurred, going back to munching on her burger. Another awkward silence descended, ripe with all their unasked questions.

'Cooper, we're out of here, let's go.' A square-faced man towered over their table, his steely eyes sweeping over the two of them as they sat, not talking to each other.

'Sure thing, boss. See you outside in a sec.' Coop didn't look at the man, but nodded his head towards the door.

'Make sure it is only a sec, *Cooper*.' He accentuated the last word, making it sound like an insult. Tara watched the dark-headed man as he threaded his way through the crowd towards the door, the rest of the team following in his wake.

'Wow, he's all heart. Who's that? Is he your boss now?'

'Yep.' Coop's tone was clipped as he stood up. The mischievous grin had been replaced with a look of sombre resignation. 'Good to see you again, Tara. Might see you around?'

Before she had a chance to ask him how long he planned to stay in Byron Bay, he'd turned on his heel and strode out of the pub.

Tara dropped the remains of the burger on her plate and watched him retreat. When the door closed behind him she hid her face in her hands and drew in deep, calming breaths. Even with all the deep breathing, she couldn't stop her shoulders starting to shake or the hot prickle of unshed tears behind her eyelids.

Damn David Cooper. Damn him to hell.

Ten minutes later she slammed the front door as she walked into her house, dropped her keys onto the hallway table and turned on a light. She'd fled the pub as soon as she was sure Coop and his teammates had left, avoiding Vlad's questions as she hurried out the door. She'd have to deal with Vlad's curiosity on Monday, but by then she would've pulled herself together. The hard outer shell of the woman the rest of the world saw would be well and truly back in place.

But tonight? Tonight all her emotions were running wild.

Marching through the living room, on her way to the kitchen to grab a beer from the fridge, Tara was brought up short by the photo nestled all by itself on top of the bookshelf. She stared into the eyes of her brother, Kane, and he stared back at her. He'd just turned fourteen when the photo was taken, and he stood in the typical stance of a couldn't-care-less teenager, shoulders slouched, hands in pockets, glowering at her from beneath lowered eyebrows. She peered at the photo for countless seconds, trying to fathom what secrets those hooded eyes held. She'd only been sixteen when he died. What would he think of the woman she'd turned into? Would he think less of her? Not able to face her fears; to face Cooper.

God, she missed Kane so much.

It was the final straw that broke her resolve, and the tears started to sting the backs of her eyes for real now. Without bothering to turn on her bedroom light, Tara collapsed onto her bed, pulling the pillow over her head to try and stop the tears from coming. She didn't cry. She didn't. But they came anyway.

And with the tears, came a memory she thought she'd buried. Of the morning she'd stormed in to drag Coop out of the male locker-room, *again*, because they were late for their shift, *again*.

Coop was right there, standing next to his locker. Shock had swept through her. He was practically naked, the only thing preserving his dignity, a crumpled t-shirt hastily draped in front of his groin.

In a heartbeat her annoyance gave way to disbelief and then incredulity. She hadn't been able to drag her eyes away from him. She already knew Coop was taller than her. She was five foot eleven and it was a nice change not to have to talk down to him like she did to most men. So she should've been expecting to see those long, nicely shaped legs, but was caught completely unawares by the sheer strength evident in his powerful thighs and calves. Her gaze fluttered upwards, taking in his chiselled chest and the rippling hardened abs, followed a fine covering of blonde curls as they dipped below the t-shirt that covered his manhood. He had a remarkable body.

This was the first time she'd seen him naked—well almost naked. And the sight of all that fine physique had made her breath freeze in her throat.

Making her movements as slow as possible, so it didn't look like she was beating a hasty retreat, Tara backed out of the room. Once safely in the corridor she exhaled loudly through pursed lips, trying to calm her rapid pulse. The corridor was empty so she turned towards the wall, resting her forehead up against the welcome coolness of the whitewashed brick. What'd she been thinking? They worked together. Coop was the best partner she'd ever had. They understood each other, functioned seamlessly as a team. They had both saved each other's butt's more than once on the job. She wasn't about to put their special partnership in jeopardy.

And she wasn't about to put herself through the hell her family had to live through, either. Tara was only fifteen when her mother left. Her mother was a successful policewoman, until she'd fallen in love with her dad—another cop—and gotten pregnant. Her mother never forgave her dad for making her give up her career. He'd said it was too dangerous, she couldn't be a mother and a policewoman at the same time. Her mother's resentment swelled silently for years, tainting every interaction with her family, until it finally drove her to leave them.

No, Tara was determined not to replay that scenario in her life. She wasn't going to get involved with another cop. Period. Relationships between partners never worked out. Even if her own family wasn't a perfect example, she'd seen it happen time and time again in her years in the force. Two cops got involved and their logical ability to think straight got all shot to hell. Their focus shifted, became more for the other person in their relationship than for themselves, or their other teammates. And then mistakes were made, people were injured, or even killed. All in the name of love.

And she'd been proved right that very same day. When Cooper had dived in front of a bullet to save her and everything she thought she knew about love had been turned on its head.

CHAPTER TWO

This town sure was trippy. Cooper sat watching the people go by on the street as he sipped his coffee. He'd heard Byron was full of people looking for the alternative lifestyle, and even though he'd been prepared, it was still a bit of an eye-opener.

'The coffee actually isn't too bad here.' Coop dragged his gaze away from the street and towards Martin and the table where the five of them sat. Grunts of acknowledgement came from Tony and Bruce, but both Coop and Graeme stared at Martin as if he'd gone mad. The coffee wasn't good. It was terrible. Perhaps if they'd been allowed to go to one of the other cafes, where all the locals congregated, they may have gotten a half-decent coffee. This café was clean, modern, full of tourists, and served really bad coffee.

Martin had chosen this coffee shop because it looked the most *normal* of all the cafés in the main street. Martin cared even less for all the *hippies* than Coop did. It was all he could do to keep the snarl of disapproval off his lips whenever they passed another guy with dreadlocks and a purple shirt on the street this morning. The sooner his boss went back to Sydney the better. Being in Byron put Martin in a bad mood.

'So, what's the plan for today, boss?' said Tony, spraying bits of muffin out of his mouth as he spoke.

'Do you have to eat like a caveman all the time?' Bruce roared in disgust. He punched Tony in the shoulder and moved his chair a few inches further away. 'Use a goddamn napkin will you. Jeez.'

Tony grinned and snatched up a paper napkin to wipe the crumbs from his chin. Tony Russo and Bruce Marchesi had been partners for over ten years. They knew each other better than they knew their own wives. Cooper often teased them, saying that next, they'd be finishing each other's sentences. They even looked alike, both clean-shaven, with a mop of dark, curly hair and brown Italian eyes. They also shared a love of gold jewellery, sporting more gold rings than Coop thought reasonable for any man to wear.

Inspector Martin Greenslade was in charge of this specialist unit, and most of the time he was a stand-up guy. Even if he was a little stiff and completely compulsive about following the rules. If there was ever a need for Martin to leave his desk and get out in the field, then Graeme Norton was his one and only choice for a partner. Graeme was close to retirement. His career had stalled at Senior Constable, but he seemed extraordinarily happy with his rank, telling Coop that he'd never had any aspirations to rise higher. Senior Constable suited him just fine. Coop was glad Graeme was here. He was a good cop to have on the ground. His experience in the field was second-to-none. Behind that grizzled face lurked one of the few purely decent men in the whole of Sydney.

Cooper would never admit it, but he was jealous of these two teams. They could depend on each other explicitly. Ever since Tara left Sydney, he'd never found another partner who was right for him. The first one his boss trialled with him, a young guy, fresh and full of enthusiasm, had moved down to Melbourne after only a couple of months to join the bomb disposal squad. The second one, Dean, had been arrogant and self-centred, and Coop made sure he didn't stay more than a couple of months. There were plans for a third trial with an older man, who'd just lost his partner in a shooting. But the poor guy had pulled out, taking early retirement, unable to cope with the aftermath of losing his long-time partner and friend. After that his boss, Chief Inspector Mike Duggan had pretty much left him alone, deciding Coop worked just as well on his own.

When Coop heard that Martin Greenslade, from counter-terrorism was looking for people to join his team, he'd volunteered for a year-long secondment straightway. Coop's excuse was he needed a change of scene. Time to get away from gun-crime and try something different. It'd seemed like fate, when only four months later, Martin's team received a tip off about a terrorism cell working near Byron Bay. Coop refused to admit, even to himself, there was another reason he was interested in Byron—a tall brunette with a kickass smile reason.

And now here he was, the odd man out in the party. The only one here without a partner.

In a way, it suited him fine. No other partner had felt right since … Nope, he'd promised himself he wasn't going there. He was going to ignore the swirling emotions the unscheduled meeting with Tara last night at the pub had dredged up. Dig a big hole in his subconscious and bury all those bloody memories way down deep. He needed to shake her off, it wouldn't do to have it affecting him. Affecting this mission.

But perhaps he should've thought about that before he came to Byron, because like it or not, she kept invading his sub-conscious now.

'This is the last time we're going to meet up as a group. I don't want us becoming too obvious. And much as I hate to say it, we stand out like dog's balls in this town,' said Martin, breaking into Coop's musing. 'Graeme and I are going over to talk to the local squad here, see if they've noticed anything suspicious. They've already been informed we're here, but it's manners to go and introduce ourselves.' Coop took another sip of his terrible coffee as he listened to Martin's orders.

'Tony and Bruce, you go and check out all the local bars, cafés and restaurants. See if anyone has seen any of these guys we're looking for. But be cool about it, will you? Try not to attract too much attention.'

'Sure thing, boss,' grinned Tony. 'We can blend in when we need to.' Coop shot a look at their black designer jeans and crisp white shirts, necks hung with thick gold chains and gave a quiet snort.

'Coop, you'll be on your own, so I want you to look into transport for us. We're going to need some 4WDs to get out into that wilderness. And have a scout around, too. There must be people here who know about the places we need to get into. See if you can ferret out some info on the country surrounding Byron. You're good at that sort of thing, ferreting, aren't you, Coop?'

'Yep, will do.' It was the only reply Cooper trusted himself with. He tried so hard to get along with the man, but Martin just seemed to rub him up the wrong way at every opportunity. If only he weren't so bloody supercilious. Coop knew one thing about Martin. No one would ever accuse him of corruption, he was always completely squared away, clothes tailored and unobtrusive. The guy was straight as a die. Just hideously annoying.

'We'll meet up at the hotel again tonight. See you all then.' Martin swigged the last of his coffee and nodded for Graeme to come with him as he stood and walked out the door. Tony and Bruce began to argue about where they should start their investigations and Coop tuned out of their conversation.

His gaze drifted back towards the main street. There was a shop across the road that pronounced in proud gold letters *Psychic readings done every half an hour*. Ha! He wouldn't be found dead in one of those places. Talking to ghosts and spirits and the afterlife. What a lot of hogwash.

His phone chirped with an incoming text. Coop picked it up off the table and glanced at the name on the screen, then groaned loudly. Bloody hell. It was Jade. The second text in two days. He'd hoped his little *chat* with her the other night had put her firmly in the picture. But she obviously hadn't got the hint. Her text said she missed him and asked when was he coming back to Sydney.

Coop uttered a noncommittal noise and shoved the phone in his pocket. He wasn't sure how to answer. So he was going to ignore it for as long as possible.

* * *

The poached eggs with kale and spinach sat congealing on her plate, as Tara stared out the window.

'Are the eggs all right, miss?' Tara turned to the waitress who had a concerned frown on her face.

'Oh, yes. Yes of course they are.' She cut a hunk from the buttered toast and eggs and shoved it in her mouth, chewing with renewed enthusiasm. It wasn't the food that was bothering her—breakfasts at the Bayleaf Café were second to none—it was her meeting with Claire half an hour ago upsetting her.

Claire was a psychic. If anyone asked Tara what she thought about psychics, she would've snorted in derision and said it was all a load of *gobbledygook*. Never admit in one-hundred years she was actually seeing a psychic. But the nightmares and odd feelings—thoughts so strange and unlike her sometimes she felt she was going insane—had forced her hand.

She'd been seeing Claire every two weeks for nearly six months now. She was still terribly unsure if she wanted to believe what Claire was telling her. It was plain ridiculous. The spirit of her brother wasn't haunting her. Once people were dead, they were dead. Tara had seen death more times than she'd care to mention, and she knew it was absolute. There was nothing left afterwards but an empty shell of a body. So why was Claire trying to convince her otherwise?

Tara had first met Claire when she'd stumbled across her little shop hidden behind one of the many surf shops in town. Tara had been wandering the street one Saturday morning, severely sleep deprived after a night filled with disturbing dreams. Dreams about her dead brother. The dreams had been coming off and on since just before she'd left Sydney. Just before Coop had been shot. But now they were gaining in frequency and clarity. And last night she hadn't had a single decent hour of sleep.

Tara stopped to lean against the wall outside the shop, to rest for a second and gather her wits, when a voice came from behind her.

'You look exhausted. Can I make you a cup of tea?' The woman with the kind eyes asked her into her shop and Tara followed her inside. She sat down in the wonderful little room, full of bright, eclectic cushions, wall hangings and deep, comfortable chairs. Tara immediately felt some of the tension drain from her shoulders, and wondered how the small woman had known there was something wrong with such unerring clarity. She needed someone to listen to her, and it seemed Claire understood.

The psychic had soft brown eyes, long curling hair and a motherly smile. For some unexplained reason, Tara felt at ease in the woman's presence. It hadn't taken much coaxing for Tara to admit she wasn't sleeping well. Claire said she might be able to help her with her problem and it'd gone from there.

But, honestly, how was she supposed to believe her younger brother, Kane, was haunting her? It was ridiculous. Today, Claire tried to convince her Kane wasn't actually haunting her, but rather trying to protect her. Like some kind of guardian angel.

The muscles in Tara's throat tightened. A piercing sense of longing went through her. She missed him so much. But Kane was dead. He'd been dead for twelve years now, and nothing anyone else did or said was going to bring him back.

'Ugh!' Tara let out a loud grunt of frustration, startling the waitress clearing the next table. 'Sorry,' she apologised, and went back to eating her cold eggs.

A sound made her turn to look out the window.

David Cooper was standing on the street, tapping on the window and beaming at her with one of his best caught-you-out-again smiles.

'I thought that was you,' he said, coming in and seating himself at her table, without even asking permission.

'Jesus Christ.' The words were out of her mouth before she could stop them. This was the second time he'd caught her by surprise. Her heart couldn't handle much more. It was too much seeing Coop twice in twenty-four hours. She shot him a look that'd curdle milk.

Ignoring her stare, he said, 'I bet the coffee here is great, isn't it? He glanced at the dregs of her cold coffee with what could only be called consummate envy.

Straightening her shoulders, she tried to pull herself together. 'Yeah, it was,' she said tersely, while sending up a silent plea he'd just go away. But he kept on sitting there, larger than life, long legs sprawled out at an angle, elbows resting on her table. Staring at her with those sky-blue eyes. The black t-shirt he wore stretched neatly over his chest, highlighting the breadth of his shoulders, fitting snug around his muscled biceps.

It was as if there was no longer enough air for Tara to breath in the little café. She had to get out of here. Standing up, she pushed the chair back, making a loud scraping noise on the floor and shoved past him to pay her bill.

'Hey, you haven't finished your breakfast.'

'Yeah, well I'm not hungry anymore,' she said as she headed out the door.

He followed her. She walked faster down the street, skirting around the Saturday morning crowds. Her mind was going a million miles an hour, wondering how she might best lose him. She thought she'd dodged a bullet last night when she'd managed to get out of the pub without Coop asking all those awkward questions. But if he kept showing up all the time, he was bound to corner her sooner or later. She'd done the right thing. The only reasonable thing under the circumstances—by leaving Sydney—but she also knew she'd never be able to explain the complexities of her headlong rush to Coop. He just wouldn't understand.

'Where are you going?'

'None of your business.' She walked a little faster.

'Hunter, wait.' He grabbed her elbow and she spun around.

'What! What do you want?' They stopped, glaring at each other like two quarrelsome cats, and the crowd on the street parted to go around them. She clenched her fists, wanting to yell at him or punch him, anything to get him to leave her alone. Something of her fury—or was it fear—must've shown in her face, because he took a step backwards, raising his hands palms upwards.

'Settle down there, girl.' He took another step backwards, widening the distance between them. A little of her anger started to ebb. 'I just wanted to say hi. Catch up with an old friend. Shoot the breeze a little, you know.'

She lowered her clenched fists. A sliver of guilt sliced through her gut. Was she overreacting?

'Why are you here then, Coop?' Even as she asked the question, she knew she wasn't going to get the answer she wanted.

'I'm not here to disrupt your perfect life, if that's what you're thinking.' Those blue eyes of his became hooded, regret and something else unfathomable clouding them.

She huffed out a long, calming breath. God, he was still infuriating, but people were starting to stare at them.

'You already are,' she replied quietly. Not waiting for his reply, she pointed down the main street, towards the beach. 'I'm going this way.' They continued side by side down the street in silence for nearly a block.

'So, you want to shoot the breeze, huh?' she finally asked, keeping her eyes on the pavement ahead. 'Tell me, how's your mum going then?'

'What?' Coop's eyes widened with surprise and he slowed, dropping behind her for a pace or two. He'd wanted conversation, well he was damn well gonna get conversation.

'Your mum, is she still living in the Blue Mountains?' She kept her tone conversational, but she knew the topic of his mother would unsettle him. Good. She didn't want him to feel settled. She didn't want him to think they could just go back to their old ways, their old friendship that easily. Coop was very protective when it came to his mother. Probably with good cause. Tara was one of only a handful of people who knew Coop's true family history. Perhaps she was being a little harsh, but the way she was feeling right now, he was lucky she hadn't just knocked his arse to the ground and left him there in the middle of the street.

'Oh, yep, she's still up there. Doing great actually. I talked to her yesterday and she told me the azaleas are all in flower at the moment.' An image of Coop's mother, Maggie, stooping over her wonderful azaleas, pointing out an especially gaudy one, came into Tara's mind. Maggie's little colonial cottage on the outskirts of Katoomba was a haven of pastel painted weatherboard and white picket fences, with a garden filled to bursting with flowers of every colour. Soft green foliage brushed the sides of the house and there were acres of cool green grass and raised beds filled with many, many different kind of vegetables. Coop had taken her to visit his mum once, when they'd been partners back in Sydney. And Tara had fallen in love with both Maggie and her magic little house nestled in one of the most scenic places in the world. She'd always meant to go back for another visit. But things just hadn't worked out that way. Tara knew Coop visited Maggie regularly, as always the dutiful son. But then, Tara couldn't really blame him for wanting to make sure his mum remained happy and healthy. Not after what'd happened. After the way Coop's father, Travis, had treated her. And him. Or after the way Travis had died.

'And she said Monty is a great help around the garden, too,' continued Coop.

Tara snorted. She was damn sure *that* wasn't true. 'Your mum's looking after Monty?'

'Yeah, I didn't trust anyone else and I didn't know how long this op would take.' A small frown formed beneath his blonde curls and Coop breathed out on a sigh. Her heart squeezed ever so slightly. Coop's sigh was genuinely heartfelt. He loved that scruffy dog more than any human. Coop was probably missing Monty as much as the dog was pining for him.

'I'm sure Monty's having a ball. He's probably got your mum wrapped around his little paw, getting fat and lazy on all the titbits she's feeding him.' The comforting words were out of her mouth before she could think.

'True.' Coop's face cleared. Coop had found Monty wandering the streets when he was only a puppy and had taken him home with him, unable to hand him over to the pound. The dog was ungainly—ugly really—patchy grey in colour, with tufts of hair that stood out at all angles, and no one could pinpoint exactly what mix of breeds made up Monty's pedigree. But Coop loved him, and the dog was insanely loyal and devoted to the man in return.

Tara counted back. Monty must be nearly five years old now. It only seemed like yesterday Coop had introduced her to the straggly adolescent dog when she'd first moved to Sydney. Tara had to fight the urge to sigh as well. It was no use rehashing the past. Or letting old regrets come back to haunt her. She had to keep looking forward.

As she thought about Monty and how it seemed Coop's life hadn't really changed much since she'd left, another memory tickled her conscience.

'Are you still volunteering at the homeless shelter?' she asked suddenly.

'Yep, every Saturday, as long as I'm not on shift.' He cast her a quick sideways glance from underneath his curls.

'That's good.' She was glad. Glad to see the things close to Coop's heart remained the same. He'd once told her volunteering at that shelter had saved his life. It put everything back into perspective, allowed him to forget most of his petty peeves and problems when he saw what other people had to face on a daily basis. She knew he'd been working there for a long time, ever since he'd been a teenager. Even when he'd had to quit school after his father died to find a job to help support himself and his mother, he'd still found the time somehow.

Coop might try to hide it, but he really did have a good heart. Bugger, this was no time to get sentimental. Time to find a new subject.

Picking up her pace a little, she asked, 'Do you know how to surf?'

'No.'

'Really? You grew up on the northern beaches of Sydney, and you don't know how to surf?'

'I never got the chance,' he replied defensively. 'But I'm a fast learner.' The corner of his mouth twitched upwards, a hint of his familiar humour returning, and she was foolish enough to smile back at him.

'Come on then, I know where we can borrow a board.'

* * *

Coop shook the wet hair out of his eyes and tried to concentrate. This was way harder than he'd ever imagined. But he was doing it. He was standing up on a surfboard. And it was fantastic. He knew he was already hooked. The fresh, tangy air. The freedom of the wide blue expanses stretching out from the beach. The unbridled power of a wave surging along underneath him. The quietude of sitting in the water waiting for the next big wave. As soon as he got home, he'd go and buy a board and start surfing.

'You always did look a little like Shaggy from Scooby Doo with your hair wet,' Tara yelled as he flashed past her on his board. The comment was enough to send him tumbling into the foaming waves.

'Come on, we've been out here for hours, it's time to go in.' Tara started paddling towards the beach, using long, relaxed strokes to propel her forwards.

'Oh, come on, Hunter, just one more wave. Please.' Even to his own ears he sounded like a pleading child, and he had to laugh at himself.

'Believe it or not, Coop, I have things I need to do today,' she called back over her shoulder. She'd just reminded him he had things he should be doing too, and wasting his time out on the ocean with a woman he thought he'd once been in love with was probably not it. He grimaced, imagining the look on Martin's face if he saw Coop now. Following Tara into the shallow water, he caught up with her as she splashed up onto the wet sand.

'That was great, Hunter. Thank you.'

'No probs.' She shot him a delighted smile. 'This is the one thing Byron has taught me, and I'm very grateful. I surf nearly every day now. I couldn't imagine not doing it.'

'I can see why.' She really did look happy. He was glad for her. That's all he'd wanted, for her to be happy. Wasn't it? So why did that knife twist in his guts every time she looked at him?

She looked great. Exactly the same. He'd been casting covert glances at her while she surfed and he had to admit he was still just as attracted to her as ever. He couldn't drag his gaze away from the way the wetsuit clung to her curves, highlighted her perfect butt and showcased her flat stomach and voluptuous breasts. He'd always liked his women tall, and Tara certainly fit that bill, with legs that seemed to go on forever. Her thick auburn hair was longer than he remembered, kept tied back in a jaunty ponytail, showing off the new earrings, which sparkled at the top of her ear. They reflected the sunshine, lent her face a little something unfathomable. A softness perhaps, or maybe it was just the glittery adornment made her seem more womanly.

The one difference he noted, out here surfing, her eyes danced with a verve for life he couldn't remember her having back in Sydney.

Once upon a time he'd wanted to drown in those liquid brown eyes.

This morning he'd almost believed their easy camaraderie was back. If only it were that simple. The truth was, it was never going to happen between them. He was more than reconciled to that fact.

'So tell me, exactly what is it you do for a living?' he asked as they put their boards down on the sand.

'What, you mean my job?' She unzipped her wetsuit and stripped it down her waist and Coop pretended to watch the other surfers still out in the ocean so he didn't get caught staring at all the bare skin her tiny bikini top exposed. Creamy olive skin, with a hint of a tan from her time spent in the sun.

Tara bent down to pick up her towel and Coop caught a flash of a tattoo, nestled next to her spine on her lower back. He was shocked. Had she had it the whole time they worked together, or was it something new? Another artefact of living in Byron? A single word running parallel to her backbone. *Kane*.

Ah, now it made sense. The name of her dead brother. Definitely not a topic for today. The midday sun was hot on his head now they were out of the water, so he decided to strip his wetsuit off as well and then sat down in the soft, white sand.

'You said you were an extreme sports guide. Exactly what is it that you do?'

'Well, let's see,' she said, slowly plopping down on the warm sand next to him. 'I work for a company called Alive and Kicking. The simplest way to put it is that we organise adventures for people who want more than just a comfy hotel room and sipping wine on the beach from their holidays. We take people skydiving, jet skiing, or kite surfing.' A faraway look entered her eyes. 'You should try that sometime, it's fantastic. Almost as good as real surfing, but on steroids.'

'I bet,' he replied.

'Yesterday I took a group out rock-climbing, that's a fairly common thing to do. There are so many good places to climb around here. We can also organise people to go jet-boating or rally driving. Sometimes they just want a bit of a wilderness experience so we take them on a two or three day hike up into the Border Ranges.' She shrugged. 'That's about it really.'

Coop couldn't stop the sudden flare of significance that made him draw in a sharp breath. She'd just mentioned wilderness and hiking. Had she offered him a solution to his problems?

'Do you take all these people out in a 4WD?'

'Yes, of course. It can get a bit hairy right up in the ranges, especially after rain. The mud holes can be two or three feet deep. You definitely need a 4WD.' She gave him a curious frown. 'Why?' There was suspicion in her voice.

'Well, it just so happens we're in the market to hire a 4WD or two, as well as a guide for a little hiking trip into the mountains.' It seemed too good to be true. Tara and her crew from Alive and Kicking might be able to aid Coop and his team in finding the people they were looking for. If they knew the area as well as it sounded like they did, Tara might save them days, or even weeks of fruitless searching, not to mention having the right gear on hand for surviving days in the jungle wilderness. Not only would he be in the good books with Martin, but this might also be the break that'd give them the edge over the assholes they were hunting.

'What do you mean?' Was she just playing dumb, or not really listening to him?

He tried again. 'Can I hire you to take us where we need to go?' The smile faded from her face, replaced by a hard glint in her eye that Coop knew could only mean one thing.

'What? No!' Her voice was loud on the quiet beach. Drawing in a deep breath, she said in a quieter tone, 'I don't think that'd be a good idea.'

He wasn't sure he didn't agree with her. It probably wasn't a good idea, but it was the only one he had, and it was growing on him by the second. Why was he pushing to spend more time with Tara? He'd satisfied himself she was happy with her new life in Byron, he should just leave her alone and go back to his own life in Sydney.

Except he couldn't. She might be the key to helping them with their case. He needed her.

* * *

He was kidding, right? There was no way she was going to get any more involved with Coop than she already was. On impulse she'd offered to take him surfing, just for old times' sake. And to banish the look of hurt self-reproach she'd seen on his face. But no more. She wasn't going to give another inch to David Cooper.

'Fine, I'll just go and find Vlad then. I'm sure he'll help me.'

She stared at him with her mouth open. 'You wouldn't dare!' She couldn't believe the gall of the man.

'You know me better than that, Hunter.' The look in his eye told her he would do exactly what he said. There was no way she was going to let him anywhere near Vlad.

'Goddamn you to hell.' She stood up, grabbed her board and stormed up the beach, kicking the sand in her fury.

'Temper, temper,' she heard him call after her.

'I am NOT helping you, David Cooper, and neither is Vlad,' she yelled back over her shoulder, and was dismayed to see him follow her up the sand. Reaching her jeep, she threw her board into the back seat and then slammed the door shut. It made a very loud, very satisfying thud that echoed through the carpark. She balled her fists and felt the blood rise up her neck. She wanted to kick the tyre, slam her fist into the side of her car. Why did Coop always know how to push her buttons? He came up and stood behind her. Close behind her.

'Come on, Hunter. This is a business opportunity now. I'm asking for your help on a professional level.' He kept his voice low and calm.

Whirling around she said, 'Well Alive and Kicking don't need your business. They don't want to get mixed up with the cops.'

'Really? Are you sure about that? Perhaps I should talk to the owner to see if that's his take on the matter as well. He might be interested to hear you want to turn down what could be weeks' worth of paid work.' He was completely unruffled. And possibly right. And that just made her madder. That, and the fact he was looking at her with those electric-blue, unreadable eyes of his again. Judging her, making her feel petty and guilty and lacking.

She could see she'd have to bring out the big guns to scare him off.

'This might come as a surprise to you and your big ego, David, but I wasn't at all pleased to see you last night.' Screwing up her eyes into little slits, she planted her hands on her hips. If she had to make it personal to keep him away from her, then so be it. 'Actually, I'd be very glad if I never saw you again. There was a reason I left Sydney. And you were it!' There, she'd said it. If that didn't push him away then nothing would. She tensed, ready for his backlash. Let it come, she'd tell him the truth. Tell him to get away from her and never come back. She didn't need him in her well-ordered life. She'd been quite happy without him.

A tiny muscle in his jaw twitched and his eyes went a steely-grey colour, but that was the only clue her comment had any effect on him.

'I need your help, Tara. You know I wouldn't ask if I didn't.' His tone remained cool. Now he was just confusing her. Why wasn't he fighting back? Her comments were intended to damage, to wound, to send him running. But he was still standing there, ignoring the fact she'd just brought up the very question they'd been skirting around all morning. Ignoring it in favour of getting her onside. The Coop she remembered would've risen to the bait, given her a tongue-lashing and then stormed off. He had a temper large enough to equal her own. What could be important enough for him to keep his cool?

'Why? What the hell could you possibly be looking for in the middle of nowhere?'

'It's a matter of national security.'

National security my ass. I'm not helping you unless you at least tell me who, or what you're after.'

She could see him weighing her up, studying her, trying to come to a decision. He'd never been a big one for protocol before. Surely he knew he could trust her. What was he waiting for?

Still he hesitated. She turned on her heel and was about to jump in the car—tell him to go to hell—when he said, in a very quiet voice, 'A terrorist cell.'

'What?' Those words were the last thing she expected to hear. The anger drained from her body.

'We're looking for a group of terrorists. Hiding out somewhere up in the hinterland here.'

'Terrorists? You must be joking. Since when have you worked for counter-terrorism?'

'Since I decided I needed a change from the gun-crime unit. They asked and I accepted.' He wasn't joking either. She felt the recognisable jolt of adrenaline course through her veins at the thought of being involved with something clandestine.

'We've been monitoring this cell for the past year and a half. We know they're planning something big. Then they suddenly disappeared off our radar. Just gone. We threw everything we had at finding them again, and then we got a tip-off last week from a credible source. They told us the people we were looking for have gone bush. It seems they've taken to hiding out in the wilderness to escape detection, while they polish off the final details on whatever they're planning.'

'Wow,' Tara said, pursing her lips. This was big. This changed things. Oh hell! What was she to do? Brad, the boss of Alive and Kicking, would indeed welcome a paid job, especially one that lasted a few weeks. The idea of being involved in a police mission again, albeit as a mere civilian with no special powers, and no gun, made her pulse quicken.

She missed being part of that world. There were times she had to physically stop herself from jumping in the car and driving back to Sydney and begging for her old job back. She thought she'd finally mastered that part of her personality. She thought the adrenaline hit she got from skydiving and rock climbing was enough. Now she knew it was a complete lie. She was desperate to take part in this mission, almost jumping out of her skin at the possible danger and the immense satisfaction when they caught these guys. It made her feel alive again. But would her heart be able to stand being in such close quarters to Coop for that long?

CHAPTER THREE

'I just want to reassure you, sir, your employees will be completely safe in this venture. We're only asking them to help us locate the ... group of individuals, nothing more. We'll send your people back the second we've pinpointed the ... individuals we're after. They'll never be in any danger, sir.' Coop was impressed at how sincere Martin could sound when the need arose. And was quietly amused when Martin seemed to find it impossible to name the group they were after as terrorists in front of a civilian.

'Thanks for your guarantee, Inspector, but I've already spoken at length to my employees and they know exactly how I feel about this assignment.' Brad Monroe, the owner and manager of Alive and Kicking, locked a clear-eyed gaze onto Martin. Coop was further impressed when his boss didn't squirm beneath Brad's unswerving scrutiny. 'And they also know exactly how far I'm prepared to let them go in this *venture*.' Brad continued to stare at Martin, thin-lipped, his bulk an imposing presence as he stood in the doorway to the Alive and Kicking warehouse. Martin stared back, and Coop was reminded of two junk-yard dogs, sizing each other up.

Coop wondered just what Brad had said to Tara and Vlad in their closed-door meeting half an hour ago. He would've loved to have been a fly on the wall during that conversation.

Brad didn't seem to be a huge fan of the police, nor of this mission. Even with all the money the Federal government was about to pay him, he was making it very obvious he'd pull the plug at a moment's notice.

'They'll definitely *not* be putting themselves in any kind of danger, and I've made it totally clear they're volunteering for this task. I'm not forcing them in any way,' Brad continued. Coop liked him. He was a big man, broad, with square shoulders and a wide jaw that matched his frame. He looked to be in his mid-sixties, but was still in great condition.

'Well, thank you again for your help,' Martin replied in his deadpan voice. 'And thank you again for your continued discretion in this matter. I'm sure I don't have to reiterate how important it is no one else knows what we're doing here.' Coop cringed inside. No matter how hard Martin tried, he couldn't make that last sentence sound anything other than a thinly veiled threat.

Brad didn't take too kindly to Martin's tone. 'No, Inspector, you don't. But don't think for one second that I'm not utterly ready to protect my employees if anything … untoward happens. I have connections in high places, and I'm not afraid to use them.' It looked like Brad was equal to Martin at playing the thinly-veiled-threat game. Coop liked him even more.

'Right you are,' Martin said, busying himself with re-adjusting the small backpack over his shoulders, neatly avoiding Brad's gaze.

'Come on, let's get this show on the road,' Vlad interjected, easing some of the tension in the air with his casual smile. 'It's already past eight, we should've been on the road half an hour ago.'

It was Monday morning. Coop had spent most of Saturday afternoon cajoling Tara into letting him talk to Brad, and then trying to convince Martin this was their best option. Martin hadn't been keen on involving civilians but in the end he'd grudgingly agreed it might work.

They'd spent all of yesterday organising the gear they were going to need, buying food and other supplies and sorting through reams and reams of maps, to pinpoint exactly where they needed to go. The informant's intelligence gave them a general area to search, but as Coop was finding out, it might be like trying to find a needle in a haystack. Even though they were surrounded by cities, towns and human habitation, the mountains were still vast and difficult to traverse.

Coop also knew if Martin found out about his history with Tara he might think twice about this operation. He was relying on the hope none of the other men in the team knew anything either. Martin knew Coop had been shot in the line of duty, but that was as far as his knowledge went. And Coop was one-hundred per cent sure Tara wouldn't say anything.

'Inspector, you and your partner, Graeme, is it? You can jump in the car with me. Tara can you take David and the other two?' Vlad was all efficiency as he balanced the last of their backpacks on top of the pile of other equipment in the back of the 4WD Land Rover. Coop was glad Vlad had volunteered to come. He was friendly, easy to get on with, strong and energetic. All qualities that might come in handy in the next few weeks.

Coop swung up into the passenger seat alongside Tara, who was driving. Tony and Bruce grumbled under their breath, but both of them got into the back seat. Tara started the car. It felt good to be under way at last. He waved to Brad, who remained standing in the doorway, watching them leave. Brad didn't return the wave, kept his hands at his side, a deep frown creasing his brows as he watched them pull out of the car park.

Coop's phone vibrated in his back pocket. A text message. The phone was on silent and he decided to ignore it. It was the third time this morning his phone had pinged. Jade. Her texts were becoming more frequent. She was worried about him. A shard of guilt snaked its way through his chest. He should answer her, at least let her know he was okay. But now was not the time, or place. Later, he promised himself.

At least he'd had time to call his mum last night, to see how she was going and make sure Monty wasn't driving her crazy. She knew by now not to ask him where he was or what he was doing. It came with the territory when your son was a cop. Especially if some of that work was undercover ops. So she hadn't been surprised when he said he'd be out of touch for a few days. And of course she readily agreed to keep Monty for however long he was gone. The softer edge to her voice when she mentioned Monty had him wondering if she wasn't getting a little too attached to the scruffy dog. It started him thinking. Perhaps he should look into getting a puppy for her birthday. The company would do her the world of good.

'Where are we headed first?' Coop asked, erasing Jade and her disapproving texts as well as his mum and loveable mutt from his mind.

'To start with, we're heading inland, to a town called Kyogle,' Tara replied.

'Great name, love the place already. How long will that take us?'

'Not too long. Around an hour and a half.' She eased the car out of the car park of the Alive and Kicking warehouse and followed Vlad's car onto the main road.

'And then?'

'Then it gets a little tricky. There's a range of mountains called the Richmond Ranges. They run pretty much north to south from the Queensland border. Because you couldn't give us much more to go on than a very vague region,' she cast him a significant glance before returning her eyes to the road, 'we're going to enter the National Park at the southern end, through a place called Doubtful Creek, and work our way north.' The look she'd just speared him with told him she thought he was withholding information. He wasn't; this was really all they had to go on. But if she knew exactly how little info they had, it might scare her.

He pursed his lips into a wry smile. 'The name is kind of appropriate don't you think?'

'What, Doubtful Creek?' She laughed. 'I hadn't really thought of it like that, but yeah, I guess so.' It was good to see her smile. There were dark smudges beneath her eyes. Like she wasn't sleeping well.

Today she was wearing denim cut-off shorts and a yellow short-sleeve button up shirt. She looked almost as good as she had on Saturday in her wetsuit and bikini. The shorts showed off her taught legs and he had to curtail a sudden urge to run his fingers over the olive skin of her exposed thigh. Would it really be as silky as it looked?

He wouldn't do it. Especially with Tony and Bruce looking on from the back seat, but the mischievous little voice in his head would've loved to see her reaction. When they were partners he'd enjoyed their informal banter. He loved provoking her just enough so her cheeks turned pink with embarrassment. He even loved the way she'd flown into a rage on the odd occasion when he'd pushed her too far. She had a temper, did Tara Hunter. But God she was beautiful, even when that temper took flight.

'The roads will start to get pretty dodgy around there, too,' she continued, bringing him back from his recollections. 'They'll be rough dirt tracks, only used by other 4WD enthusiasts. They probably haven't been graded in years. Just pray it doesn't rain, or we might be stuck in these mountains for a long, long time.'

'Glad you're driving then. Takes the pressure off me.' He raised an eyebrow in her direction, but she never took her eyes off the road.

'I'd much rather her drive than you any day, Cooper,' Tony said from the back seat. 'You're a terrible driver.'

'Yeah, the last thing we need is to be stuck in these mountains with you for weeks on end,' Bruce teased loudly.

'Although I wouldn't mind being stuck for weeks out here with *her*,' replied Tony, a predatory grin on his face. 'Now that'd be fun!'

Tara didn't hesitate. 'I'd be careful what you say, Tony,' she warned, her eyes narrowing to slits. 'You might find yourself sleeping with one of the Richmond Rangers' nastier bedfellows. There are scorpions and large spiders *galore* out there and I know where to find each and every one of them.' She glared at him in the rear-view mirror and Coop saw Tony's grin fade.

That's the girl. Put them in their place early on. Tony and Bruce were about to learn Tara was no easy target. She had a rough tongue, a sharp wit, and was used to putting lascivious cops in their places. The funny thing was, the more she threw it back in their faces, the more they'd respect her in the end. Cops were a strange bunch like that.

Something about what Tara just said niggled him.

'Spiders?' he asked, trying, and failing, to keep his voice from going squeaky.

'Yep.' She gave him a huge grin. 'Big hairy ones.' Her gaze locked onto his for a second before she turned back to the road. But that twinkle in her eye told him everything. He groaned under his breath. Of course she hadn't forgotten. God, he wished he'd never told her he was scared of spiders back when they'd first partnered up. From that day on she'd made it her mission to leave plastic spiders around for him to find, in his locker, on top of his bullet proof vest, inside his shoe, even on his sandwich once. It didn't matter how many times he told her in icy tones how childish and immature it was, she still exploded in gales of laughter every time he squealed like a girl at the sight of one of those deadly little eight-legged fiends.

His skin prickled at the mere thought of coming face to face with a real spider monstrosity in the jungle, and his palms became suddenly sweaty. Gritting his teeth he steeled his features and pretended to be studying the countryside.

* * *

'So this is Doubtful Creek?' Tony asked as he stepped out of the car.

Tara got out from behind the wheel and rubbed the kinks out of her neck. 'Yep. This is the bottom end of the Richmond Ranges.' It'd been a long drive, nearly three hours from Kyogle, over dirt tracks that'd gotten progressively rougher. Tara could feel the start of a mammoth headache coming on. The pot-holed roads had required one-hundred per cent of her concentration.

'It's a lot more beautiful than the name suggests,' said Coop, unwinding his long legs and stretching his arms high above his head as he exited the other side of the car.

'There's not much here,' grumbled Bruce, eyeing the surroundings balefully.

Tara had to laugh. 'What were you expecting? This is just a daytime picnic spot.'

There was a rough-hewn wooden picnic table with two benches and a concrete fire pit nestled into the small clearing. That was as far as the amenities went. The dense jungle closed in on all sides, creating a living green wall around them. Bruce's comment worried her a little. This expedition was going to get very rough and very dirty. She hoped they were up to it.

'Make the most of it guys, this is the flattest piece of ground you're going to see for a while.'

'Good driving, Tara.' Vlad appeared from around the side of his vehicle, giving her a quick high-five on the way past. She gave him a sideways glare. He looked as fresh as a daisy. Seemed none the worse for having endured a five-hour drive, still cheerful and buoyant as always. 'Lets get these cars unpacked guys, we need to make the most of the daylight hours we have left,' he said, yanking the back of his Land Rover open and starting to fling bags to the ground.

Coop was quick to follow Vlad's lead, opening the rear door and pulling out a backpack. She stood and watched, taking small sips from her water bottle, while contemplating his jean-clad backside. Coop had always looked great in a pair of jeans. Relaxed and confident.

Coop had filled her in on as much as he knew about their mission during the drive. Or as much as he was allowed to tell her anyway. Tara was sure Coop was under instruction to only give the information that was absolutely necessary. Even so, his words had been a little daunting and Tara was still digesting the significance of who and what they were hunting.

'We think this group have ties to ISIS,' Coop had said in the car.

'Oh my God.' Her voice had been quiet. The hairs on her arms stood up at his words. Slivers of ice settled in her spine at the mere thought ISIS could be here. On Australian soil. She'd never had to deal with anything on such a global scale when she'd been in the police force. This would be a brand new experience for her.

'That's big stuff. Are you sure?' She'd cast him a worried frown.

'I've only been with this team for a few months, but Martin, Tony and Bruce have all worked in counter-terrorism for nearly ten years now.' Tara threw a quick glance at the two men in the back seat. Tony winked at her. It was hard to reconcile these two men as hardened terrorist trackers, they just seemed too self-indulgent, too soft. But her years in the force had taught her never to jump to conclusions. She'd been wrong about people's characters before. She'd reserve her judgement until she knew more about them.

'Counter-terrorism have been following this particular cell for nearly two years,' Coop continued. 'They first picked up the group through increased chatter on the internet. The original group consisted of only three men, but over the years it seems that two or perhaps three others have joined them.' Coop must've noticed her eyebrow raised in question, because he continued on in a hurry. 'It's not what you think. Counter-terrorism is nothing like gun-control or undercover work. We have to stay very low key, keep our distance, otherwise we might spook the cell. That's why we're not exactly sure how many men we're after.'

'Why, what would happen if we spooked the cell? Can't you just swoop in and arrest the ones you know about now and be done with it?' she asked.

'It's not that easy, Hunter. This cell may be connected to one, two or even more other cells. If we panic them, it could set off a chain reaction and they'd all scatter, go into hiding, never to be seen again. Then we'd never know what they were been planning. Problem is, another cell would soon take their place, and we'd be back to the drawing board. Have to start from scratch.'

Tara guessed it all made sense. It still made her uneasy, not knowing how many men they might encounter out here in the jungle. 'So what do you think this cell is planning? Why are they hiding out here? In the middle of no-where.'

Coop cast a quick glance into the back of the car and Tara saw Bruce frown at him and give a slight shake of his head.

'She deserves to know.' There was an awkward silence in the car. 'We can trust her, she's an ex-cop,' Coop added, his nostrils flaring.

Bruce shrugged and said, 'Go on, tell her then.' But she could see the warning glint in his eye as he watched the back of her head.

'We don't really know, but we think it's something big.' Coop paused to let his words sink in. 'They may be planning an attack here in Australia. In Sydney. Perhaps a bombing of a Sydney icon.' Her entire body felt like there were ants crawling beneath her skin. She thought she might be sick. Tara could hardly believe what she was hearing.

'They're very close to executing their plan. We believe they've gone dark. That means they're no longer using modern technology. As you know, Tara, it's easy to track people using their mobile phones and computers, or internet connections. Easy to gain information on who they're contacting, how often and when. Hell, we can even intercept their texts, voicemails and emails. By going dark, we no longer have access to any of that. Without concrete evidence, we're no longer sure what they're up to. Now they'll be using old-fashioned methods of communication, ones that're much harder to track. Human couriers, letter drops, that kind of thing. That's why they've gone bush. To gather the rest of their cell together, get their supplies sorted and receive their final orders.'

Tara stared at the road ahead, knuckles going white on the steering wheel, unable to speak. Unable to form a rational thought. She could feel Coop's gaze on her. Weighing her up. She had to keep it together, not let him see how rattled she was by their revelations.

'The other reason they might've gone bush is because they caught wind of the fact we're on to them. That's why we need to be extra careful,' said Tony, his tone holding a gruff warning.

Tara finally found her voice. 'Wow. That's scary stuff. Terrifying actually.' A shiver of trepidation ran through her. 'Which Sydney icons do you think they have in mind?'

'Perhaps the Sydney Opera House. Or even the Sydney Harbour Bridge,' Coop replied despondently, as if saying those words out loud pained him.

'No. Really?' she whispered. The logical part of Tara's brain knew the Sydney Harbour Bridge would be a target. But a much larger part of her wanted to shout, *how dare they!*

'We have analysts back at HQ sorting through all the different scenarios, going through any big events due to be held in Sydney over the next month or so, that kind of thing,' Bruce interjected. 'They'll let us know if they come up with anything new.'

'In the meantime, we've been tasked with finding the group. Which is where you come in.' Coop glared at Bruce and took up the conversation again. 'You and Vlad know this area like the backs of your hands. You'll give us a better-than-even chance of finding these bastards.'

'What happens when we do?' Tara asked.

'HQ will send updated orders once we find them. Most probably we'll just hunker down and watch and wait. If they do want us to move in, they'll send more reinforcements first,' Coop replied.

'But don't make a mistake, Tara, these are very dangerous people,' Tony interrupted again. 'They won't hesitate to kill any of us. Most of these jihadists are willing to sacrifice their own lives, which makes them even more unpredictable and harder to monitor.' Tony's face in her rear-view mirror was stony and unreadable. He was trying to scare her. Well, he'd soon find out she didn't scare that easily. She glared back at him.

'He's right, this is serious stuff, Hunter.' Coop's voice drew her focus back to him. 'I just want you and Vlad to be aware of it. And to know you can opt out whenever you want, no questions asked.' His blue eyes were grave and the normally jovial Coop smile was replaced by lips drawn into a severe line. She almost didn't recognise this serious version. But he should know her better than that. She didn't back down from a challenge.

'I know, Coop. Thanks for the warning, I'll keep it in mind.' She hoped her voice sounded just the right amount subdued.

'You'll let Vlad know as well?'

'Sure thing,' she said, eyes on the road, her critical mind already churning with all the different permutations, sifting through the information. That was one of the reasons she'd been such a good cop. She was good at finding a logical solution for almost every problem. Didn't let emotions rule her decisions. Until Coop took a bullet for her and turned everything on its head.

Tara's attention returned back to Doubtful Creek and this perilous operation. They'd leave the cars parked here, hidden from the road and any prying eyes. Tara stood next to Coop, at the end of a semicircle surrounding Vlad and waited for him to speak.

'Come on, what's the hold-up? We need to get going.' Martin exuded the air of a caged lion as he hefted his large backpack higher onto his shoulders. His khaki shirt was already showing damp marks under his arms. The air was thick and humid here in the jungle. Even Tara felt the prickle of perspiration starting on her brow. At least Martin was smart enough to dress in a pair of hard-wearing cargo shorts and some sturdy boots, with a black cap finishing off his sensible outfit.

Graeme had on similar practical attire, his craggy face nearly hidden by the old brown Akubra hat pulled down low over his brow. Both men looked competent and squared-away. It'd be one less thing for her and Vlad to worry about.

Tony and Bruce, however, were another matter completely. They both wore tight, white t-shirts, that seemed to have been worn more to show off their pecs than to be of any real sensible use. The material was lightweight and wouldn't protect them from the tearing branches and leaves of the underbrush once they started walking. Bruce had a pair of tiny shorts on which only touched the top of his thighs. Probably designed to display his taut quads to their best advantage. And he did have nice legs, she decided as her gaze flicked over him. He must spend a fair bit of time in the gym to get that kind of definition.

Instead of shorts, Tony wore long black dress pants, which Tara knew would become unbearably hot very soon. She hid a tight smile. He'd find out the hard way. The final straw was the heavy gold jewellery they both wore. Did they think they were going to spend their time in a nightclub?

Tara bit her tongue. She was used to dealing with tourists, who more often than not turned up in completely impractical attire. A large closet of spare clothes was kept at the Alive and Kicking warehouse, for just such occasions. But she wasn't about to tell two seasoned cops what they should wear. They'd figure it out for themselves soon enough.

Coop was wearing an old pair of faded jeans and a black t-shirt, with a baseball cap turned backwards on his head. His style hadn't changed since she'd last seen him. Still coolly casual. And also incredibly sexy. He was standing close, waiting for Vlad to speak. His arm dangled down by his side, so close she'd only have to twitch her wrist to touch him. The tiny hairs on her arm stood up at the thought. There was no doubting Coop still had the same effect on her now as he'd had two years ago. She closed her eyes for a millisecond, willing her body back under control. This was going to be a long couple of weeks if she had to fight these feelings the whole time. She needed some kind of strategy to protect herself. Steeling her features, she took a tiny step away from him.

'Well, it looks like we're all ready to go then.' Although Vlad was smiling, he paused to stare at Martin hard for a second or two before he continued. 'Just a few pointers before we head out. We should walk in single file, that way we'll be less likely to lose anyone. If you need a breather, just let me know and we'll stop.' A loud sound of derision from Martin's direction made Vlad direct another meaningful glare his way. 'I don't care if you're the toughest cop in the whole of Australia, this'll be a lot harder than you can imagine. It's hot and humid and you'll need to drink a lot, at least three or four litres of water a day to make up for all the sweat you'll lose. Most of the time we won't be following a track. To get to the positions you've identified as potential places the terrorists might be hiding, we'll need to bash directly though the bush. There are no roads, or tracks out here. There'll be no showers or toilets or beds or soft pillows or running water. You'll be experiencing the jungle wilderness at its worst.'

* * *

'What the hell was that?' Bruce turned towards the jungle and was already reaching for his gun holster. Tara's laugh broke the clammy air, lightening the sombre mood surrounding them.

'You must be joking, Bruce,' she chortled. 'You can't honestly tell me you were about to pull your gun and shoot a poor innocent paddymelon, were you?'

'No, of course not. Jeez, whad'ya take me for?' Bruce scratched his head, not completely hiding his embarrassment. 'What the hell is a paddymelon? Sounds like some kind of horrible fruit. Fruits don't make that kind of noise,' Bruce blustered.

Coop smothered a grin as he listened to Tara explain that a paddymelon was much like a wallaby, or a small kangaroo, and that they were very cute, placid creatures who didn't deserve to be terrorised by gun-toting cops.

They'd been walking for a little over three hours now, and dusk was starting to creep its soft fingers over the horizon.

'Just so you're prepared, soon there'll be fruit bats flying overhead. Don't try and shoot those either, will you, Bruce.'

'We need to find a campsite soon,' said Vlad from the front of the line, his voice low, muffled somewhat by the dense underbrush.

Coop was silently glad Vlad was calling a halt to their search. His clothes were drenched with sweat, he was covered in tiny scratches and he could feel blisters starting to rise on his feet.

Tara was just ahead of him, her yellow shirt emphasizing the colour of her olive skin. She'd changed out of those cut-off shorts, into a much hardier pair of cargo shorts, but he'd still found himself struggling not to stare at her legs the whole afternoon. They were so long and shapely. He couldn't remember a time back in the force where she'd ever worn shorts. They hugged the curve of her buttocks. Smooth, rounded buttocks, shaped and toned by all the climbing and outdoor exercise. It was an arse worth staring at. It was having an adverse effect on his concentration, and more than once he'd had to catch himself mid-stumble because he wasn't looking where he was going.

'Keep your eyes open for any flat ground,' said Vlad. 'Or any small clearing. It doesn't matter if you think it's too small, we can always make it bigger. But we need to stop soon.' Coop followed Vlad's voice, brushing aside some low-hanging vines and stepping over a large strangler fig root spread across his path.

After another ten minutes of fighting their way through the scrub, Tara suddenly stopped in front of him. 'There. Over there. I think I can see a bit of a clearing.'

Coop traced the arc of her outstretched arm, staring into the mounting gloom.

'Really?' He couldn't see what she was talking about. It all just looked like thick, unending jungle to his untrained eyes. Vlad made his way back towards them.

'Show us the way, Tara,' Vlad said with a nod of his head. She pushed her way through a large, prickly bush Coop just knew would score him with more fresh scratches. How come she didn't seem to be covered in scratches? There must be a knack to wending your way through this God-forsaken place.

Following the yellow colour of her shirt, Coop was surprised when he lurched into a small clearing. She'd been right.

'It's small, but we can clear away this bush here, and flatten some of this grass right down and we should be able to fit our tents in quite nicely.' Satisfaction washed through Vlad's voice. Coop was glad he could see the potential of the spot. It looked tiny to him.

As soon as they stopped, a swarm of midges gathered around Coop's head, buzzing softly in his ear. He battered ineffectively at the insects. 'Bloody hell,' he muttered to himself. The look on Tony and Bruce's faces mirrored his own when they stumbled in next to him. Disbelief mixed with something akin to determined resignation. This was going to be a long night.

Dusk was falling quickly now, lending soft edges to the trees and undergrowth around them.

'Come on, no time to waste. We don't want to be setting tents up in the dark,' said Tara, already throwing her pack on the ground and unclipping the small, one-man hiking tent attached to the bottom. Bruce was watching Tara unpack her tent. A sneer formed on his lips, beneath his sheen of perspiration. Coop had seen this look before. It meant Bruce was about to turn either mulish or childish, or both.

'Why bother with the tents? I might just sleep under the stars tonight. Get closer to nature, you know.' He gave Tara an expressive wink, clicking his fingers together in a dismissive gesture. What he was really saying was he couldn't be bothered setting up the little one-man tent. Coop could almost sympathise with him. All he wanted to do right now was sit down in a comfy chair and chug back a cold beer.

Tara stopped unpacking her tent, stood up to her full height and looked Bruce directly in the eye.

'You can do what you like, Bruce. But if you don't set up your tent you'll be eaten alive by the mosquitoes and possibly wake up like a drowned rat when that tropical night-time downpour comes bucketing down all over your unprotected ass.' She gave a delicate shrug and returned to kneel on the ground, pulling a lightweight sleeping bag from within the depths of her backpack.

Coop gave a cough to smother a smirk behind his hand. God he loved it when Tara took Bruce down a peg or two. She'd certainly wiped that smug, self-indulgent look off his face. Coop didn't mind Bruce most of the time but every now and then he acted like an immature prick. It was great to see him put in his place for once. He wanted to give Tara a high-five, congratulate her the way they might've done when they were partners. Instead he dropped his pack on the ground, rubbed his sore shoulders and went to help Vlad flatten out the grass.

'Come on guys, get to it,' Martin's voice rang out. He shot Tony and Bruce a punitive glance. They grumbled quietly to themselves, but started setting up their little one-man bivouacs.

'No fires tonight. We can't have any tell-tale smoke giving us away,' Vlad said way too cheerily.

'What? What the hell we gonna eat then?' Bruce said loudly.

'Keep your panties on, boys, I've got a little methylated spirits stove we can heat the ration packs up with. Don't worry, we won't let you starve,' Vlad replied.

Coop turned his back on the three of them. Taking his tent out of its small cover he walked over to where Tara already had hers almost set up.

'Can you give me a hint or two? I'm a city boy you know. Not used to this roughing it in the jungle.' He rolled his bivouac out, right next to Tara's and started fumbling with the aluminium struts.

'You don't fool me, Coop.' She stared at him with those deep, unfathomable brown eyes of hers.

'What?' He gave her one of his best little-boy grins, offering his hands palms upwards in surrender.

'I know you're just trying to set your tent up next to mine. I can read you like a book. Always could.'

Damn.

'Nothing of the sort, Hunter. I just know Tony snores like a steam train. I want to get as far away from that noise as I can. In this tiny clearing anyway.'

'Really?' She didn't sound like she believed him for even a second. But she knelt down next to him in the underbrush and showed him how to join the slender poles together, threading them through the special hidden tabs in the tent material. Her deft hands moved over the shelter and his heart gave a gentle tug in his chest. Her face, so familiar. Those beautiful high cheekbones, so soft he wanted to run the pad of his thumb down her face. Those sexy earrings sitting at the top of her earlobe, making him wonder if they would be cold against his cheek if he leant in close to whisper something in her ear. He'd missed her so much over the last two years.

He was still no closer to finding out exactly why she'd run away from him. It'd taken him a long time, but he'd built up some strong fortifications around his heart after she left. He was determined never to be hurt again like that. He was equally determined to get an answer from her before he returned to Sydney. He needed closure. To be able to move on again with his life. Something about the fact he'd been willing to take a bullet for her had spooked her, sent her running. But what? What'd she been so afraid of? Was it a fear of commitment? If it was he might understand that. But was that enough to send someone fleeing for the hills? He just didn't know.

'Are you even listening to me?' The sharp edge to her voice brought him back from his musings.

'Sure. This black pole goes through this black tab, so they match up,' he replied, voice even and measured. Showing none of the turmoil pulsating through his insides.

'Whad'ya feel like for dinner tonight?' Vlad's friendly face appeared between Coop and Tara. 'We've got all sorts of gourmet food.'

'Like what?' piped up Bruce.

'Lemme see.' Vlad rifled through a canvas bag at his feet. I've got a beef Massaman curry, a pasta bolognese, a cheese, corn and vegetable risotto. I've got instant noodles, freeze dried mashed potato, chicken and vegetable soup.'

'Wow, were you carrying all that food in your pack?' asked Coop. The food bag must've weighed four or five kilos, at least.

'Yep,' Vlad's cheeks split in a wide grin. 'Someone has to keep us fed. And we don't know how long we're going to be out here.' Coop was impressed. Vlad had been carrying all that extra food, plus the metho stove, and made it look easy. While Coop struggled with his much lighter pack.

'I'll have the chicken soup thanks,' said Tara, standing up and casting a shrewd gaze around the area. 'I'm going to head over to that gully over there.' She pointed to a spot where the terrain fell away. 'See if I can find us some water. There might be a creek running at the bottom.'

'Have you got your head torch?' Vlad asked. When she pointed to her pocket he just nodded and went back to raking through the food sack. Coop was alarmed. He stood up. Reached towards her as if to stop her. The protective instinct he always had around Tara suddenly kicked in.

'Wait, should I come with you? Should you be going off on your own like that?'

Tara made a rude sound. 'You'd be more of a hindrance than a help. Stay here, Coop. I'll be back before you know it.'

Coop looked to Vlad for support, but all he got was a cocked eyebrow. Vlad trusted Tara to do what she needed to do. Blood pounded in his ears. Tara walked off into the scrub and it was all Coop could do not to take a step after her.

'Fine,' he spluttered. But he watched her figure move though the bush, staring at the spot well after she'd disappeared from view.

'I'll keep an eye out for any of those killer spiders.' Tara's voice drifted back to him through the trees.

'Very funny,' he yelled. Then he went back to putting up his tent, nearly snapping one of aluminium poles in half when he tried to force it to bend at an unnecessary angle. 'Bloody woman,' he muttered to himself. Always had to be so bloody independent. But wasn't that one of the traits he'd been attracted to in the first place? Her sheer resourcefulness. The ferocious self-reliance she exuded. She was so perplexing, even now.

He knew first-hand how much she didn't want his protection. His mind flew back to the night of the jewellery heist. The night he'd been shot. They were both there as undercover security for the Tiffany and Co auction. Tara was wearing one of the diamond creations, showcasing it and safeguarding it at the same time.

Earlier that day, Tara had walked in on him in the locker room as he'd been getting dressed for the night and caught him naked. He'd been gratified to see the words of rebuke—telling him to hurry up—die on her lips as he hurriedly covered himself with a t-shirt. She'd backed out of there faster than a startled deer. He grinned at the memory.

Then later that night, she'd walked into the hotel ballroom of one of Sydney's flashiest hotels and taken his breath away.

'Wow, you look … amazing! That dress is … amazing.' Cooper's gaze roved over her and a prickling heat rippled beneath his skin.

'Really.' Cynicism dripped from her words. She didn't believe him.

'No really, Hunter, you do.'

She considered him warily. 'Well, thanks, I guess.'

Tucking a strand of hair behind her ear, he studied her as she looked around the crowded ballroom. Tonight her long hair had been left loose to flow like a wave of dark velvet over her shoulders. Her simple little black dress also showed off her womanly curves to their best advantage. And the dangerously high heels made her long, slim legs look irresistible. The marvellous diamond and sapphire creation nestled in the hollow at the base of her throat.

Wow.

Just wow.

Words failed him. He stared at her.

'Where've you hidden that tough, ruthless killer-cop I know and love so well?' He took a few steps towards her, his gaze never stopping its intense scrutiny. 'I don't think I've ever seen you in a *dress* before. And certainly not in anything like this dress.' It was true. Well-worn jeans and snug button up shirts were all she normally wore to work. This was a completely different woman to the one he was used to. The dress made her look imminently more beautiful … and more vulnerable, than ever before.

'Dance with me?' Before she could say no, he grabbed her left hand, placing it on his shoulder and cupped her right in his own.

'I don't think so, Coop …' He wouldn't let her break his hold. The immediate, searing friction of her palm on his was almost unbearable. He tucked her hand against his chest and all ordinary thoughts fled.

'Just one little dance, it can't hurt.'

'Everyone will be watching,' she said, her eyes darting around the room, checking where the rest of their undercover buddies were.

'So what? We're just staying in character, that's all.' His body hummed with a slow, spreading heat. Ever so gradually, he pulled her towards him, and she no longer resisted.

They danced, slow and sensuous, drifting through a set of French doors, open to the let the balmy night air in, and out onto a darkened patio. They were alone, only one other couple giggling quietly in a far corner. The music still throbbed through Coop, deliberate and luxurious. He couldn't help himself, he dipped his head and kissed the curve of her neck. She sighed and closed her eyes.

He'd ached to kiss her for so long, but never truly acknowledged how deeply he lusted after her. Until now. In one single instant, she'd brought his whole body alive. Coop's lips rasped down the edge of her jaw and his stomach clenched with wanting her.

A low groan escaped her lips. Then she tensed beneath his shoulder.

'Oh no you don't,' he said. Taking her chin in his hand he pulled her hard against his chest. 'I've been desperately trying to ignore this … this thing that's growing between us, and now finally, I seem to have run out of strength to fight it. I can't fight it anymore, Tara. I don't want to fight it anymore.'

He watched as her eyes clouded over. 'Don't, Coop. You know we can't—'

'I would do anything for you, Tara.'

'That's the problem, Coop. That's why this would never work. If we got together, if we allowed ourselves to care, then we'd become a liability. To ourselves and to the rest of the force. If I let myself fall for you, I'd never know if my decisions to take down a target were made out of logic, or fear. Fear you might get hurt because of my actions.'

Coop dropped his head. She didn't want to destroy this partnership, this friendship they'd worked so hard to perfect. But he couldn't agree with her, not when every cell in his body screamed to take her back into his arms.

'I'll do anything you want, Tara. I'll leave the force if I have to.' Even as the words left his lips, he knew them to be true.

'No.'

'Yes, whatever it takes.'

'You'd never be happy.' Her hand clenched on the lapel of his jacket. 'I'd never be happy.'

'You make me happy,' he growled. Capturing her lips, his mouth trapped hers. Then he broke the kiss and said, 'Yes. Just say yes, Tara. We can work everything out later.'

She opened her mouth to speak, but no words would come. She looked like a painted statue, paralyzed with indecision.

'I'm in love with you, Tara.'

'I—'

Suddenly, shouts sounded from inside. She and Coop broke apart and they both sprinted back into the brightly lit ballroom. Men with guns, lots of them, were herding the auction crowd like sheep. People were screaming and crying. Shots rang out. One of their operatives dropped to the floor, limp as a rag doll.

Shit. Shit. Shit. What was going on?

He pulled his gun out of the shoulder holster. And that's when he saw him. A big ugly fucker came around the huge double doors at the front of the room and took aim—straight at Tara. She was fumbling to release her own gun, hidden in a leg-holster under her dress.

He was going to shoot her. She had no time.

Coop reacted on instinct, running towards her, firing at the ugly fucker as he went. He and Tara came crashing to the floor.

He saved her life, and took a bullet for his troubles.

And then she left.

It made no sense to him. Something she'd said, about the fact partners could never be lovers, someone always got hurt, rang in his head for months afterwards. But he never truly understood.

Coop shook his head and stood up, bringing himself back to the present. His tent was set up now, and his eyes flickered back to where Tara had disappeared into the jungle. She owed him an explanation. And he was damn-well going to get one.

CHAPTER FOUR

'That's it. We're heading back tomorrow.' Martin's voice was tight with barely-reigned-in frustration. Various noises issued from the rest of the team, all clustered around Martin in a tight semi-circle. There were muttered grumbles and even one conceivable grunt of delight. Tara thought that might have come from Graeme.

She approved of Martin's choice. It'd be nice to be clean again, and her comfy, king-size bed back in her little cottage would feel glorious after four nights sleeping on the ground. Not that she wouldn't have continued trekking for uncounted days, if it'd been required. But a long, hot soak in her bubble bath would be more than pleasant to look forward to. And God only knew all these men badly needed a wash. Especially Tony and Bruce. It was all she could do not to hold her nose every time they came close.

'Don't give me any of your grief, boys.' Martin gave a pointed stare towards Bruce and Tony. 'Even if you don't believe me, it's become damned obvious we're just chasing our tails out here. We may as well go back to town and see if we can get some more up-to-date information.'

'Not arguing, boss.' Tony held Martin's glare. 'But are you absolutely sure?'

'Yes, I'm sure.' Martin's jaw whitened with tension. 'You may not have been paying attention to where we've been going, but I have.' He drew an arc with his hand in the air. 'We've just made a huge loop through this God-forsaken wilderness.' Martin glanced at Vlad and received a nod of agreement. 'It's fair to say there's nothing and no one out here. We're looking in the wrong spot.'

Martin was right. He'd spoken with both her and Vlad an hour and a half ago, when they'd stopped for water and a breather. At Martin's bidding, over the last four days, Vlad had lead them in a circuit, taking them to the two highest peaks, giving them a panoramic view. They'd come across no evidence of any human trace; no smoke streaming from a campfire, no giveaway flash of colour, no freshly trampled trails through the dense bush, no dings or bangs, or voices in the dead of night. Nothing. The only signs were of native animals and birds. The wild animals would give a hint if anybody was camped nearby. They would've been uneasy. The brightly coloured parakeets didn't like their territory invaded, and would screech loudly if humans occupied their space. Most other native animals temporarily vacated their territories, especially at night, leaving a vacuum of quietude in their wake if humans were nearby. The jungle would become too silent, too still.

'I don't want to go back empty handed any more than you do. But we all knew this might be a needle in a haystack mission,' said Martin.

'Righto then,' replied Graeme. 'How long till we get back to the cars?' Surprisingly, he directed his question to Tara.

Over the past four days, Tara had come to respect Graeme. He didn't say much, but he took everything in. And he analysed it, quietly and efficiently. Then formed his own opinion. The other three cops, Martin, Tony and Bruce made it obvious they'd listen to whatever Vlad had to say, but frequently either talked over the top of Tara, or totally disregarded what she said. She sure as hell wasn't going out of her way to prove her worth to these guys. She'd encountered their kind of prejudice many, many times while working in the force. But it'd only taken Graeme one day to go against the tide of machismo and treat her like an equal. Tara liked his unobtrusive strength, his astuteness born of wisdom and experience. He'd be a good guy to have on her side in a tight spot.

Of course, Coop treated her with the respect she deserved, too. He knew what she was capable of. He gave her a conspiratorial grin, waggling his eyebrows at her and waited for her to answer Graeme's question.

'We'll make a campsite in the next hour or so. Then, if we can get an early start, we'll be able to pick up a proper walking track and be back at the cars before sundown tomorrow,' she said.

'Lead on then.' Graeme gestured to Vlad and proceeded to place his Akubra hat with much care back on his head. Tara readjusted her backpack, took one last sip of water and slotted in at the rear of the line. It was her job to make sure everyone was accounted for and didn't wander off the barely-there trail Vlad was making through the bush.

* * *

'Wanna drink?' Coop gave her a sly smile, reminiscent of an errant schoolboy.

'What? Do you mean alcohol?' She was lounging against the trunk of a tree, watching the others clean up from their meagre dinner. It was just coming on dusk and the mosquitoes were emerging to forage for warm, human blood, the cicadas starting to wind down from their daily deafening din. This was about the time they usually settled in around their campsite, to chat, drink coffee and work out their plan of attack for the next day, before turning in for an early night. Coop's offer was breaking the routine.

'Sure do.' With a flourish, Coop withdrew a half-bottle of Bundaberg Rum from his backpack.

'Have you been carrying that around the whole time?' Bundy Rum. Apart from a cold beer, it was her favourite alcoholic beverage. It was even better mixed with cola and a few ice cubes, but she'd drink it neat if she had to.

'Yep. You never know when a medicinal quaff will be needed.' Coop tucked the bottle down the back of his pants, giving the other men a surreptitious glance. 'Come on, before anyone else sees us. I don't want to share.' He grabbed a fistful of her t-shirt and towed her behind him as he made his way out of the camp. Tara suppressed a giggle. It felt like she was fifteen again, sneaking out of a school camp to steal an illicit drink.

'Where are we going?' she asked, a little breathless.

'Not far. Don't worry.' He let go of her shirt, but grabbed her hand instead. For a second she tensed at his touch. He'd done it on pure instinct, a friend leading a friend. That was the way Coop was. He wouldn't have thought for even a second about the ramifications of them holding hands. Or about what it might do to her pulse.

Up till now she'd made a conscious effort to stay away from him. When they were having a group debrief, she'd make sure there was at least one other person between her and Coop in the huddle. Or she'd bring up the back of the line as they tramped through the jungle, keeping a suitable distance from Coop and his jean-clad backside up the front of the line. That way he couldn't accidentally brush against her while they were walking. And she kept to the opposite side of the campsite when they held their nightly discussions. But no matter how hard she tried, he'd still catch her unaware. She'd suddenly feel his breath tickling her neck while they were stooped over, studying a map. Or he'd lightly tap her arm to show her a rocky outcrop that might make a good vantage point. The tip of his finger would graze fleetingly over her palm as he handed her a plate of food. And his touch still had the same effect on her, all these years later. Like a flame had just licked over her skin.

All these thoughts made her hesitate, resist his pull. Coop felt her hesitation and turned back towards her. Their eyes met for one strained moment.

Perhaps it was time to mend some fences. Repair old wounds. This mission could end tomorrow. This might be the last time they'd have together. Wouldn't it be better for them to part with no hard feelings? She smiled and let him lead her. Wading through thigh deep grass for a few hundred feet, they wended in and out of the sparse jungle and into a small clearing where a panoramic view of the Toonumbar Ranges spread out before them.

'Wow. It's so beautiful.' Tara drew in a deep lungful of air. 'We should've set up camp here instead,' she sighed.

'Then we wouldn't be able to use it as our little escape,' he said, patting a length of fallen log.

The sun had already faded, just a trace of orange light faded to indigo around the horizon to hint at what must've been a glorious sunset. Soft, rolling hills unfolded around them, turning dark blue-grey in the waning light. Silhouettes of darkening trees nearby formed a frame around the vista in front of them. It was so peaceful.

She could still hear a low murmur of voices from their campsite, but she was able to fade them out. A dainty breeze ruffled the leaves, making the branches sigh as it passed through. Her soul lifted, the same way it did when she'd just finished a great morning surf. As if she'd been freed from a cage.

Coop tipped his head back and took a long swig from the bottle. He handed it to her without tearing his gaze from the mountains. Holding the bottle to her chest, she didn't drink. Not yet.

'This makes everything we're doing seem all so insignificant. Don't you think?'

He looked at her, surprise in his furrowed brow. 'I guess so. Never really thought about it before.' For a second she almost forgot she'd lived here for years. Learned to appreciate this place. While Coop was back in the city.

She took a swig of Bundy. The liquid burned the back of her throat, but it was nice, the way it warmed all the way down to her stomach. Wiping the top of the bottle she handed it back to Coop.

'You gotta admit, this is better than any view you get in Sydney.' There was challenge in her tone.

Coop shot her a devastating smile. 'You don't have to convince me. I can see why you love it here.'

'Yeah, I never intended to stay long …' She'd been going to say, *after I left Sydney,* but changed her mind. 'Byron really gets under your skin.' What the hell was she thinking? It was dangerous ground. She snatched the bottle from him and took a deep drink.

'This lifestyle suits you, Tara.'

'Mmm hmm.' She grunted, taking another sip of amber liquid. What was he implying? That she made a better tourist guide than she did a cop?

'You just look … I don't know … More at ease or something.'

Did she? Now she thought about it, she guessed she was less stressed. The surfing had definitely helped. Taking one more quick sip, she handed the bottle back to Coop. A lassitude invaded her veins, the heat of the alcohol smouldering deep in her gut. The back of his hand brushed against hers as she passed him the bottle.

'And the tan definitely suits you. Brings out your eyes.' Now he was throwing compliments her way. She needed to take evasive action.

'Yeah, well you still look like shit,' she retorted.

'And there it is. Some things never change huh, Hunter?' He sighed gently. 'At least that was one thing we could always do well.'

'What?'

'Talk to each other. Even if it did mean resorting to sarcasm most of the time.'

Curious, she chanced a quick glance at him, trying to gauge his mood. His features had become undefined, melting into the darkening background. In the shadows, she could see his curling, unruly hair falling down over his eyes. A gently humorous curve tugged his lips upwards. Yep, they'd been good friends. The best of friends. It was one thing she missed, his warm, reliable, rock-solid friendship. The fact she could trust him implicitly. Well, until he'd pulled that stunt at the Tiffany's auction. Two stunts actually. First, kissing her. Then nearly dying for her.

'So, do you miss being in the force?' His question brought her back to the present. Swatting thoughtfully at a mosquito, she considered his question. Of course she missed it. It'd been her dream job, something she did instinctively. But how did she answer Coop? With the truth, or a version of it at least.

'Yes. Yes, I do.' Raising her chin, she kept her face turned away from his. 'But I don't miss the city. Or that cramped little flat I lived in. Or the pollution, and the endless traffic jams.'

'So I take it that means you're not coming back?'

'No, Coop, I'm not.' Her voice was quiet. It felt odd to say those words aloud. A small part of her had known all along she'd never go back, but this was the first time she'd said the words aloud. It was if a door had clicked shut at her admission. No, she was never going back. The realisation made her feel both lighter and heavier all at the same time.

'What about going back to LA?' he asked.

'I … I don't really know.' It was another question she'd been skirting around the edges of for a while now. Because she wasn't sure what her answer would be. And she wasn't sure of the ramifications to her life if she did finally come up with an answer. Her family was in LA. But what else was there for her in LA? She was definitely planning a trip back to see her brothers and her father soon, but as for moving back there for good … Much as she hated to admit it, Byron was working its way into her bones, cementing her to the place.

The world had gone completely dark now, not even a hint of grey sky to lend any depth. Coop was a dense presence beside her. She could feel him more than see him. One by one, stars appeared onto the black fabric of the sky. Glints of light, getting brighter the darker the background became. Her mood mellowed as she watched the stars come out. They sat in silence. The alcohol working its way through her veins probably had something to do with her state of mind. The edges of reality blurred ever so slightly, as the liquor took effect. A gentle buzz started in her brain, and she liked the way it felt. She'd have to stop drinking soon. She needed her head to be clear for the day ahead.

'Want some more?' he asked, voice deep in the murky jungle. One more sip wouldn't hurt. She fumbled for the bottle in the dark, until he curled warm fingers around her hand and helped her feel her way to the bottle.

'What about you, Coop? Are you thinking about moving to the terrorism unit for good?'

'Nah, I don't think so. Not sure I could put up with Tony and Bruce long-term.' Tara chuckled along with him at the thought.

'Me neither,' she agreed.

They continued to sledge the bad habits of both Tony and Bruce for the next ten minutes, all the while passing the bottle slowly backwards and forwards between them. He asked about her family, about her brothers, Keith and Dylan, and what they were up to now. She told him Dylan was doing fine, loving his job as prosecutor in the DA's office in Los Angeles. And Keith's surf gear and clothing brand were fast becoming a must-have item in LA. Who would've thought her brother could become such a self-styled entrepreneur, Tara joked with him. Coop laughed out loud when she told him Dylan was now having to cope with two precocious little girls who were running his life. Coop knew her well enough not to ask after her mother. But he prodded her gently about how her father, Vincent, was doing. Mainly because the bourbon had mellowed her mood, she told him he was going well, only a few years off retirement from his life-time career with the LAPD.

'So, Coop, are you seeing anyone?' The words slipped out before she could censor them. Shit. Why had she said that? Because she was dying to know, that's why. And the booze had loosened her tongue.

'Not really,' he replied. Then he drew in a deep breath, and said, 'Well … maybe … kinda. You remember Jade?' His answer filled her with a swirling tornado of mixed emotions and confusion.

Of course she remembered Jade, how could she forget the bright bubbly, petite blond with doe-like eyes. 'Yes. You were going out when I first started working with you.'

And wasn't that an understatement. Coop and Jade had been serious. Living together, when she first started working with Coop. Back then they hadn't known each other well enough to confide their deepest secrets, but Tara was aware, even as early as her first week, there was trouble in paradise. Coop didn't say much, but she got the feeling he was carrying a heavy weight around on his shoulders. Carla, one of the dispatchers at their precinct had whispered to Tara that Coop wasn't happy with Jade, he was feeling suffocated and judged, and had been for a while. Then, after only two months working as Coop's partner, Tara had seen him come in one morning with dark shadows under his eyes and hair even more scruffy than normal. But there was a lightness around him, too, as if a weight had finally lifted from his shoulders. She knew he'd broken up with Jade even before he told her.

Back then she hadn't been jealous of Jade. But that was before things between her and Coop had gotten … complicated.

Was she jealous of Jade now?

'Yeah, that's right,' Coop replied.

'So you've started seeing her again?' she prompted.

'Not really.' He raised his shoulders in resignation. 'She wants to start things up again. Go back to where we left off.'

'Doesn't sound like you're sure,' she said, and was surprised at how gentle her voice sounded, not giving away any of how the green-eyed monster was afflicting her right now.

'She wants kids. Always has.'

'And you don't.' It wasn't a question. She already knew the answer to that one.

'Nah. I'd be a terrible father.' He was completely wrong, and she was just about to argue with him when he said, 'I don't have such a good track record with dads.' He'd only told her once what'd happened between himself and his father, but Tara was smart enough to put two and two together and realise his relationship with his own father had tainted all his ideas of families and happiness. It was sad, because Coop really would make a great dad. But how could she tell him that without making it sound like she cared?

She stared at him in mute silence until he finally handed her the bottle and asked, 'What about you? Are you seeing anyone?'

'Me? Nah.'

'Figures,' he replied.

'What do you mean,' she asked, wanting to put a sharp edge into her voice, but unable to get past the pleasant buzzing in her head.

'You're about as keen on commitment and marriage as I am on kids.'

'Ha.' He knew her too well. During one of their many stakeouts, where they'd sat in a car into the small hours of the night, she'd finally revealed to him she was determined that she'd never marry. Marriage ruined a good relationship.

But she wasn't going to take the bait, wasn't going to argue with him. Not tonight. She just wanted to sit here and enjoy the evening.

Tara gave the bottle a gentle swish and was surprised to find it nearly empty. They couldn't have finished it already. Could they? But as soon as the thought registered it was replaced by the distraction of a warm waft of breeze against her skin, smooth and balmy. Her mind swam upwards to the stars, cocooned in a fuzzy warmth as she stared thoughtfully into the sky.

'Isn't thss just gorgeousss,' she sighed. Had she just slurred her words? That wasn't like her. She never got drunk, or lost control. But what the hell, she didn't really care at this particular moment. Her body tingled from head to toe, and for once she felt totally uninhibited and lost in the ambiance of the tropical night. Tara slid off the log until her bottom hit the ground, her back came to rest up against the warm wood. Coop followed suite. Sleepily she lay her head back on the log and stared up at the stars.

'Are you drunk?' he asked quietly.

'No.'

'Me either,' he replied, but she could hear the thickening in his voice. 'I wish we could stay here all night,' he sighed. They sat in silence for a while, bathing in each other's uncomplicated company.

Then Coop took up her hand, threading his fingers easily through hers. His touch set off a quivering deep inside her. 'I miss you, Tara.' His voice held a quiet longing, sending a wrench of remorse through her gut.

Before she knew what she was saying, she replied, 'I miss you, too.'

Coop angled his body towards her. His legs stretched out along the length of hers. The heat of his thigh radiated through the jeans fabric where he pressed it into her own. Tiny points of light, a reflection from the stars, flickered in his eyes. She hadn't remembered him being this close before. Her alcohol-muddled brain was taking too long to work out what was happening.

He raised his other hand and cupped her chin with his palm, ran his thumb slowly over the curve of her cheekbone. Her heart stilled in her chest, and then began hammering double-time, as his thumb rasped again over her skin. The starlight was just bright enough for her to trace the outline of his face, so close to hers. To make out the tightened set of his jaw, the hunger burning in his eyes. Her gaze slid down to his lips, craving their touch, silently entreating him to draw closer. Terrified of what might happen at the same time. The urge to pull his mouth down onto hers hit her like a physical blow. Her body was reacting to his exactly the same way it had two years ago, when he'd kissed her at the jewellery auction. The tangle of emotions when she was near him still caused an ache at the centre of her chest. Nothing had changed.

His lips took hers. Nothing tentative or inquiring about his kiss this time. Heat uncurled in her gut and spread outwards. No one had ever touched her like he did. As if he could see deep down inside her, to something no one else could know. To where she sheltered the best part of herself, a wholesome, perfect Tara. Unspoilt by her fears and petty preoccupations. She tasted his lips, hot and delicious, and her breath mingled with his.

Cooper deepened the kiss, pushing her hard up against the solid wall of the tree trunk, pinning her there. His chest was a wall of sleek, unyielding muscle beneath his t-shirt, and her breasts tightened. Tara's head spun at her boldness, reacting to him the way she was. Her brain, dulled by the effect of the rum, swirled with a mix of emotions.

Memories of Coop came flooding back. Of the way he'd watched her when he thought she didn't know; with a look filled with craving. How he showed up with donuts on the morning after a long night's stake-out, or invited her to join him at the pub for a beer to take her mind off how the Sargent had reamed her out for not handing in her paperwork on time. How he made her laugh out loud at his silly jokes. How tenderly he'd looked at her the first time he opened his eyes in hospital. How much she'd hurt him when she'd betrayed his faith and fled.

It was this final thought that ultimately brought her mind crashing back to reality.

* * *

This was real. *Real.* He'd dreamt of kissing Tara many times since she'd left. But this was no dream. She was here, returning his kiss, touching his face, wrapping her arms around his neck. He could feel how much she wanted him and it filled him with a tentative hope.

Their connection was still there, as strong as it'd been the last time he'd seen her. Every part of him fed on the sensation that she was here, revelling in her lips on his mouth. Her fingers running over his skin. A flash of desire laced through him. The intensity of it threatened to steal his breath. God, let her be feeling this too! The thought caused a stab of pain so hard in his chest he almost winced.

Her fingers trailed up his spine, coming to rest at the base of his neck, pulling him in even closer. Her touch ignited a fire deep within. Craving coursed through him in waves. He wanted to crush her to his chest, devour her mouth.

He ran a hand over the curve of her hip and slowly brought it up to trace the outline of her breast beneath her shirt. Her nipples were hard behind her bra, and a throaty groan escaped her when his hand cupped her fullness. She was so beautiful. Wild and untameable. Full of fire and life. He tangled one hand in the length of her hair, the silky strands long and thick against his fingers.

He deepened their kiss further, his tongue probing the heated, wet recess of her mouth, feeling her teeth nip at his bottom lip and her tongue, inviting him even deeper. She was nothing but darkness and warmth, a shadow of a woman, but God, she ignited his desire. The ache in his groin became hot and heavy, filling him with an urgency that cried out to be satiated. He laid his weight against her, their bodies moulding together, becoming one. Nothing else existed except him and Tara. Out here under the stars.

The last thing he expected was her quick intake of breath or the stiffening of her hands on his neck. Before he could stop her, she'd broken the kiss and pushed him away from her. He tried to lean in, to close the gap that'd opened between them, but her hands braced against his biceps.

An awful truth started to penetrate his fogged senses.

'Did I do something—'

'I'm sorry, Coop.' It was hard to make out Tara's features in the starlight, but the tone of her voice told him everything he needed to know. She couldn't be doing this to him. Not again. His stomach clenched as if he were expecting a direct hit.

'I thought you … I thought we …' He didn't know how to finish his sentence and his voice rasped painfully in his throat.

'I'm sorry. So sorry.' she repeated, still holding him at arm's length.

'Will you stop saying that.' Anger replaced the wrenching despair in his gut. He rose to his feet, reaching out for the fallen log to steady himself. His fingernails dug into the rough bark until it hurt. All the moisture left his mouth. He licked his suddenly dry lips, trying to find the right words.

She got slowly got to her feet as well, and stood a few paces away, regarding him.

'I shouldn't have let this happen, Coop. Blame it on the alcohol, but I never intended to do this again with you.' Tara took another step away from him, widening the gap.

'Never intended to do what?' he growled. Her words caused a slice of hurt so deep in his belly he was afraid it would leave a scar, but he needed her to spell it out for him. Clenching his jaw tight, he waited for her answer.

'Kiss you,' she said faintly. He wasn't sure, but he thought he caught a slight tremble in her voice. 'We'll never be more than friends, Coop, and it wasn't fair of me. I'm sorry.'

'I told you, stop saying you're sorry. It's a false platitude.' The words almost stuck in his throat, making his voice sound like a threatening growl.

'Okay, I won't say it again.' She knelt down, retrieved the bottle from the ground and stood up. 'Besides, you have Jade to think about now.'

He grabbed her by the arm, his fingers digging into the muscles of her bicep. 'Oh no you don't. You don't get away that easy this time, Hunter. And this has absolutely nothing at all to do with Jade.' A barely contained rage was starting to burn in his stomach. 'I need more of an answer from you than *we were only meant to be friends*. That's bullshit and you know it. Tonight you wanted me just as much as I wanted you.' Her arm stiffened beneath his hand, tension radiating between them. He wasn't going to let her off the hook tonight. He needed an answer from her once and for all. He deserved an answer. If she truly didn't care for him then let her say it out loud. But he knew she couldn't deny the heat, the mutual hunger they'd just shared.

Tara shook her head in denial. 'I'm not going to do this with you tonight, we're both—'

He cut her off with a harsh laugh. 'Drunk? So what? It doesn't change anything. There's always going to be an excuse with you. Well, I want to know when you'll be prepared to talk about your feelings for me? When Tara?'

She stared at him, mutely, a dark shape in the jungle night. He nearly cursed out loud at the darkness. He was behaving badly by forcing the issue, but he couldn't seem to stop himself. If only he could see her face clearly, he might be able to comprehend a little better what was going on in her head. But he couldn't see her, so he'd have to rely on the power of his words alone.

Drawing in a deep breath, he squared his shoulders and made a decision. He was going to tell her how it was for him, whether she wanted to hear the words or not.

'I'll never get over you walking away the way you did, Tara.' He let go of her arm and dropped his hand down by his side. 'You'll never know how much it hurt, losing what could have been between us.' There was a sharp intake of breath at his revelation. Good. His words had hit their intended target.

He'd had years and years of practice at keeping his feelings hidden beneath layers of learned fortifications. A good cop needed to have a poker face, not let anything show that might give him away to a would-be criminal. Not feel anything too deeply in case he suddenly couldn't turn the feelings off. Maybe it was time to tell the truth for once.

'I used to think being strong meant never letting go of self-control. But look where that got me. Well, tonight I might just be drunk enough to let my feelings out.'

'Coop, don't,' she pleaded. He almost gave in to the desperation in her plea. Instead he stepped in closer to her. So close he could feel her breath coming out in ragged gasps over his neck. So close he would've been able to see the hint of gold highlights in her eyes if there'd been enough light to see by. So close he could feel the mixture of anger and desperation emanating from her.

Keeping his voice low and tight, he said, 'Our connection was more than just a sexual one, and you know it.' A silence spread between them. He could almost hear the blood pounding through her veins and her heart hammering in her chest. He waited. She needed to answer him. He shouldn't be enjoying the pain he knew he was inflicting on her, but right at this very moment he didn't care. A part of him wanted to hurt her as much as she'd hurt him.

'Partners can never be lovers, Coop. I learned that lesson the hard way.' Her voice was breathy and low, the strength of emotion so clear in her voice it was like a punch to his solar plexus. She really believed the words she'd just uttered. He scrubbed his hands over his face.

'That's fucking rhetoric, and you know it. You owe me an explanation, Tara Hunter.' The words burst out of him loud and unrestrained. He was accustomed to being able to control his temper. But tonight there was a boiling rage rising in him which threatened to obliterate all reason and composure within. Perhaps it was the alcohol loosening his reserves, combined with the weight of the question years in the waiting for an answer. Whatever it was, he wasn't leaving until he knew. 'Why did you leave me like that?'

She took a step backwards at the menace in his voice.

'I don't owe you anything, David.' Her breath came in short, sharp inhalations as she spoke, her rising anger equal to his own. 'I didn't ask you to take that damn bullet for me, and I sure as hell didn't want you to.'

'I did it to protect you,' he snorted. 'And that's not what I was talking about. I'm talking about the fact I admitted I wanted you—cared about you. And you had feelings for me, too. I know you did.'

'Well I don't need your or anyone else's protection. I'm quite capable of looking after myself.' She skirted the question and realisation slowly dawned on him. He knew what the crux of the matter was now.

'What are you scared of, Tara?'

'I'm not scared of anything, least of all you!' She was yelling at him now and he could feel the hot rush of air past his face. 'Just face it, David, you and I weren't meant to be together.' She crossed her arms in front of her chest and rocked back on her heels. He could just make out the angry creases furrowing her brow, like dark slashes against her pale skin in the starlight. 'We'll never be together.' She lowered her voice as she spoke. He could tell she was struggling to regain some composure, but there was a distinct edge of finality in her statement.

'Are you saying you don't have feelings for me? That you never had feelings for me?' All the anger drained out of him in that instant.

'That's exactly what I'm saying.' She turned away from him, but not before he caught what might've been the shimmer of unshed tears in her eyes. He let her go, watching as she walked back towards the campsite. Hands clenched at his sides, he stared out into the black space in front of him.

She'd said the words he'd dreaded. And she'd sounded sincere when she uttered them. But something inside him wouldn't bow down, wouldn't believe it. His heart hadn't shattered into a thousand pieces as he'd expected. Either he'd somehow become much stronger than he could've imagined, or his heart had heard something in her words that her mouth hadn't said.

Gritting his teeth together he turned to follow the same path back to campsite. It was going to be a long, long night.

CHAPTER FIVE

Tara's head throbbed. And she needed more water. She'd emptied the last of her bottle over an hour ago. But she could see a white glint of metal through the dwindling jungle fronds and knew her torment was almost over. They'd made it back to the cars at last.

Vlad set a blistering pace on the trek back this morning, shaking them all out of their bivouacs before the sun had even thought about tickling the sky. He was punishing her. He didn't say a word when she'd returned to camp last night, but he must've smelled the rum on her breath. And he must've heard at least some of the conversation, she'd been yelling by the end. He also knew her well enough to see how livid she was when she'd stormed back into camp. At least he'd been discreet enough not to ask what she and Coop had been fighting about. Not that she would've told him anyway.

Her one consolation on the four-hour hike back was Coop looked as if he was feeling just as bad as her. Face pale, he was sweating profusely, but none-the-less he kept his head down and didn't complain at the gruelling pace.

She'd managed to avoid talking to Coop for the whole hike back, and intended to do the same on the ride home in the car. David Cooper could go to hell. And she didn't care what the rest of his team thought about their silence. Bruce tried to make a few droll comments around camp that morning but she'd shut him down with a couple of death-stares and a promise he'd be walking home with a limp if he kept it up.

'Thank the Lord that's over,' growled Tony. 'You sure know how to walk when you want to, big guy.' His words were directed at Vlad, who was already shucking his pack onto the ground and fumbling inside it for the car keys.

'No use in dilly-dallying, when we have things to do and places to be,' Vlad replied, lips pulled together in a thin line.

Coop dropped his bag on the ground and sat down heavily next to it, emitting a small groan. 'Kill me now.'

With pleasure. Tara managed to keep the thought to herself. Just. She turned to help Vlad drag out the extra bottles of water from the back of the car and hand them around. Tony, Bruce and Graeme sat down at the little picnic table in the clearing and drank deeply from their bottles. Martin took his bottle and found a spot away from the rest of them in the shade of a large camphor laurel tree, where he started pressing buttons on his Satellite Phone.

Tara crawled into the back seat of the Land Rover to see if some of those muesli bars she'd stashed in the side pocket were still there. Martin's raised voice caught her off-guard, and she thunked her head on the car door as she backed out too quickly.

'Shut up all of you, I'm calling headquarters and I can't hear a damn thing.' Martin waved an arm at them all. He screwed his eyes shut in an effort to concentrate.

'Yeah, sorry. We've been outta range for a day or so. It's pretty wild country out here, you know. Over.' There was a long, drawn-out silence, in which Martin made a few grunts but said nothing intelligible. And then he said, 'That's great news. We'll head back to town immediately. Over.'

Tara released a silent sigh of gratitude, not wanting anyone else to guess just how badly she was looking forward to a shower and some clean clothes.

Martin rang off and walked over to the picnic table, beckoning the others to gather around.

'Headquarters has just gotten some new info,' he said without preamble. 'This is a solid lead. They've got some pretty good directions this time.'

'Great, so no more needle-in-a-haystack stuff then?' asked Tony.

'They said it's somewhere near the Edinburg Castle,' Martin continued, as if Tony hadn't spoken. 'We're going to head back into town and replenish supplies and then go straight back out again tomorrow morning. You guys okay with that?' Martin shot an inquiring glance towards Vlad. Then, belatedly at Tara as well. Vlad said nothing, but turned his blue gaze towards her. She locked eyes with him and nodded once, completely ignoring Martin. Two could play at his game.

'Yep, we're good to go,' Vlad replied. 'We know Edinburg Castle. Should only take us a day to get there. We'll have to drive around the back of the National Park first though. That'll take four or five hours.'

'Righto. We can work out the details on the way back in the cars. I'll ride with you again, Vlad.' Martin was already heading towards the car and shoved his backpack unceremoniously into the rear. 'Cooper, you, Tony and Bruce can go with Tara, same as last time.'

Tara grimaced at Martin's order. Great, that was going to make for a very long, very silent trip home. She sent up a soundless entreaty Coop might ask if he could ride along with Martin. But no, he just ambled over to the cars and plonked his jean-clad arse into the front passenger seat, shooting her a challenging stare.

Tara huffed with annoyance and ground her teeth together. She was a professional, she'd handle this with her usual cool, calm demeanour. Pretend he wasn't there. Drive with the music turned up loud and ignore the whole damn lot of them.

She spent the five hours on the drive back to Byron Bay trying to figure out a strategy to help her through the next few days. She wouldn't be able to continue this not-speaking thing with Coop, even she knew it was getting childish.

By the time they pulled into the Alive and Kicking carpark, it was just coming on dusk and she had a plan ready and her game-face on.

'I guess if we're going to be working together, we should at least be civil towards each other,' she said to Coop, using the fact she was backing the car into a parking spot as an excuse not to look him directly in the eye.

There was a moment's silence. Tara guessed Coop was taken by surprise that she'd actually spoken to him.

'Okay,' he drawled, in that bloody familiar wisecrack tone of his.

'Not that all is forgiven, or anything like that, David.' She used his first name, just so he knew exactly how mad she was. 'But I'm happy to be back on speaking terms, if you are.'

'Of course,' he bit back. 'And ditto. To all that.' She nearly took back her words at his insinuation she had any blame in last night's debacle. The man was insufferable. He'd been the one in the wrong last night, thinking he could just start right back up where they'd left off. She'd told the truth last night. And if he couldn't handle the truth it wasn't her problem.

Without looking back, she jumped out of the car, stalked over to her Jeep and hopped in, starting it up with a vicious jab on the accelerator. She wasn't going to hang around and help them empty the cars. She needed a shower and to get away from all their testosterone-fuelled problems.

Winding down the window, she drove up next to Vlad, saying, 'Give me a call and let me know what time you want me back in the morning.' Then she relented, and added, 'Sorry, I've just got to get home. You'll be okay to unpack all this, won't you?'

'I guess so.' His tight smile told her all was not yet forgiven.

'I'll make it up to you later, I promise.' Guilt at leaving Vlad to do all the work was making her gut squirm, but dark anger was still the overpowering emotion. She couldn't stay.

'Sure,' he sighed. 'You go do what you gotta do.' Vlad would understand. He always did.

'Thanks,' she mouthed as she gunned the car and drove out of the carpark at full speed.

The road up to her house was narrow and winding, but Tara flew around the corners, pushing the poor old car to its limit. She was still seething at the gall of the man. How dare he. How dare he try and put any of what happened last night onto her. She'd never led him to believe he'd ever have a second chance with her. She'd acted completely professionally and kept it cool and on the down-low the whole time.

Hadn't she?

Well, maybe the getting drunk part had been a little bit foolish. But the kiss? That'd all been on him.

Pulling into her driveway, Tara slammed her door hard and stomped round to her letterbox to collect the mail. She let herself in and flicked on lights, then did a quick tour of the house. A leftover habit from her life as a cop; one that seemed to have stuck with her.

The light was flashing on her answering machine and Tara pushed the button. It was her mother, Francisca. With an angry stab of her finger, Tara deleted it as soon as she heard who it was, not bothering to listen to the rest of the message.

Cass

God only knew how her mother had gotten Tara's home phone number. Probably from her dad. He was always telling her, 'She's the only mother you've got,' in a sad kind of voice. He also used to tell her she got all of her wilful stubbornness and wild nature from her mother too, but Tara didn't want to hear she had anything in common with Francisca. So she'd shout at her father, tell him she was nothing like her, until he finally stopped saying it.

The only good thing her mother had given Tara was the ability to stay in Australia for as long as she wanted. Her mother was an Australian citizen, although this was almost by default. Francisca was born in Australia when her parents visited. Her father was on a two year academic secondment to the University of Sydney. They'd returned back to LA at the end of his secondment, with their baby, Francisca, now an honorary Aussie. This happy state of affairs in turn gave Tara dual citizenship.

She could count the number of times she'd spoken to her mother since Kane's death on one hand. Francisca lived in Spain now, with her second husband, Steven Callaghan. From the little she knew about Steven, he was a well-off business man who owned houses in the south of France and Corsica, and Francisca spent her time jet-setting between the three countries.

Tara sat down on the couch, the wad of unopened letters in her hand. She owed her mother nothing and she was damn sure she wasn't going to return her calls. Francisca had made her choice, now she could live with it. She'd chosen to leave her family behind and that's the way it was going to stay.

Her mother had been a successful policewoman, until she'd fallen in love with her dad and gotten pregnant. Her mother had never forgiven her dad for making her give up her career.

Suzanne Cass

84

It was only now, as an adult Tara had the wisdom to understand her mother blamed her family for what she called her life of unfulfilled dreams. Perhaps Francisca could've been a good cop; a great cop even. But having a family had got in the way of that. When she'd met their dad, Vincent, they'd both been young, full of ambition and eager to be the best cops they could. Then Francisca fell pregnant. She agreed to marry Vincent, still hoping things would somehow work out. But she'd never gone back to her police career after Dylan was born. Then Keith came along soon afterwards, and then Tara and finally Kane. Her mother had been saddled with the career of a *mere housewife*, as she put it.

Tara threw the letters onto the couch and stood up to pace around the room, too agitated to sit still as memories of her adolescence came back to haunt her, of the day her mother left.

It was exactly a week after Tara's fifteenth birthday and she'd walked into the kitchen that morning to grab a banana on her way out to school, when she'd found her mother's note lying on the Formica bench top. The note had been short and to the point. No sentimentality or tenderness in the blunt prose. It said she just couldn't do it anymore. They were better off without her.

Tara hadn't exactly been in shock at her mother's disappearance, they all knew how unhappy Francisca was. She'd made it abundantly evident. But it wasn't till many weeks after her mother had gone Tara realised just how much of a cloud of bitterness and regret they'd all been living under. It was almost a relief to be able to claw her way out from beneath that blanket of shadowy accusations and recriminations her mother had draped over them. In some ways, for Tara at least, it was a good thing her mother was gone. No more walking around on eggshells, feeling like she needed to apologise for being a burden, for even being born.

But one thing Tara would never forgive her mother for was leaving Kane at such an impressionable age. Kane had been thirteen when Francisca absconded. The baby of the family, he relied more heavily on his mother than the rest of them. He was also Francisca's favourite. She never lost her temper with him and was always buying him little gifts, slipping him an extra donut, helping him with his homework. Tara's older brothers, Keith and Dylan—two and four years older than her —had both coped well with Francisca's departure. Dylan had left home by that stage and Keith was fast becoming an independent adult as well. Both of them stepped in to help where they could to fill the gap Francisca left.

Kane had pined for his mother terribly. And it seemed Tara was the only one to see it. She tried talking to her dad about it, but he couldn't, or wouldn't, see the problem, too lost in his own grief and hurt to see what was going on around him. 'He'll just have to survive, like the rest of us,' he decreed in his pragmatic way and that'd been the end of the matter in his eyes. Vincent threw himself into his work as a way of coping. He still loved his kids, and went through the physical motions of caring for them day to day, but Tara knew he wasn't emotionally strong enough to support them. Not the way she needed him. Not the way Kane needed him.

By the time Kane got involved with the local street gang, it'd been too late. He'd been shot dead in a drive-by shooting three weeks before his fifteenth birthday, and there wasn't a thing Tara could've done to stop it.

Tara's contempt for her mother turned to fully-fledged hatred that day. In her naive, adolescent mind, the blame rested squarely on her mother's shoulders for Kane's death.

And she was in no mood to change her mind now.

Her mother could go to hell.

Along with David Cooper.

She stopped her pacing and went over to the photo on the bookshelf, as if the picture of her brother was calling to her. Trailing a finger lovingly over the frame, she stared into her dead brother's face. What are you trying to tell me little bro?

The dreams of her brother were still coming. Becoming more intense every day. And it scared her.

* * *

Coop's breath came in short, sharp gasps. Each lungful made his chest expand and contract in great heaves. Sweat ran freely down his face. But he was nearly there. He could see the expanse of blue sky growing with every pump of his thighs. He stopped, balanced his weight through both of his legs and grabbed a nearby knob of rock for stability. He looked up to see Tara's pert backside disappearing over the lip of the huge boulder blocking his path.

The worst part was Tara was scarcely breathing hard at all, while it was all he could do to keep putting one foot after the other and suck in life-giving air at the same time. Damn. He wasn't as fit as he'd thought. Either that, or she was fitter. Which rankled just as much.

Up ahead, Vlad announced they'd made it to the top. Vlad's head, a dark shape against the bright sky, appeared over the edge of the craggy boulder.

'Come on guys, little bit more and you're there. Don't give up now.' Coop had to smother an urge to throw something. Why did that man have to sound so cheery all the goddamn time? Coop knew Vlad was aiming his comment at Tony and Bruce, who'd both given up a good hundred or so metres below them. Coop chanced a glance back down the trail—if it could be called a trail. A mountain goat would've had trouble climbing this rocky cliff-face. He took in Tony and Bruce, both sitting on their arses in the dirt, refusing to go another step. At least he wasn't as unfit as some. Vlad could deal with them.

'Get moving, Cooper,' said Martin, breathing heavily and prodding him with a blunt finger. 'Let's get this damnable climb over with.' Martin and Graeme were just below him on the trail, waiting for him to get going again.

'Yeah, yeah,' he grumbled. But his thirty-second rest had done the trick, allowing his screaming lungs to drag in just enough air to get him the rest of the way up. He began to scramble upwards again, finding footholds, now needing to use his hands to help him as well.

Vlad's hand descended, seemingly from out of the sky, and Coop reached up to grasp it, to let the big man haul him the last few metres over the top.

'Welcome to Edinburg Castle.' Vlad spread his arms wide and pointed with his chin at the vista below them.

'Wow.' It was a sorely lacking response to the view spread in front of him, but all he was capable of right now. They could see for miles and miles from up here. Coop was sure he could even see the glint of the ocean, hundreds of kilometres to the east. Hills and valleys rolled away from The Castle in every direction, forming a green carpet around its feet. He could get used to this view. Even get used to living here, like this.

Vlad was helping Martin up over the top and was still calling encouragement down to the other two lazy bastards, who were refusing to move. Coop dumped his pack onto the rocks and moved away to give them more room.

His gaze found Tara, hunkered down on a flat rock twenty metres away, rummaging around in her backpack. For the tenth time today he had to stop himself from going over there. To say he was sorry. Tell her he'd been an idiot. But of course he wasn't going to do that, because his pride wouldn't let him. And his ego wasn't up for another rejection just yet, either. So he stood drinking in the view from The Castle and pretending to ignore her.

He'd been more than surprised when she'd apologised yesterday. He wasn't used to Tara Hunter apologising. To anyone. Did that mean she'd softened ever so slightly in the past two years? But then it hadn't been a true apology, more of an olive branch really, to make it bearable for them to work together.

Again, he wished he hadn't been so stupid the other night. Why had he drunk so much? He'd lost his temper. Things hadn't worked out the way he'd envisioned. Words hadn't come out of his mouth the right way. In some ways, Tara had been completely correct. She was a strong, smart, determined woman, very capable of looking after herself. It was *his* problem he had this primal urge to protect her. As if he were some kind of caveman and she a helpless maiden. He couldn't explain the feelings he had for Tara, and he knew if he tried, she'd call him a chauvinist pig. And she'd probably be right.

He cast a furtive glance in Tara's direction. She was still rummaging in her bag. Nodding his head at his own stupidity, he admitted even though he was still determined to get an answer from Tara, perhaps his bull-at-a-gate methodology hadn't been the best idea at the time.

'Found them,' Tara said in Vlad's direction, brandishing a pair of expensive looking binoculars. 'This should help us spot them.'

'Great,' Vlad said with a grunt. 'Start looking then.' He'd just hauled Graeme up onto the rock. Coop watched Graeme cast his knowing gaze slowly around the top of The Castle, sizing up the area. Spotting the escape routes, checking for any likely ambush positions. Coop was glad to have Graeme along, his knowledge and experience coupled with his quiet, no-nonsense attitude helped keep them all on a more even keel. Graeme removed his Akubra and dusted it off against his thigh, running a hand through his sweat-dampened hair.

'Are we camping up here?' he asked Vlad in his low gravelly voice.

'Yep.' Vlad and Tara both answered in unison.

'You must be joking. Won't it be like flying a red flag? Let the terrorists know where we are?' Martin butted in.

'Nope, there's a bit of a depression over there. It'll hide us from all prying eyes,' Tara replied. 'There're even a few low-growing bushes which manage to survive on the non-existent soil up here that'll shelter us from the wind. As long as we don't light a fire or do a rain dance we should be pretty much undetectable.'

'Okay,' said Graeme, as always unruffled by the news. 'Point us in the right direction and we'll start making camp.'

'Over that way.' She extended a slender arm towards where the top of the rock seemed to curve gently away from them. 'See the black trig point way over there?' When Graeme nodded, she continued, 'Well if you get to that, you've gone too far.' Graeme nodded again, adding a grunt for good measure. Coop laughed. But then, maybe Graeme had the right attitude. Why waste breath on words, when a grunt would do?

'I'll come with you,' Coop interjected. No use in him hanging around here, waiting for tweedle-dee and tweedle-dum to finally drag their backsides up top. Vlad had the patience of monk.

He picked up his bag and followed Graeme down the gentle slope, stifling a yawn as he marched along. Last night hadn't been the best nights sleep he'd ever had. Tossing and turning, he'd twisted his sweat soaked sheets up into knots. Reliving the fight with Tara from the night before, his mind refused to go blank. Trying to find a better solution, to find a way he could've done it differently. In the end, he'd left his mussed up bed and prowled around the small hotel room like a caged tiger. He'd still been wide awake when the golden touch of the sun painted the horizon, so he'd thrown on his running shoes and loped for miles, right down the beach and back. The same beach he and Tara had surfed together not quite a week ago. All he'd managed to achieve was to make himself even more fatigued. The questions about Tara still roiled around in his head, unanswered.

To make matters worse, as soon as they'd got back to civilisation—back within mobile range—his phone had lit up like a Christmas tree, with at least ten texts from Jade. *Where are you? Why won't you answer me?*

Jade. What to do about Jade? He'd loved Jade once. Well he thought he had. Enough to move in with her. They'd met at the homeless shelter where he volunteered most Saturday mornings. She was so full of energy, a bustling pocket rocket, with long blonde hair and a ready smile for everyone. She served the meals while he cleaned the bathrooms and the kitchen. It'd been a whirlwind romance and because she'd been hard up for a place to stay, Coop had suggested she move in with him. As a temporary measure of course. They'd only been together for one month. Two years later she was still there, but things had changed. For Coop they had anyway. He'd moved onwards and upwards in his police career, but Jade had stayed the same girlish free spirit with an agenda for righting all the world's wrongs, but with no real job or ambition.

Coop became frustrated with her attitude, her lack of purpose. The fact she spent too many days and nights drifting from the couch to the bedroom and back again. And when she did actually go out, it was usually to smoke joints with her friends and talk about organising protests over somebody cutting down some tree somewhere. Their fights had become more and more frequent.

Then he was partnered up with Tara, and it was as if he'd been hit by a lightening bolt. It suddenly became crystal clear Jade wasn't right for him.

He hadn't left her because he wanted to be with Tara—that infatuation had grown later—it was more that Tara had shown him what a real woman looked like. And he knew Jade would never be enough for him. He'd broken up with her over four years ago now.

Then out of the blue, Coop ran into Jade again. She was working as a barmaid at a pub Coop had been staking out. They'd got talking and Jade asked him out for a drink. Coop was never sure what made him agree to her request. Loneliness probably. He only had two, very short, very unsatisfactory *hook-ups* since Tara fled. He'd been starting to think perhaps he was never going to find the right woman; his job had become his mistress. Jade had caught him when he was feeling vulnerable.

They'd been out a few times, and Jade even managed to coax him back to her apartment one night, but something, the voice of reason perhaps, had stopped him from sleeping with her. That same little voice told him she wasn't—and never would be—what he was looking for. Sometimes he wondered if he was his own worst enemy.

Then he was sent up to Byron. Because it was a top-secret operation, he'd left without telling Jade where he was going or when he'd be back. And all it'd taken was one look into Tara's beautiful fudge-brown eyes and he knew it was over with Jade—if indeed it'd ever really started again. The way his body responded to seeing Tara sitting there in the pub, had brought clarity to his fogged mind. He'd never felt that way about Jade and he never would.

So straight after his run on the beach, he'd sat down to answer her texts, his lungs still burning with the fresh salty air, giving him the courage he needed to do what had to be done. As gently as he could—if you can be gentle breaking up with someone over a text message—he told Jade it just wasn't meant to be between them, and how terribly, terribly sorry he was.

The phone had been silent ever since. Which was a good thing. He hoped. It didn't make him feel any less of a bastard, though.

The drive into Edinburg Castle had been harder than into Doubtful Creek. The road was churned up from some less-than-careful 4WD enthusiasts in the last downpour, which made it nearly impassable. Coop was impressed by the way Tara handled the 4WD over the rough terrain, never once getting the car bogged or baulking at any of the steep climbs. But of course he dare not say anything. The heavy going had slowed them down, so even though they'd left Byron Bay at dawn, they were running behind schedule when they finally found a flat spot to leave the cars. Vlad insisted they needed to get to the top of The Castle before dark, and now Coop could see why. It would've been impossible to climb that path in the dark, even with head-torches on. The end result of their running late was Vlad setting another cracking pace to get to the top.

Coop couldn't stifle the next yawn, it was so huge it threatened to crack his face in two. He was dog-tired. What he really needed was some hot food and then to be allowed to crawl into his bivouac to sleep the whole night through. He knew he shouldn't want this, but he sent a silent entreaty up anyway. *Please don't let Tara spot any bad guys this evening.* Give him one night of peace.

He stopped and turned back. Tara was silhouetted against the setting sun, holding the binoculars up to her eyes. Coop studied her. She cut a stunning figure, the orange sun highlighting her from behind made her legs seem impossibly long, her figure impossibly willowy. The rounded curve of her hip was accentuated as she thrust one leg forward to balance herself. Hair pulled back in a ponytail so it bared the back of her neck, olive skin exposed. The angle of her neck, tilted to get the best view of the land below, made it look as if she was offering her throat up to be kissed. His heart jolted at the idea. What she'd said to him the night before last came back to him with a thump. Yes, she was a fierce, strong woman. Standing there now, he might even be tempted to call her magnificent. She was right, she didn't need his protection. He should trust her enough to look out for herself. But that was easier said than done. The voice in his head told him now he'd seen she was safe, doing well up here in her new home, he should leave her to it. Go home and let her get on with her own life. But the tightness in his chest was telling him something different. There was a darkness in him that'd taken over after she'd left Sydney. A feeling that tore a little deeper every day they were apart, as if a light had been switched off in his soul.

When he'd seen her for the first time, sitting at that table in the pub back in Byron, his heart had stopped beating. But when she'd smiled his heart had taken flight again, thundering in his chest so hard he thought people around him must surely hear it. That few seconds had brought clarity back to his life. Had showed him how he'd only been half-alive, having to pass each day without her in it.

Tara shifted her stance slightly, aiming the binoculars away from the setting sun, all her focus intent on the view down the lens. Now her face was in profile and he could see the outline of her high forehead, the jut of her chin as she concentrated. At that particular moment he was incapable of withdrawing his gaze, even if there'd been twenty terrorists storming over the top of the cliff. He was held by some gossamer thread of veracious truth, unable to look away. She was so beautiful. And so utterly determined. He knew now, if he could, he'd grasp at any opportunity to kiss her again. Their last kiss had left too many things unsaid. Unanswered. Heat surged through him, his blood running hotter with every second he watched her. He shifted uncomfortably to ease the ache in his groin. God he wanted her. Wanted her like he'd wanted no other woman before. Just looking at her for too long nearly sent him over the edge. The tension in his gut told him this was nowhere near over, this thing between them.

* * *

A strong arm gripped her in a headlock. She struggled to free herself, in vain. She was bound too tightly against his chest by his other arm.

The arms, although firm, were also gentle. Not allowing her to pull away, but not hurting her either. A low rumble of mirth erupted from him, and Tara could feel the laughter judder though his body. She started to laugh too.

'Come on, Kane, let me go you big oaf.'

'Not until you give,' her brother replied.

'Just because you're dead, don't think you can still boss me around.'

'I can do whatever I like.' His voice held the faintest hint of defiance. 'I know things you don't.' He let her go, and she swivelled around and punched him in the shoulder. His dark eyes fixed on her, a winning smile turning up the corners of his mouth. They were sitting on her bed in her old bedroom. Pink and purple horses galloped on the bedspread below her hands. The colours swirled and mingled, changing to browns and then reds and then back again. The walls were covered with posters of more horses, interspersed with the occasional one of Micky Mouse. Mickey had always been her favourite. Nothing had changed. It all looked exactly the same as when she'd been twelve.

'You shouldn't pick on your little bro like that.' He stood up, grinning as if he knew a secret. He was wearing that old, ratty green jumper, with the frayed sleeves he loved so much. His black hair was long and tousled, half hidden by the grey beanie slouching over his forehead and pulled down over his ears. Kane always wore the same clothes in her dreams. The clothes he'd been wearing the day he died.

She leaned in and hugged him, just because she could. It felt so real. She breathed in his scent, earthy and musky, with a light tang of smoke.

'Hey.' He pushed her away. 'Don't be doing that, sis.'

'I know, I know, I won't do it again.'

The room suddenly morphed in the way of dreams. Now they were standing in Kane's untidy bedroom. The shades were drawn and it was dark and dingy. Just the way he'd liked it. Shadows hung in every corner. A chill ran through Tara and uneasiness carved its way down her spine.

In an instant the smile drained from Kane's face.

'I've got to tell you this, sis. Something I know, and you don't.'

'Okay,' she sighed. She didn't want to hear it, but if she wanted to keep Kane here, in the dream with her, she'd have to listen.

'You need to look where the horses are always running.'

'What?' That didn't make any sense to her, but Kane rarely did in her dreams.

'They're down there. Sleeping in their bags. You need to get there soon, or they'll move.'

'Who's down there?' Tara tried not to sound weary. But she was feeling tired, her eyelids drooping.

Kane grabbed her by the arm and she jerked upright. 'You have to stay here, with me, sis. You have to look. You have to see him.' It was then she noticed the posters on Kane's wall suddenly move, the photos shifting and morphing. One in particular drew her attention. It was up high, on the wall way above his bed. She peered at it, trying to see, going in closer. A room coalesced from out of the kaleidoscope of lines and shapes in the poster. A dank, dark room. A basement perhaps. Something was there, in the corner of the room, writhing against the wall. A human figure, half naked and bound tightly. The rest of Kane's room disappeared. There was only the poster in front of her, filling her entire vision, her entire world. Nothing else existed except that image in front of her. The person—it was a man, that much she could tell now from the bared chest—had their arms stretched, spread-eagled out against the wall. Wrists bound tightly. His head flopped on his chest and blood-splattered hair hung down in front of his face.

A low moan escaped the man, and Tara felt the hairs on the back of her neck raise up. A weight settled, heavy in her gut, as if she'd swallowed a load of concrete. Fear. The sound was so full of pain and anguish, desperate. She wanted to reach out and touch him, help him somehow. Relieve his suffering.

A harsh laugh cut through the man's moaning. Tara drew back, away from the sound, but couldn't see anyone else. There was only this one person in the poster. The man stopped moaning and tensed, as if waiting for something. Ever so slowly, he raised his head. It took a few seconds for Tara to focus on his face. Both his eyes were puffed and bloodied. One was swollen completely shut, but through the other Tara could make out the flash of piercing blue as he stared defiantly ahead. His lips were bruised and cut, and he spat out a glob of blood at he continued to stare. There were dark welts covering the right side of his face, as if he'd been beaten with something long and thin. Something about that sky-blue eye tickled at the back of Tara's mind. The man tried to move, tried to stand up straighter, as far as his bindings would allow. He drew in a shallow breath, gritting his teeth, as if even the act of breathing was painful.

'Fuck you,' he said. The words were more like a grunt, coming out thick and almost unintelligible from his battered mouth.

It was then, at the sound of his voice a cold realisation slid through her. She knew that voice. The man spat more blood and tried to grin horribly at the unseen man with the harsh laugh. Deep in her belly, fear stretched out its claws. A spasm of cold slid down her spine.

It was in that smile that she finally recognised him. It was Coop, tied up and beaten. Bound like a pig waiting for slaughter. She made a sound in her throat. It welled up through her, forcing its way out of her chest. It was half scream, half roar of fear.

She lunged at the poster, but only found cool, smooth paper beneath her fingers.

'David.' She battered at the wall with her fists.

'David.' His face stared back at her from the poster, unable to see her, unable to hear her screaming for him. At him.

'David!'

'Tara, I'm right here.' A warm hand cupped her face, then a strong arm held her and shook her awake.

The world slowly swam back into focus. Coop's face hovered mere inches from hers, lit from below by the filtered light of a torch.

'You're okay, it was just a dream.' Coop's voice was low and soothing, as if talking to a frightened child. 'Take some deep breaths. I'm here, babe. I'm here.'

Belatedly, she realised she was trembling, shaking from head to foot.

'That must've been a helluva dream. You were yelling my name. What's the matter?'

'David, are you hurt?' She ran her hands over his face, feverishly feeling for cuts and abrasions. 'God, it was so real,' she said, her breath came in short, sharp gasps, her lungs clamping in her chest. She could still feel the fear, the cold dread that'd flooded her soul when she'd seen him like that.

'It's okay,' Coop repeated softly. 'I'm here.'

'What's going on?' Martin's face appeared over the top of Coop's left shoulder. She could just make out the serious frown hovering on his brow in the dim light of the torch. He looked worried, but she wasn't sure if his concern was for her mental wellbeing or for the fact she was causing a disturbance. When she gave a sharp nod in reply, he said, 'Right. You two need to keep it down then.' And there it was. Of course the safety of the mission would always be paramount in his mind. 'And turn that light off, Cooper. We can't take any chances.' Coop just grunted in reply, but he covered the torch up, so there was only the faintest hint of light seeping out from around the edges of his jumper. Martin made his way back to his own bivouac, the sound of the zipper quietly being done up announcing he was safely back in his tent.

'What was all that about?' Coop whispered as he hunkered down on the ground next to her. He hadn't let go of her. His arm was still wrapped protectively around her shoulder. She absorbed his warmth. Welcomed his closeness. His presence helped drive away some of the raging fear that'd threatened to consume her. He took his hand away from her face and the air was cool and damp against her skin. An insane voice inside her head said she wanted him to put his hand back there and never take it away again.

'You were yelling my name. Really loud.' He gave a low chuckle and she could imagine the mischievous smile that accompanied that laugh. The sound of his voice slowed her heart rate even more. His deep, oh-so-familiar voice wrapped around her like a warm blanket. 'And much as I love it when you yell my name ....' He stopped and she could feel him trying to contain another chuckle of glee. 'Even I was a little worried.'

'Jesus, was I really that loud?' she whispered back, worried now she may well have given them away to the men they were hunting.

'Pfff. Don't worry about old cranky-pants boss there. Yeah, he's probably worried you're going to bring the terrorists descending down on us like the hounds of hell. I think it just sounded loud up here because we're all camping in this little amphitheatre and the sound is amplified. But your face was muffled by your sleeping bag, so I'm pretty sure the sound didn't carry.'

She didn't want to tell him about the dream. If she did, it might make it come true. Even though every logical bone in her body was telling her it was just a dream and to stop being such a superstitious old woman, her heart was telling her something different.

There was a small part of her that wanted to believe her brother really was communicating with her from the grave. But if she let herself believe that, then she'd have to believe the dark, terrifying nightmare she'd just encountered also held some truth. She needed to talk to Claire. She'd understand the meaning of Kane's dream better than Tara could. Tara drew her thoughts up short. When had she started believing what Claire, the psychic, was trying to tell her? This was just a dream. Wasn't it?

Tara blew out a loud breath between her teeth.

'I get it, you don't want to talk about it. That's okay. I'm not really sure I want to know why you were yelling my name anyway. The way you screamed made the hairs on the back of my neck stand up. If I'm being devoured by a three-headed monster in your dreams I don't really need to know.'

She was grateful he didn't probe. He could've demanded an answer, and rightly so. But then she would've had to lie to him.

'It was nothing really,' she said, lifting her shoulders in a small shrug.

'Good,' he whispered back, but his tone told her otherwise. His gaze stayed fixed on her face. He understood her well enough to know this dream was something out of the ordinary, but he wasn't going to press her on it, and right at that particular moment, she loved him for that.

His voice was low and husky in her ear. Intimate. He was still crouched down next to her, his body sheltering her, his arm solid behind her neck. Tender, attentive. Now the shivers had subsided she should probably push him away, tell him he should go back to bed. But it felt so nice to be held, treasured. To feel safe. Tara knew she didn't need a man around to make her feel safe. But, God, it felt good, to surrender just this once. To let his arms enfold her and keep her safe from the dark. Safe from her demons. Her body suddenly became aware of his proximity. She became acutely aware of the parts of her skin that were touching his. The back of her neck, the skin of her palm where it lay against his thigh. The way his breath whispered over her cheek as he hovered near. Something uncurled deep in her belly, like a cat stretching after a long sleep.

Her mind returned to their kiss, two nights ago. Funny, but she couldn't seem to summon the heights of that self-righteous rage tonight. Her anger had evaporated. If he tried to kiss her tonight, her reaction might be very different. The dream had stripped away her defences, showing her what was truly important. Coop. He was important to her. Now, if he leant in, she might even meet him halfway.

'I guess I'd better get back to bed then.' His voice held a note of regret. 'Otherwise we'll have Martin back over here poking around, asking what we're up to again.' But he still hadn't moved, hadn't withdrawn even a millimetre. She hesitated. The silence drew out between them, the darkness cocooning them.

'Go.' Her voice was barely audible, even to her own ears. 'Go back to bed, Coop.' She forced her tone to a steady calmness she didn't feel.

'Whatever you want, Tara.' Then he was gone, disappearing into the dark like a wraith. The cold air rushed in around her. She felt naked and alone as he stripped her of his wonderful, earnest concern.

Lying back down, she snuggled as deep into her sleeping bag as she could go, pulling it up to cover her ears. Like she'd done whenever she'd had a nightmare as a little child. In her warm cocoon, she could hear the sound of her own heart thudding, and she listened as it slowed, returning back to its normal rhythm.

She probably wouldn't sleep any more tonight. Images from the dream circled round and round in her head.

Kane had never given her such a vivid message in any of her dreams before. What did it mean? What if the dream were to come true? If only Claire were here to help her decipher it.

The visions brought on by dreams could rarely be interpreted literally. She very much doubted Kane was trying to tell her Coop was going to be tortured and beaten by the group of terrorists they were tracking. So then, what was Kane trying to tell her? Was he trying to show her how she'd feel if Coop was in danger? Force her to confront her true feelings about him?

When she allowed the image of Coop, tied up and beaten, to float again before her mind's eye, the icy, claustrophobic fear came back with a vengeance. Her gut twisted and she broke out into a cold sweat at the mere allusion he might be hurt in some way. It was exactly the same feeling she'd had two years ago, when she'd seen him lying on the floor of the hotel lobby, bleeding profusely. The squeezing of her heart so it stopped beating, the sudden sense of powerlessness, as if her limbs were weighed down with lead. That feeling had remained while she'd watched him being carted off in the ambulance, and when she'd forced herself to walk through the double glass doors into the hospital. It'd only eased once the harried nurse told her he wasn't going to die. Eased, but not gone away. The pressure of that feeling weighed down on her until the only option was to run away.

The truth hit her like a lightning bolt. She *did* care about what happened to him. Cared about him more than she wanted to admit. She always had. Running away hadn't changed any of her feelings for him. If anything they'd grown stronger over the past few years.

She pondered the answers to that revelation long into the night.

CHAPTER SIX

'I see something.' Tara's voice was slightly muffled behind the large pair of binoculars.

'What?' Martin's voice cracked the air like a whip. They'd been scanning the dense carpet of jungle below for hours now, with no sign of any movement. Coop raised his head from where he lay on the flat rocks and squinted at Tara through the bright midday sun. She held the binoculars rigid against her face, strain evident in the muscles of her neck and shoulders from the effort of holding the heavy glasses up for so long. There were more dark shadows under her eyes. He guessed she hadn't gone back to sleep after her dream last night.

'A flash of something. I'm not sure … Wanna take a look?' Martin jumped up from where he'd been sitting in the shade of a small bush, and hurried over to Tara. Vlad appeared from the shady spot he'd been occupying, also eager to look through the binoculars.

Coop let his head flop back down the folded jacket he'd been using as a pillow and watched the leaves above his head flick and shimmer as a slight breeze caressed them. Flashes of blue were replaced by the dark olive green of the leaves, the yellow sunlight sparkling through the openings and partially blinding him as it shimmered and danced. Lying on the sun-baked rocks, the warmth of the day made him drowsy and content. It was nice not to be rushing off somewhere for a change. To have time to think.

If Tara *had* seen something, they'd all know soon enough. Bruce emitted a loud grunting kind of snore, half-woke up, and then rolled over and went straight back to sleep. Tony sat dozing, his back against a scraggly tree next to Bruce. Graeme was awake, sitting on a rock and whittling away at something with his pocket knife.

This morning had been something of a Godsend for Coop. They'd all arisen with the dawn and packed up camp, ready to move as soon as they had a target. But then, nothing had happened. Not a sign. Not a whiff of smoke. No sounds of conversation or clang of a dropped pan. Nothing. Perhaps it had something to do with the constant, annoying buzz of cicadas, which even up here on top of the rock prevailed over every other noise. It was more than a noise, Coop decided. It was a deep vibration that went right through to his bones, fading and then rising again to a crescendo fit to break his eardrums. Even so, these terrorists seemed to know their stuff. If they were out there, they were keeping well hidden.

So Coop had taken the luxury of spare time and used it to get some more, much-needed rest, store up some reserves for the coming days. He'd slept well last night. Deep, and for once, dreamless. At least he had until Tara had woken him in the small hours of the morning with her muffled screaming.

What'd that been all about? Unease ate at the edges of his conscience. He could tell she'd been frightened. Really frightened. And it took a lot to shake up Tara Hunter. He'd wanted to ask her why she'd been dreaming about him. What'd he done to deserve a place in her nightmares? But a little voice of caution warned him not to push her too far last night, and for once he'd actually listened.

He could still remember how it'd felt to cradle her in his arms. She'd never surrendered to him like that before. That's how he knew her fear was genuine. She'd been so frightened she let him hold her. Now that was one for the books. And something he'd savour for a long time to come.

There'd been one positive outcome from Tara's violent dream, from Coop's point of view anyway. Something in Tara softened towards him last night. That impenetrable wall she'd put up after the kiss was no longer there. It'd shattered the second he'd taken her in his arms. He'd felt it almost as a physical thing, her change of heart, intertwined with the shuddering that'd run through her body. The harsh animosity left her, replaced with a hesitant kind of tenderness. Her body welcomed him, yielded to his arm around her shoulder. Their bond was renewed. Whatever she'd dreamed about had been enough to make her forget about her righteous anger towards him.

'I saw it too,' Martin's voice split the redolent hum of the cicadas, breaking Coop's train of thought. 'Everyone up. We've got to go.'

Coop groaned and heard Bruce give a loud grunt as Tony punched him in the leg to wake him up. Pulling on his backpack, Coop went to stand next to Tara, who was shading her eyes with a hand and peering out into the verdant green field below them.

'What did you see?' He leaned ever so gently against her shoulder. A test really, to see what she'd do. If she pulled away, then he knew the connection he'd thought he'd felt last night was gone. Just a lie he'd told himself.

She didn't move away. Indeed, she even turned and touched him lightly on the forearm as she spoke. He hardly heard her words for the thrumming pulse her touch sent through his veins. Trying to suppress a smile of satisfaction, he tuned into what she was saying.

'I definitely saw a flash of something metal. Down there in Brumby Plains. See that patch of darker green in the small valley over there?' Coop followed her pointed finger to locate the spot. 'There's a couple of really large palm trees growing there. You can see the tops of them, they look like a fountain of leaves.' He nodded, squinting against the sun, concentrating hard. Yep, he could see the tall palms, although they were tiny from their vantage point up here. He nodded again, pushing a curl of disorderly hair away from his forehead to see more clearly.

'Well, those palms indicate there might be a creek bed, or at least some kind of water down there. They like to keep their roots damp all the time.'

'Aha. Camping next to a water would be desirable, I assume.' It was her turn to nod her head.

'Got it in one, Coop. See, you do have some detective skills. Don't let anyone tell you otherwise.' She laughed and nudged him, her eyes sparking with mirth. The smile she offered was the most perfect thing he'd seen in days. A small ray of hope pierced his heart. He'd been right after all. She was back. At the very least, their camaraderie was back.

* * *

Brumby Plains. Had that been what Kane meant last night when he'd told her to look where the horses were always running? Because that's exactly where she'd spotted the campsite. Tara shook her head to clear the idle thought away. It'd do her no good to let last night's dream shake her focus on what she needed to do today. They needed to confirm if it really was the bunch of fanatics, or just a family enjoying a bit of peace and quiet to themselves.

'What's the fastest way down there,' Martin snapped, the strain of having to sit idly by for a whole wasted morning obviously grating on him. Tara had known Martin Greenslade less than a week, but it hadn't taken her long to figure out he was a man of action. He was an A-type personality, who always needed to be in control and hated leaving anything to chance. When he hadn't been able to control how quickly they found the targets, he'd become irritable and spent most of the morning scowling, those dark brows drawn down over his eyes, lending him an almost prehistoric look.

Vlad walked over to where the flat top of rocks sloped away at a dangerous angle. His hand shaded his eyes and there was an evaluating look on his face. He spoke suddenly, interrupting whatever Tara had been about to say. She snapped her mouth shut with a click.

'If you want the fastest way down, it's straight down this cliff-face.' He was right, but Tara wasn't sure it was the best plan for Martin and his team, none of whom knew a thing about rock climbing. Tara held her tongue. She and Vlad were prepared for this kind of occurrence and they'd handle it in the professional manner they always did. She'd just have to pretend this was a group of eager tourists, rather than a bunch of irritated, burly cops.

'Right, let's do it then,' Martin replied, without a second of hesitation.

He was already picking up his backpack when Tony said, 'Now hold on just a second. What did you just say? First you made me crawl up onto this God-forsaken rock, up some non-existent goat track, and now you're telling me the only way down is to jump off a cliff?' His swarthy face had paled slightly as he eyed the drop-off in front of them.

'Don't tell me you're afraid of heights, Russo?' Martin stared at him, a cynical gleam in his eye. 'Because if you are, you can damn well walk back home. I didn't come out here to pander to nancy-boys. This is serious business. We're out here to catch a bunch of extremists who're planning to blow up Sydney. If you can't hack the pace, go back to HQ and tell them to send me someone who can.' There was a full five seconds of silence as everyone stood around not saying anything.

Tony's face quickly lost its pallor as red infused up his neck. His bushy eyebrows drew down into a glower, the dark eyes going hard as flint.

'What did you just call me?' He took a step towards Martin.

'Alright, alright, everyone calm down.' Graeme stepped between the two men, palms raised in appeal.

Coop moved in to stand next to her. Whether it was to protect her in case there was an altercation, or to help Graeme intercede, she never knew.

Vlad said, 'We won't be jumping, we'll be abseiling down. Tara and I'll talk you all through it. It's as easy as pie. Don't forget, boys, this is what we do for a living. This is the reason you asked us along, isn't it?'

'You make it sound so easy,' said Bruce with a growl, a pessimistic lift to one eyebrow. 'But I'm sure we can all handle it. Can't we?' His last question was directed straight at his partner, Tony, who still glowered at everyone, but finally conceded by nodding his head.

'The only minor glitch is, because of the recent rain, the creek is running fast and full, and the last part of the abseil will take us close to a waterfall at the bottom. So we might get a little wet.' No one bothered to give a comment. Martin lifted his shoulders in a shrug that indicated there was no problem. 'Or we could just go back down the path we came up,' Vlad continued in a helpful tone. 'But it'd take us over a day to traverse around the base of The Castle here.'

'Nope, we're climbing down. I want to capture these bastards, and I don't want to give them any more time to get away than we absolutely have to.' Martin stood, legs akimbo, backpack slung across one shoulder, gaze boring into each one of them. 'Like I said, we're here to do a job. A very important job. People could die if we don't catch these fuckers before they implement their scheme. And I for one, don't plan on letting that happen.'

'Righto, boss,' replied Graeme, heading towards the cliff-face. 'Let's get this show on the road.' His blunt words and confident strides seemed to kick-start them all into action.

Tara hauled her pack over to a large tree near the edge of the drop-off and started to unclip the seventy five-metre rope she'd strapped to the side of her bag for just such a scenario. Vlad joined her, unstrapping his identical rope and pulling out two harnesses from a pocket in the top of his bag.

'We only have two harnesses, so I'll talk each of you down one at a time,' Vlad said, loud enough for everyone to hear. Then a little more quietly he said to Tara, 'You can go down first and belay them from the bottom. You okay with that?'

'Sure,' she replied, knowing he was giving her the easy job.

'You'll have to be careful though. The rocks might be slippery down there because of the spray from the waterfall. See if you can drag the ropes as far away as possible, without compromising the climb of course.' His fingers toyed with the end of the rope, his eyes darting towards the brink and back again. She knew Vlad was feeling the burden of this climb with five inexperienced men. Neither she nor Vlad had ever abseiled down from The Castle before, but they'd walked the area countless times and traversed the base of the cliff a few times as well. They had a pretty good idea of what to expect. But Tara understood Vlad's apprehension. He needed it to go well, for both their sakes.

'It'll be okay, Vlad.' She grabbed his hand to stop the nervous fidgeting and waited until his gaze lifted to hers. His eyes stopped flickering and focussed on her and some of the tension left his square features.

'You're right. Of course. I just need to treat this like any other abseil.'

'Exactly,' she murmured. 'We can take turns coming down with each one of them if you like.'

'Thanks, Tara. That's a great idea.' The last of the frown lines left his forehead and he gave her that wide-open, cheeky grin. She felt a wave of affection wash over her. She was glad he was along on this adventure. His dependable nature and familiar air helped ease some of her own fears.

All of a sudden the thought hit her. She actually enjoyed what she did for a living. Up until now she'd always thought of her job at Alive and Kicking as a stop-gap, until she could find something better. Go back to being a cop, the small voice in her head had said. But now, as she prepared the rope and harness ready to go over the edge, it hit her like a sledgehammer to the head. She loved this lifestyle. Loved the kick of adrenaline every time she climbed, or water-skied, or parachuted. Loved being out in the vivid, clean sunshine, breathing the crisp mountain air. This was what she wanted to do. This was where her heart lay now.

She'd always miss the heart-stopping, blood-pounding fear of hearing a bullet hiss past her ear. Miss the satisfaction of grounding the bad guy's face into the dirt after she'd chased him down, then snapping the cuffs on his wrists.

But she wouldn't be going back.

The thought was both exhilarating and a reality check all at the same time.

'How're you going with that harness?'

She gave a guilty grin as she slipped first one leg and then the other into the harness. 'Sorry,' she said, not bothering to offer any reason for her preoccupation. At the same time she made sure the straps were fastened snug and tight over her hips. Then she grabbed the end of the rope Vlad held out, putting a loop through the belay device and clipping it into the carabiner at the front of her harness. Vlad already had his harness fitted. Creating a precise figure eight knot, he was tying the rope off to the robust tree on the edge of the cliff.

Coop came over to stand next to her, his eyes on her fingers as she checked and re-checked the belay and carabiner, making sure they were locked in and secure. He regarded her with blue eyes that seemed serene, but she knew him well enough to notice the give-away tightness around his mouth. He also seemed to be actively avoiding looking over the edge of the cliff, kept his eyes fixed on her instead. She had to stifle a laugh when she realised he was nervous. She'd been doing this so long now, she'd almost forgotten what it felt like. That apprehensive feeling low down in your gut, when your stomach clenched hard and your brain tried desperately to talk you out of putting your body in such danger.

'You'll be fine, Coop. You're at more risk of being hit by a bus crossing the street than falling from here. I'll look after you.' Instinct made her lay her hand on his upper arm, to reassure him. Now she was touching him, she could feel the nervous tension thrumming him, his bicep tight as a drum. He was more anxious than she'd first thought.

The idea that Coop was on the back foot appealed to Tara in a twisted kind of way. It gave her an advantage over him, something she wasn't used to. He stared down at her, something else besides unease igniting in his eyes. She couldn't look away. A tiny quiver of warmth shimmered through her as her body recognised his nearness. The heat of his skin gave a tingle of awareness through her fingertips. Why did her body always react this way when he was around?

'You'll be fine,' she said again. 'I'll be waiting at the bottom to catch you if you fall.' Her eyes held his blue ones. He gave her a tight smile and stepped away.

'Well don't spend so much time ogling my butt while you're down there you forget to hold onto my rope.' He gave a rumbling, familiar chuckle at his own wisecrack.

'Pfft.' She waved him away, but her tsk of exasperation held an edge of humor. She felt his low, deep laugh all the way down to the backs of her knees and it threatened to set her legs trembling. What was happening to her?

'Are you ready?' asked Vlad, walking over to join her.

'Yes.' Tara took a deep, steadying breath. A fine sheen of sweat broke out on her forehead and her stomach flipped gently as she looked over the edge, planning her route of descent. The adrenaline rush was slight, but familiar; her muscles already anticipating the free fall of the abseil. This was the best part. Some said it was the hardest part, taking those first few steps over the edge, that leap of faith. But she loved those few seconds of heightened aliveness.

'Everyone come over here and watch how Tara does this. I'll talk you through what she's doing as she goes.' The other men all clustered around her, as Vlad explained how the belay device worked to slow their descent and how they needed to keep their legs straight and body parallel to the ground to make it easier. She felt Coop press into her elbow as he leaned forward with the rest of them to study the climbing gear. She gave him what she hoped was an encouraging wink.

'The only difference you guys will notice is that we'll be getting you to use a prusik knot as an extra safety device. But Tara's an old hand at this, so she won't need it today.'

'One last note of caution, men,' said Martin. 'We need to keep this on the down-low. We don't want those bastards to know we're coming. So, while Vlad has advised me they won't hear us if we speak normally, and they shouldn't be able to see us through the tall gum trees sheltering the climb, they might possibly hear us if we start shouting.' Martin fixed each one of them with his steely glare. 'Got it?' They all nodded agreement. 'I don't care what happens down there, no one is to make a sound above a dull whisper.'

'Got it, boss,' replied Graeme.

'Right, Tara, off you go,' Vlad said.

Her left hand held the rope and she tucked it into the small of her back. Giving a curt nod in Vlad's direction, she went over. The curve was gradual to start with, the limestone smooth and pebbled. After a few metres, the grey rock fell away beneath her and she was walking backwards down a vertical slope. Below her was a fifty-five metre drop. Leaning back into the harness she surrendered all her weight to the rope, having complete faith in both the strength of the rope and in her abseiling ability, and walked quickly downwards. Started to take little hops when she was sure of her footing. This didn't compare to the sense of freedom she got from skydiving, but it wasn't bad. This was more like Spiderman must have felt. She took another large leap into space, suspended by the gossamer thread of the rope.

Out in the full blazing sun now, the sweat started to trickle down her back and between her breasts. Making sure she mapped the best route for the other less experienced guys to come later, she nevertheless made the descent in less than three minutes.

The last ten metres or so was a little tricky. As Vlad had predicted the wet rocks were slippery, even when she tried to steer herself over to the left, away from the worst of the spray. She couldn't go too far to the left, however, as two large eucalyptus trees barred her way. Throwing their limbs towards the sky, they waited to tangle any unwary climber in their branches. Her shoes were walking boots, not climbing shoes, and while they provided some grip, her feet slipped more than once, even though she took it slowly.

Her boots finally hit the ground and she let the line go slack. Shading her eyes, she looked up.

She could just see Vlad's head and neck as he craned out over the drop-off. She gave him the thumbs up to let him know she was safe. His voice drifted down to her, barely loud enough for her to hear. 'I'm going to lower the backpacks down first, one at a time. And then I'll let you know when Coop's ready to start the descent.' So it was going to be Coop first over the edge. A small smile played over her lips. If he was nervous about this, he was doing a good job at hiding it, putting himself first.

She had a few minutes to spare while Vlad tied on the first backpack and he and Graeme lowered it down, so she surveyed the lie of the land. The waterfall discharged from a cleft in the rocks about half way down the cliff-face. It was a thin, wispy film of water that swayed and bent with each gust of wind. Even though the stream of water looked insubstantial, it was enough to fill a depression, creating a small waterhole four metres across at the bottom. Various ferns and other water-loving plants sprouted from precarious footholds in the rock wall nearby, enjoying the moist surroundings. She was standing on a jumble of brownish-grey basalt rocks that littered the bottom of the cliff. The bare rocks stopped anything growing, but the jungle soon closed in around the small clearing, shrouding her with shady greenery.

All in all, it was a beautiful spot. An oasis.

Finally, Vlad said, 'We're on our way, Tara,' but he kept his tone so low she almost didn't hear him. Now it was Coop's turn. Taking up the slack on the rope she'd just climbed down, she waited. Vlad's legs appeared first, his lengthy, powerful thighs, revealed beneath his khaki shorts, flexing with each step backwards. He was talking to Coop, his voice low and calm, showing him what to do. Then Coop was over the edge too, taking slow jerky steps backwards. She couldn't see his face, so there was no way for her to know what was going on in his mind, but it didn't take him long before he was leaning further back into his harness, starting to trust his rope. Tara kept a firm grip on his line as he came down. At the moment Coop was controlling his rate of descent, but if he did happen to slip or lose his grip on the rope, just by pulling the end of the rope tight, she could stop him from falling.

He was nearly half-way down now, and doing extremely well for an amateur. She was proud of him. And now he was closer she was starting to enjoy the view. She took the time to survey his well-defined legs, visible through the jeans drawn extra tight from the harness, muscles bulging and contracting with each step he took. Her gaze travelled further up his body, to his broad shoulders, drawn tight with the strain of holding the rope. The ridges of his back muscles clearly visible beneath his body-hugging t-shirt. He certainly was a delicious male specimen. Physically perfect in every way.

'You're doing great,' she said, unsure if he could hear her at this distance.

Vlad answered for him. 'Yes, he is. He's a natural.' Coop just grunted in reply.

'Just make sure to stay well clear of those branches to your left, Coop,' she said, keeping her voice nonchalant. Coop was less aware of his surroundings and had veered a little too close for her liking. Vlad turned and gave her a quick look, knowing the warning was really for him.

'Let's just see if we can swing a little to our right, Coop. Yep that's good, keep coming a little further.' Vlad talked him over the rock face, closer to the wet rocks. Tara knew the wet rocks were preferable to entangling branches, but being an abseiling virgin, Coop wouldn't understand that.

Before she knew it, Coop was lowering himself the last few metres to stand next to her, barely containing his sigh of relief. Vlad jumped down on a flat rock a few metres away.

'One down, four more to go,' he said, giving her one of his quick grins, eyes flashing. He was enjoying this now. Vlad shot a quick look at Coop, who was preoccupied with releasing his harness, and beckoned her closer. 'I'm going to bring Tony down next,' he said quietly in her ear. 'He's doing a good job of being all macho and tough up there, but he's just about to shit his pants. The quicker we get him down the less time he has to get himself worked up about it all.'

'Righto,' she replied, keeping her tone low and light, to match his. 'We've handled plenty of his type before, nothing to worry about. I'll go up and get Martin after that if you like?'

'Yep.' He gave her a hasty wink and then nodded to indicate Coop was coming over, ending their quiet conversation. 'Got that harness ready?' he asked, as Tara took a step away from him and pretended to fiddle with the ropes in front of her.

'Here you go.' Coop handed the harness over for Vlad to take back up the cliff for Tony to use.

'At least there's enough of them up there to haul you back up, so you don't have to make this climb too many times,' said Tara in a cheerful voice.

Vlad tugged on the rope three times and Graeme's face soon appeared over the edge. Vlad gave him the thumbs up, letting them know he was ready to be pulled up.

Tara and Coop stood and watched Vlad slowly ascend the cliff, going up in fits and starts as the men at the top hauled on the rope.

'Wow, this place is amazing,' said Coop, finally taking a look around.

'It is, isn't it,' she agreed. 'One of the perks of this job is you get to see some of these wonderful hidden places. Not too many other people have ever been here.'

A few minutes later, Vlad's voice finally floated down to them. 'We're on our way down again.'

'At last,' muttered Tara under her breath, taking up the slack on the end of the rope. She cast a quick, envious glance over at Coop, who'd perched himself on a rock in the shade of the huge eucalyptus trees. It was hot here, standing in the blazing sun, she'd rather be under the shade with him. Tony came over the edge. He was keeping his body too upright, almost parallel to the rock face, a typical rookie mistake, and Vlad tried to coax him into leaning back into the harness, to let the rope do the work for him.

After a few aborted attempts Tony eventually did as he was told, but remained stiff as a board, walking backwards in slow jerky movements.

'Come on you pussy, you aint gonna let that upstart Cooper show you up, are you?' It was Bruce. Taunting Tony.

'Shut up, you idiot,' she muttered under her breath. Didn't Bruce realise how serious this was? He probably thought he was helping. But they didn't need any of this male macho bullshit going on in the middle of an abseil. And they didn't need him giving away their location by raising his voice. She was pretty sure Martin would remind him of that fact damn quick.

'Don't listen to him,' Vlad said, his voice strangely authoritative. He hadn't been keen on Bruce's comment either.

But the damage had been done. Even from this distance, Tara could see Tony's shoulders hunch, his neck bulge with fury. He started to walk backwards faster, even resorting to taking a few hopping jumps, swinging wildly when he did, descending dangerously fast. Coop came out from the shelter of the trees and shaded his eyes, looking up at the climbers.

'Tara,' Vlad said quietly, at exactly the same time as she reacted, pulling firmly on the rope, slowing Tony down until he came almost to a standstill.

'Hey, watcha doing?' Tony glared down at her. 'I've got this, I don't need no woman controlling me.' Tara didn't bother to reply. And she didn't loosen the rope either.

* * *

'Just wait until I get level with you again, will you?' Vlad said. Tony waited, but Coop could tell Tony was fuming. He fidgeted and jiggled, playing with the ropes holding him up.

'What's going on?' he asked, even though he was pretty sure he knew. Tony was being a dumb arse. Again. Tara turned to look at him.

'Tony's just trying to show us all how fearless he really is,' she answered with a sly grin. He pursed his lips at her comment, at her unsaid words. But he knew what she was probably thinking. After all, she'd told him often enough when they'd been partners. The one thing she couldn't stand about being a cop, was putting up with all the male testosterone and masculine posing that went on in a bid to show how intrepid they all were. Coop gave a nonchalant shrug. There wasn't really a lot he could do about Tony right now, but he meant to have a little chat with him later. Come to think of it, he'd probably have to get in line after Martin and Graeme. The thought brought a twist of mirth to his lips and he could see the question form in Tara's russet-brown eyes as she continued to stare at him.

Tony started to move again and she looked back up, shaking her long ponytail back over her shoulder and out of the way.

'Okay, Tara, you can let him go now,' Vlad said, somehow managing to keep his voice controlled and calm. Coop watched her loosen her hold on the rope, her gaze never leaving the two men. Tony's normally pristine white t-shirt was now drenched with sweat and covered with smudges of dirt. The climb was taking its toll on him and his unsuitable clothing.

Tony seemed to be descending a little more steadily now, taking it easy but adding in a longer jump here and there.

Soon they drew level with the spreading branches of the largest eucalyptus tree. These trees were amazing, tall and statuesque, their green crowns feathering the top of the cliff face further around to the right. He was glad the trees grew here, as they camouflaged the group's descent. But they also added another element of danger, with their long entangling branches, which looked as if they wanted to reach out and grab an unwary climber. If Tony kept going on the path he was taking he'd end up right underneath the waterfall.

He was just about to give a warning when Tara said quietly, 'You need to move over to your left a little, Tony, otherwise you're going to get wet and it's very slippery there.'

Tony merely grunted in reply, and took a big jump downwards, while at the same time trying to correct his direction away from the waterfall. His legs flailed violently in the air as he went out too far from the rock face, and miss-stepped the landing, banging hard into the rock wall while also slipping quickly down the rope. He gave a yell of fright, taking his hand off the rope, scrabbling for a hold in order to stop himself undulating on the rope. Before Tara or Vlad had a chance to react, he'd kicked away from the rock and swung wildly on his rope, pushing himself way too far over to the left.

'Tony, watch—' Coop remembered too late not to yell, just as Tony crashed into the topmost branches of the tree.

'Jesus Christ.' Tara's quiet expletive hissed out between clenched teeth. He gave her a quick glance and saw her hauling on the rope as hard as she could, her face pale and set like stone. Scrambling over the rocks as fast as he dared, he ran to Tara and grabbed the rope as well. She never took her eyes from the disaster unfolding above.

Coop couldn't really see what was going on up there, it was all flashes of colour as the branches swayed and thrashed. It looked like Tony was hanging upside down, but he couldn't be sure. One thing he could be sure of was the noise. Tony was wailing like a frightened child, and Vlad was hissing at him to shut up. The dumb arse was going to give them all away if he didn't shut the fuck up.

'How bad is it?' Coop asked Tara.

'I don't know. I can't really see,' she replied, tipping her head backwards in a vain attempt to make out the scene above. 'Something went wrong, I couldn't seem to slow him down enough.' Every line of her body was drawn taught as a bowstring and he knew she was desperate to get up there and help Vlad. 'If Tony's rope is badly tangled we might have to unclip him to get it free.' Deep lines furrowed her brow as she stared up. 'And if Vlad gets tangled too ...' she let the rest of her thought go unsaid, but Coop knew it wouldn't be good.

'You go up. I've got this end,' he said.

'What? No. You don't know what you're doing,' she replied. Her gaze flickered onto his face for a second before returning the tree.

'Come on, Tara, how hard can it be to hold onto the end of a rope?' He was a little miffed she didn't trust him to do that much, but he waited out her hesitation, knowing not to push too hard.

Her face suddenly became smooth, her dark eyes clearing. 'Vlad, I'm coming up,' she said as loudly as she dared. There was no answer, and it was hard to know if Vlad had heard. At least Tony's girly wailing has subsided, but the branches were still thrashing to and fro.

'I'm going to use Vlad's rope to climb up,' she said, eyes focusing back on his face. 'All you need to do is keep a good hold of the end of Tony's rope. Don't let go, no matter what happens.'

'Right,' he said.

'I'm going to get you to move over this way more, so you're more or less directly under Tony.'

'You can let go of the rope, Tara, I've got it,' he said quietly. She removed her hands, one at a time.

'Vlad, I'm coming up to give you a hand,' she called again.

This time he seemed to hear her, and called back down, 'That might be a good idea, Tara.' A quick ripple of fear crossed her face and Coop knew it was worse than they'd first imagined.

Tara looped the end of Vlad's rope around her waist to use as a makeshift harness and clipped a carabiner into Vlad's rope, then made a quick ascent up the rock face, finding handholds with nimble fingers, her long legs pushing her up the cliff in record time. At any other time, Coop would've enjoyed the spectacle, her supple body flexing and straining as she pulled herself up. But the situation was too dire for him to take much of that in.

Countless minutes passed as he waited at the bottom, his arms bulging with the strain of holding the rope tight. Lactic acid started to build up. He didn't dare take a hand off to ease the ache. He tried hard to hear what was going on up there, but could only catch a word or two.

'Tony, move your leg ….'

'I got this part over … branch in the … wait …'

'… you're hurting my …' That last one was definitely Tony.

All of a sudden Coop heard scrabbling and a small shower of rocks and dirt rained down on him. He dropped his head and shook his hair, trying to dislodge the debris. Lucky none of it had gone in his eyes.

'Tony, relax, goddamn you,' Vlad said, but at the same time there was more scrabbling and more rocks came tumbling down on top of him. A couple of larger ones landed on the ground around him, bouncing and rolling down the jumble of boulders. Instinct screamed at him to get out of the trajectory of the falling rocks, but he couldn't let go of that rope.

'Tony, stop it, you bloody idiot.' Coop chanced a glance upwards and was just in time to see a rock the size of a fist heading straight for him. Ducking to the right, pain seared through his left shoulder as the rock glanced off him and he stifled a yell of agony. But somehow he managed to hold onto the rope. Then something hit his topmost hand, breaking his grasp, and at the same time a hail of rocks rained down on him, a larger one striking him on the head, followed by more hitting his body.

He let out a bellow of pain, everything going black for uncounted seconds as he fought for consciousness.

'Watch out!' The cry from above brought him back to his senses. He looked up in time to see Tony abseiling down way too fast. He was out of control. Realising too late he'd let go of the rope in the hail of rocks, Coop lunged for a snaking loop of rope as it twisted in front of him, but it flailed out of his reach. Tony was nearly down

'Get out of the way, Cooper.' He ignored Tara's desperate cry, instead making one more grab for the rope. He could stop Tony's out-of-control plunge, if only he could—

Tony landed on top of him with the force of a ten-ton truck, sending them both tumbling down the rocks in a tangle of whirling limbs.

CHAPTER SEVEN

'David!' Tara's strangled shriek rang out through the small clearing. She couldn't hold it back, the visceral sound erupted from her throat with no thought to containing the noise. Craning her neck to see down to the rocks below, she desperately searched for signs of movement. Signs of life. There was nothing. Oh God, Coop was dead. They were both dead. Her heart hammered so loud in her chest she thought it might burst. Adrenaline surged around her body, making her feel superhuman.

'Shit. Shit. Shit!'

'Tara, take it easy,' Vlad said from above her, his voice laced with anxiety and fear.

She ignored him completely. Dropping like a stone, she let herself free-fall downwards, until, mere inches from the bottom she yanked the rope so hard it burned her hand. But it stopped her dead in her tracks and she ignored her rope-burn, too busy unclipping her belay device from the rope to notice. Letting out a loud expletive when her fingers fumbled with the cord, she finally managed to free herself and turned to peer over the jumble of boulders beneath her.

'Fuck, Tara,' Vlad swore as he abseiled down behind her, descending nearly as fast as she had.

'Coop,' she called down into the gloom cast by the shadows of the trees. Her eyes were taking too long to adjust after the glare of the afternoon sun and she swiped a hand across her face to try and clear them. 'Can you hear me?' Vlad landed beside her and started to unclip himself. His breathing rasped in and out, as ragged as her own.

Was that a movement? She focussed hard, squinting her eyes into slits. Yes, one of the shapes she'd thought was just another boulder had definitely moved. Then she heard a low groan. It was Coop. It had to be. He blended into the basalt because he was wearing a black t-shirt, but now he moved she could make out the lightness of his bare arm. He must've rolled over, because his pale features appeared out of the murky dusk.

'Coop, talk to me. Are you okay?'

'Oh God,' Coop groaned again.

'Don't move, I'm coming down to you.' Tara was already bracing her legs, looking for the quickest way to scramble down the jumble of basalt boulders, when Vlad's hand landed on her shoulder. His grip was like iron.

'Settle down, Tara.' His hand forced her shoulder sideways until she had to turn and look at him. The intensity behind his stare shocked her. Gone was his easy-going persona, replaced by a Vlad Tara wasn't sure she'd seen before. His eyes were blue-steel. 'It won't do you, or any of us any good if you hurt yourself too.'

He was right. She took a deep breath. And then another. Vlad was still staring at her.

'Fine,' she snapped. 'What's your plan then?' He exhaled loudly and released her shoulder. Tara had the grace to feel a little abashed. Here she was, letting all her training and practice fly out the window, while Vlad was the only one keeping a level head. She should know better. But it was

Coop down there. Just the thought had her brain all in a scramble.

'There's a track leading down to the waterhole off to the left. It'll be just as quick, and half as treacherous as climbing willy-nilly straight down.'

'Okay. You'd better tell Martin what's going on, I think I can hear him having a conniption. I'll get the first aid kit and meet you down there.' She set off without bothering to see if he'd agreed with her or not.

Making it down the track in jaw-jarring leaps, Tara scrambled over to where Coop lay in the gloom. As she headed towards him, she saw another human-shaped lump appear amongst the rocks next to Coop. It was Tony. He wasn't moving.

'He's alive, I got a pulse,' said Coop. 'But he's got a broken arm at the very least.' Tara saw Tony's left arm was folded at an impossible angle beneath his body.

'Check him first, I'm okay.' Coop levered himself up onto his knees, wincing as he did so.

'You're not okay,' Tara snapped. Even in the gloomy shadows, she could see blood trailing down his temple. She desperately wanted to go to him. Hold him.

But her wayward training, that'd so far been sorely lacking, finally kicked in and she realised the unconscious patient needed immediate attention. At least Coop was conscious and moving. Kneeling next to Tony, she dropped the first aid kit and checked for breathing and a pulse. He was alive. How bad his injuries were remained to be seen. As gently as she could, she put Tony into the recovery position. He didn't even rouse when she moved him. Which wasn't a good sign. Then she patted him down, looking for other broken bones or cuts.

Vlad appeared at her side. 'I've got him, you go see to Coop.' Tara could've hugged Vlad.

Coop was sitting, knees drawn up, one hand clamped over the top of his head. His face was so pale. For once he lacked his normal verve and swagger. Instead, he looked at her with an almost childlike innocence streaked with pain and fear.

'Let me see.' She dragged his hand away from the back of his skull. There was a fair amount of blood matted in his hair, but that was often the case with a head wound. Ever so gently, she probed with tender fingers. There was a large bump, but only a small gash, hidden beneath his mop of hair.

'Oww,' he complained, but it was only a half-hearted protest. 'That's where the rock hit me, when old shit-for-brains over there started kicking them down on top of me.'

'Yeah, he's a fucking idiot,' she agreed vehemently. 'He's supposed to be a cop,' she added. 'How the hell did he end up in the force with that kind of attitude?' That was the least of what she wanted to say about Tony. If he hadn't been lying there unconscious right now, she'd be reaming him out like there was no tomorrow, broken arm or not.

'Tony can be quite ... hot-headed at times, but I've never seen him react like that,' Coop replied. 'He must be *really* scared of heights for him to go that apeshit.'

'Well, he should've told us. If we'd known, we could've been more prepared. I'm not sure anything can account for the fact he completely ignored everything Vlad and I told him, though.' Vlad and Tara had plenty of experience dealing with nervous clientele before. If they'd only suspected, they would've spent more time talking him through it at the top, and Vlad would've stuck to him like glue every step of the way down. But they'd both been lulled into a false sense of security. Tony was a cop for Christ's sake. He'd been trained to handle his fear, to handle any situation. Well, that was the theory anyway. They'd learned the hard way it wasn't always so.

'The stupid bastard unclipped the prusik knot,' Tara admitted. 'That's how he was able to slip down the rope. Why he landed on top of you.' She still couldn't quite believe it herself. But she'd seen it with her own eyes. It'd been a nightmare scene when she'd first arrived to help Vlad untangle him from the tree. Tony had been hanging practically upside down, his face an exquisite shade of beetroot. His eyes wide with fear, and sweat streaming off him.

'Get me outta here,' he'd wailed at her.

'Stay still, goddamn you,' Vlad ground out between clenched teeth, but Tony continued to struggle, making it almost impossible for Vlad to free him from the ropes. Their last resort would be to cut Tony out of the huge twisted mess he'd made, but they really didn't want to do that. It'd leave them with only one viable rope, and that wasn't really an option.

Before she even had time to ask, Vlad had said, 'He undid his prusik knot. So he could get down faster.' Vlad's mouth twisted into an ironic grimace, and his eyebrows lifted so high Tara thought they might disappear off the top of his forehead.

When her eyes followed the rope up to where the prusik knot should be, curled around the climbing rope a foot or so down from the belay device, it was indeed hanging loose. The arrogance of the man. She couldn't find words to express her fury. She'd worked alongside Vlad to free Tony, both of them in complete and stony silence. Then he'd fallen on top of Coop.

'He's just so … ohhh!' She let out an inarticulate grunt. The sheer idiocy of what Tony had done still made her want to hit something.

'He makes me feel like that sometimes, too,' Coop said, a little of his humor returning. His comment brought her back to the task at hand, and she took a few calming breaths. Unclenching her fists, she let them drop to her sides for a few seconds. She needed to check Coop over.

'But I guess everyone is human after all, hey?' He had his back to her, but she heard the rasp in his voice, saw the hunch in his strong shoulders. He sounded battle-worn and incredibly tired, reminding her he was probably in a lot of pain. The words echoed in her ears and it seemed as if there was another message for her in his statement. Was he trying to tell her he was human too? Was it some kind of veiled apology? She gave a tiny shrug, letting the thought go. She could dissect it later.

'Yeah, I guess so.' Tara released some of her anger with her words, focussing instead on Coop.

'Stay still, I need to check the rest of you. Did you get hit anywhere else?'

'I don't really remember. It all happened so fast.'

Running her hands over the rest of his head to make sure there were no more lumps, she had to quell the sudden flip in her stomach as his blonde locks slid between her fingers. It was long enough for her to catch her fingers in the curls. She picked out the odd leaf or stick as she worked over his head, the act strangely intimate. Helpfully, he tipped his head forward so she could cover every inch, right down to the nape of his neck, where the hair turned a darker shade of blonde. How many times has she envisaged doing this exact same thing?

What if she'd lost him today? What if he'd broken his neck in the fall? The thought was unbearable.

'I remember getting smashed on the shoulder,' he said, his voice coming out muffled because his chin was tucked down onto his chest.

'Let me look.' She used her best official tone, trying to gain back some of her equilibrium. She couldn't let him know how rattled the mere act of running her hands through his hair made her.

He got slowly to his knees, sucking in a sharp breath as he did so. He lifted one knee, ready to stand up and then swayed. Tara was quick to get herself under his arm, helping him to stand. Holding him around the waist, she didn't let him go until she was absolutely certain he could stand on his own. His breathing was ragged, teeth clenched together. She gave him a few moments to gather himself.

'I'm good.' He sounded anything but good. Tara knew he probably had a concussion at the very least.

'Can I have a look at the rest of you then?'

'Go ahead.' He lifted the hem of his t-shirt. She helped him, pulling up the black material to expose his stomach and then chest. Oh God. He was covered in bruises and scrapes. For Coop's sake she needed to assess his injuries properly. His life could depend on it. She forced herself to look at him in a cold, clinical light, as if he were just another warm body. Not David Cooper.

There were a lot of bruises and a gash on his left shoulder where a rock had hit him, but there was no swelling or any sign of major damage. The gash would probably need stitches. Gently she felt his stomach, abdomen, and around his back, over where his kidneys and spleen would sit.

'Does this hurt when I push here?' she asked.

'No.' He shook his head. Thank you Lord. It meant there weren't any internal injuries.

'Tara.' Vlad's sharp command made her look up from where she'd been studying Coop's lower back. 'I need your help.'

Tony was awake.

* * *

'If you've given us away, you fucker, I'll break your other fucking arm.' These were the first words Martin uttered when he saw Tony. Coop didn't blame him. He'd had the exact same sentiments when he'd first woken up at the bottom of the cliff. But after he'd spent the last hour or so sitting next to the man, watching him sweat and shake with agony as Vlad and Tara splinted his broken arm, his temper cooled. After all, Coop had a pretty good idea how bad Tony was hurting. He wasn't letting on to Tara or Vlad, but every movement was encompassed with pain. His body felt as if a hundred baseball bats had battered him all at once. It even hurt to breathe. And he didn't even have a cracked rib, like Tony. No, his anger towards Tony had turned to exasperation, coloured with grudging sympathy.

In between bouts of gritting his teeth and trying not to howl like a little girl, Tony revealed how absolutely terrified of heights he was. He'd had a childhood misadventure, where his older brother thought it might be fun to dangle little Tony from a three-story balcony; head first. If only he'd told them, instead of letting his ego get the better of him. But then they were all guilty of doing that at some time in their lives.

'What's the damage,' Martin growled, directing his question to Vlad.

'He's broken his arm in two places and got some cracked ribs,' he replied, standing up to face Martin, putting himself between Tony and the irate man. 'Plus lots of bruising and scratches.'

'Fuck!' Martin swore loudly. He swung away from Vlad and started pacing across the small clearing. 'Fuck, fuck, fuck.'

Graeme stood a few metres off to the left, taking in the whole scene with his normal, calm acceptance. Bruce was hunkered down next to the white-faced Tony, hovering over him protectively. Even though Bruce knew his partner had stuffed up big time, he was still prepared to stand by him.

'He can't continue,' said Vlad, voice deceptively calm.

'Yeah, I get that,' Martin replied and waved him away, resuming his pacing. No one else spoke. 'I don't suppose we can leave him here?' Coop was pretty sure Martin was only half-joking, but Vlad shook his head anyway in a flat no. 'What about Sat Phone reception?'

'Not down here,' Vlad replied. 'You might get it back up the top of The Castle.' Vlad tipped his head skywards. 'But it'd take another team at least a day to get out here, not to mention the extra attention it might attract.' Martin nodded his head, brows drawn down in the scowl that seemed to have become a permanent fixture on his face.

'You'll have to take him back to the car then,' Martin said at last. Vlad drew in a deep breath, as if he were about to argue. But Coop had come to the same conclusion. While they couldn't really spare Vlad, he was the only one capable of navigating back to the car. Out of the corner of his eye, Coop saw Tara make a small movement, as if she were about to step forward. She wouldn't like this any more than Vlad did. One glance at her face told him her blood was boiling with suppressed rage. Silently he prayed she'd keep her mouth shut, just this once. Martin wouldn't welcome any argument. Coop had seen him in this kind of mood only once before and anyone who'd gone near him that day had been flayed to within an inch of their life by his vicious tongue.

'Just leave me here, I'll be fine till you can get a team to come and collect me,' Tony broke into the conversation.

'Shut the fuck up, Russo.' Martin didn't even so much as glance his way, but his attitude held all the menace of a snarling, leashed lion, just waiting for any excuse to pounce.

'I'd rather send Tara, but what if Tony collapses? At least you'd stand a chance of getting him up on your shoulder or something,' Martin continued, after he'd taken a deep, controlling breath. 'And much as I'd love to be able to go on alone from here, I have no idea which way is north. I can't take the risk of the rest of us getting lost and stumbling around in this God-forsaken wilderness for days. We need Tara to show us the way.'

In the end Vlad gave a desultory nod. He was a smart guy, he'd done the maths. It was the right answer.

'Tara?' Vlad locked eyes with her. That single word, together with their glance held so many questions. Coop was a little jealous when he understood there was some kind of wordless exchange going on between them.

'It's the only way, Vlad,' she said coming towards the big man and putting a hand on his shoulder. Damn, that was definitely jealousy stabbing through his gut as Tara touched Vlad. He looked down at the ground, hoping no one else had seen the flare of hot emotion in his eyes. 'I've given him the strongest painkillers we've got in the first aid kit. It should keep the edge off for a good while,' she continued. 'You'd better get going. You've still got a couple of hours of decent light left, you should be able to make it more than half way back to the car by then.'

'What happens when it gets dark?' Tony's question was low and desultory.

'We keep going by torchlight,' Vlad replied. 'We can't spend a night out here with you in this condition. It's too dangerous. Anyway, it's a good way to keep you awake for the next six or so hours. You've had a concussion, so we would've had to do that anyway.'

Tony released a groan.

'Are you sure?' Bruce stood up, concern written in the hunch of his shoulders. When Vlad nodded, he said, 'Then I should come with you. I can make my own way back after we get to the car.'

'Not if you value your life, Marchesi.' Martin's voice was deep and gravelly. Coop knew it wouldn't bode well for

Bruce if he disobeyed. 'You're needed here. On this mission. Remember the mission?'

Bruce and Martin glared at each other for a full ten seconds before Bruce finally dropped his gaze.

'Good,' was all Martin said.

Vlad pulled some maps from the top pocket of his backpack and he and Tara put their heads together over them. Vlad pointed out landmarks and Tara nodded, her dark auburn ponytail bobbing in time with her head.

She hadn't said much in the past half an hour, but Coop knew how hard she must've been biting her tongue. She'd never been one to take a back seat when they'd been in the force together. Especially when it came to ego-driven, chauvinistic guys like Martin, Tony and Bruce. Come to think of it, she must've been biting her tongue this whole week. Which just went to prove she *had* changed. Her ideals weren't quite so hard-edged and black and white as they used to be. Another piece of evidence to uphold his theory this two years away from the force *had* been good for her.

She squatted down to peer intently at what Vlad was showing her and he was drawn again to her features. Such an angelic face. His breath almost caught in his throat at her beauty. And those eyes, a rich, dark chocolate, so deep a man could easily drown in them. Even hunkered down like that, her legs curled underneath, it was obvious how tall and statuesque she was. Then she smiled at something Vlad said, flashing that hundred-watt grin, and Coop was suddenly reminded of that exact same smile he'd seen on a woman on TV the other night. Megan Gale, an Australian model. Nah, come to think of it, Megan wasn't a patch on the woman in front of him now, Tara was the most beautiful woman he'd ever laid eyes on.

He'd been of two minds when he'd heard Tara would be continuing on with them. He'd get to stay near her for just a little longer. But more importantly he was worried. The voice of doubt was speaking double time, telling him he needed to make sure she didn't put herself in any danger. But of course she'd do whatever she damn well pleased, no matter what he told her to do. This was intended to be a search and locate mission only, and once they'd found the terrorist camp they were supposed to contact HQ and let them send in the cavalry. *Supposed to.* Coop knew missions often didn't turn out how they were *supposed* to.

He'd managed to convince Tara his injuries were superficial and he was fine to continue. It was a lie. Given a few days he would've been okay. But right now he ached from head to foot. That worried him. Not because he mightn't be able to look after himself if the need arose, but because he might not be able to look after Tara.

Tara stood up, folded the map and continued to listen to Vlad. Coop went to move, to lever himself off the ground, and had to bite back a bark of pain. Goddamnit, this wasn't good. But he'd have to conquer this, not let it show. There was no way he was going to let them send him back too. No way in hell.

* * *

'Oww!' Coop winced. Tara pretended to ignore him.

'Stop being such a baby,' she replied, dipping the rag back into the cool water.

'What? I'm not ....' He stopped complaining and gritted his teeth, glaring daggers at her. God, his eyes were blue. Not dark blue like the ocean, well not today at least. More like the clear crystalline blue of cut glass, light and luminescent. When he looked up at her it was like shards of steel piercing right through her soul. Shaking off the distracting thought, she bent over and continued working on his back, cleaning all the dried blood away from his wounds.

'I'm being as careful as I can.'

'Really.' His tone dripped sarcasm.

'Yes, really. If you like, I could get Martin to come and do it instead?'

'No thanks,' he replied quickly.

Coop was sitting on a small boulder at the edge of the waterhole while she washed his cuts and bruises. She'd already cleaned and dressed the gash on his head as best she could through his thick hair.

'This place has lost all its appeal now,' he said. It took her a few seconds to grasp his meaning. Tara stopped what she was doing to look around.

'It's still beautiful, though. Just because Tony's a complete arsehole, you can't blame it on this place,' she replied. She was using the sparkling clear water from the waterhole to wash him. The water was safe she'd assured him, clean and parasite free this far from human habitation. She might even take a swim afterwards to wash two days' worth of sweat and grime from her body.

It was early evening, the golden rays of the setting sun slanted through the trees and lent an orange hue to their trunks. The suffocating heat of midday was slowly abating, leaving behind a balmy humidity that was almost enjoyable. Martin, Graeme and Bruce were resting back at the camp they'd set up a few hundred metres downstream, on a flat grassy area.

Hopefully they didn't sit on their butts the whole time she and Coop were away. Now Vlad was gone, she needed them to pick up some of the slack. Which meant putting up their own tents and helping with the food.

She'd cajoled Coop into coming back to the waterhole to tend to his wounds. It'd be better for him if Martin wasn't watching the whole procedure with his rapacious gaze. And she could relax a little too. This job was going to be hard enough as it was. Being so close to Coop. Having to touch him. The last thing she needed was the other men scrutinising her. To see how much self-control she had to expend to keep her fingers doing what they were supposed to. All this exposed flesh was making her hands itch. She wanted to run them over the taught expanse of his impressive trapezoid muscle and across his shoulder. Instead she took to exploring him with her eyes.

Apart from the new bruises running down his left side—which must've been where he landed when Tony knocked him down—and pockmarking the breadth of his back, there were plenty of older scars as well. An impressive one four or five inches long ran across his upper bicep. A knife wound perhaps. She winced at the sight. Another ragged one just beneath his left scapula, also looked like he'd been cut with something. These scars were a part of Coop, part of the dangerous life he lived as a cop. Some cops she'd known wore them as a badge of honour; flaunted them. But not Coop. He never made a fuss. In fact he'd dismiss them with self-deprecating humour, saying they were nothing. But they weren't nothing.

Then her gaze dropped lower and she saw it. The scar from the gunshot wound. From the bullet he'd taken protecting her. Her eyes were drawn to it like a moth to a flame. It was ragged and round, about six or seven centimetres across, but well healed. The bullet had passed through his oblique abdominal muscle just above his pelvis—thank God—not doing too much internal damage. It'd nicked his small intestine, but not much else. She knew this because she'd drilled the attending doctor for every last detail while Coop lay in his hospital bed recovering. While the guilt ate through her own guts like acid.

This was the exit wound around the back, and if she tuned him around she'd see the much smaller entry wound above his hip. Her finger reached out and traced the raised skin of the scar, gentle on his skin, just a whisper. Images came of Coop, lying on the floor at the hotel after he'd been shot, blood pooling in a thick viscous mass beneath him. Coop lying in a hospital bed, deathly pale and unmoving. God, she couldn't go there, not now. She thought she'd dealt with this, got over the fact she was the cause of Coop nearly dying. *Shit.*

'Are you ever going to finish back there?' His half-question, half-accusation had her rocking back on her heels in guilty shock.

'What?' She recovered quickly. 'Yep, all done.' Tara put on her most nurse-like voice, not wanting him to know how much the sight of that scar affected her. 'Now let me have a better look at your shoulder.'

'Do you have to?'

'Well, we could leave it the way it is, let it get infected, which will make it hurt ten times worse than it does now, and possibly end up in blood poisoning. Would you rather do that?'

'No.' His response was that of a resigned man being led off to the gallows, but he did turn around and offer her his shoulder. It was a nasty gash, the skin ragged and torn, but at least it wasn't deep.

'You were lucky. More of a glancing blow,' she said, using tender fingers to check for any underlying lumps or broken bones.

'Yeah, that's my middle name all right. Lucky.'

'It should probably have stitches to tidy it up, but I'm not going to do that out here, so I'll just put some steri-strips on it and a good bandage. That'll have to do until we get back to town.'

'Oh, I love it when you talk dirty.' He turned around and gave her a very Coop-like leer. 'Actually, now I think of it ....' His gaze flickered up and down her body. 'You'd look damned good in a nurses uniform.' He had the audacity to wink at her.

'Oh you ....' She swatted at his sore shoulder, just hard enough to get a reaction.

'Oww. Sorry, sorry, I'll be good,' he said in feigned sincerity.

She bent down and rummaged in the first aid kit for the steri-strips, hiding her smile. One thing was for sure, at least she knew the concussion hadn't affected him. He was back to his normal self. It felt right somehow, this familiar banter with Coop. Tara drew in a deep breath and was surprised to discover a weight lifting off her shoulders. A weight she'd been carrying around for the past few days.

'This might hurt a bit,' she warned, as she got ready to clean his wound.

'Yeah, yeah,' his reply was deceptively blithe. 'Get on with it, woman.' But as she touched the antiseptic to his skin, his body tensed beneath her, his back muscles going rigid. No sound left his lips, however.

She was as gentle as possible, but still a sheen of perspiration broke out on the back of his neck. Gritting her teeth, she continued her ministrations. She didn't want to do this. She didn't want to be hurting him. Every instinct was screaming at her to stop. It was tearing her apart every time he flinched. But it had to be done, and she was the best person to do it. Taking a deep breath, she willed the trembling in her hand to stop. Where was that hard-nosed, impersonal Tara when she needed her? Her mind wouldn't allow her to shut off the fact that it was Coop she was tending to.

At last she put the final piece of adhesive tape over the edge of the sterile dressing and leaned backwards.

'Finished, Coop.'

He exhaled loudly and his shoulders drooped. 'Thanks, Tara. You did a great job.' He stood up and turned around, taking both her shoulders in each hand. 'I know that was hard for you.'

Was he a mind reader now? She raised an eyebrow, ready to give some kind of scathing reply, but something in his gaze stilled the words on her lips. Those blue eyes were boring into her again and her heartbeat ratcheted up a few notches.

He was standing mere inches away. With no shirt on. His solid male chest in full view, right in front of her. The look he gave her made her breath stop in her throat. It was like being caught by a large fishhook right in the centre of her chest.

The sun had set over the horizon now, and in the deep valley a grey dusk descended quickly, engulfing them with the softness of nightfall. Things started to blur around the edges.

Everything but Coop, that was.

He was a tangible, physical presence. And he was touching her, holding her.

'I haven't checked the front of you yet,' she managed to push the words through lips that for some reason didn't work properly. That sounded wrong. 'I mean … I need to ….'

'Go ahead, babe, I won't stop you.' His voice took on a gravelly resonance that stirred something deep in her belly. Lip's curling up in a smile, he stared down at her with growing amusement. He took hold of her hand and brought it to his chest, pressing her palm over the top of his heart.

'Well, examine me then,' he said softly. Taking his hand from hers he placed it back on her shoulder again, and waited. To see what she'd do. Her hand lay over the hard muscle of his pec, the warmth of his skin burning a brand into her palm. Logic screamed at her to move, snatch her hand away and step backwards out of his grasp. But it was as if invisible walls held her against her will. She was ensnared by the sudden darkening in his eyes, from sky blue to indigo. By the flare of heat igniting within them.

Lowering her gaze, she stared at her hand laying against his chest. Of their own accord her fingers moved against his skin, trailing over his chest. Silky blond hairs curled beneath her fingertips. She heard his intake of breath as her fingers caressed, a sharp hissing sound. He watched her as she explored him.

Lower and lower, her fingers traced the outline of each muscle on his stomach. He sure did have an impressive six-pack. It was even more well-defined than she remembered. He was fit and toned, a striking specimen of a male. If anything, the years had given him more solidity, a gravitas that made him seem even more powerful.

The awareness of his firm flesh beneath her fingertips was doing odd things to her insides. A fluttery feeling invaded her stomach. A heat spread outwards from her abdomen, making her limbs feel languorous and rubbery. This was how Coop had made her feel the other night, when he'd kissed her. Only this time it felt much more … dangerous. She no longer had complete control over her reactions to him. Her body was taking over, dispelling her mind's misgivings.

This time, if things got out of control, she wasn't sure she could stop them. Wasn't sure she wanted to.

One of his hands came up underneath her chin, tipping it up, forcing her lips towards his.

'Tell me to stop and I will.' His words flowed over her like a feather trailing over exposed skin, raising goose bumps as it went. Giving an almost imperceptible shake of her head, she stared at his lips, so close in front of her face. Slightly parted, and no longer smiling.

He closed the gap, his mouth taking hers, rough and demanding, no longer waiting for permission. He took what he wanted. And she gave it to him. The blonde stubble from his three-day growth rasped her chin, down her cheek, igniting tremors of sensation that drilled down to her legs, making her unsteady on her feet. Taking her breath away.

Tara couldn't believe Coop was willing to do this again, after the way she'd treated him only a few nights ago. After the horrible things she'd said to him. But he'd always been able to see through her bullshit. She'd been so desperate to drive him away, but he knew better. He'd been willing to wait for her to sort through her feelings and come back to her senses.

And now she was desperately scrambling to remember the reasons she'd wanted to drive him away in the first place. Back then it'd been because Coop was her partner. Because she hadn't wanted to jeopardise their partnership in any way. Because partners couldn't be lovers. But he wasn't her partner any more. And after her little epiphany this afternoon, she knew she was never going back to being a cop. There was no chance of Coop ever becoming her police partner again. So that reason, which'd seemed so solid before, now leant no weight to the reason why she should keep her distance from Coop.

He pulled back from their kiss, his breath rasping, eyes dark pools in the dying light, asking the question that was also on his lips.

'Tara?'

The way he said her name, all husky and slow, felt like it's own form of foreplay. Igniting her from the inside out.

It was now almost dark, a grey gloaming left over from the departed sun gave just enough light so Tara was able to make out the solid forms of the boulders around the clearing and the length of the tall tree trunks reaching for the sky. And Coop. She could see Coop right there in front of her.

And right now, right here, she could come up with no sensible reason to say no. Especially not when her body was screaming, making her want to press herself along his chest, feel the heat of his skin against hers. Right now, nothing else seemed to matter. All her petty reasons to push Coop away seemed exactly that. Petty.

Standing on tiptoe she dragged his mouth back to hers in way of an answer. *Yes.* She didn't know where this was going, but her answer was *yes.*

Without breaking their kiss, he walked her slowly backwards until she felt the long grass lick around her legs. Pausing just long enough to kneel, he pulled her down in the ferns and undergrowth with him, the musky scent of the damp earth filling her nostrils, mingling with the scent of Coop, hovering above her. A spicy scent, reminding her of newly-cut straw drying in the sun, mixed with the sweat of this afternoon's misadventure. She'd never minded the smell of fresh sweat on a man.

'What if they come looking for us?' The sudden intrusive thought made her try and sit up.

'They won't.' Tara relaxed back down, believing him. He was right, Martin would be too caught up in worrying about whether Tony had jeopardised the mission. Bruce would be worrying about the exact same thing, but for different reasons. And Graeme ... Well Graeme would respect their privacy if nothing else.

Using his arms, he lowered himself down with her, laying the length of his body over hers. It was then she noticed him wince, closing his eyes for a second, holding back the pain.

Oh God, how could she have forgotten so quickly? He was hurt, he shouldn't be doing this. She started to push him away.

'Your shoulder, Coop.'

'It's fine,' he growled. 'You can worry about my shoulder later, Tara.' He hadn't budged an inch when she'd pushed him, and now he settled his body more securely above hers, hips extending over the planes of her stomach, chest crushing her breasts.

'I've never felt better,' he murmured as his lips came down to claim hers once more.

CHAPTER EIGHT

Coop sensed it the instant she stopped fighting her misgivings. In between one heartbeat and the next, she made a decision. He couldn't quite believe his luck. But he wasn't going to stop and analyse the moment; to wonder what'd made her change her mind.

Kissing her was a risk. A calculated one, but a risk nonetheless. And God he was glad he'd taken it. The sheer torture of Tara's presence while she bent over him, her fingers so gentle and tender on his skin, had rubbed his nerves raw until he couldn't stand it any longer. He'd hardly even noticed the pain as she'd dabbed on the antiseptic, all his senses attuned instead to Tara and her lithe, luscious body standing so close to him.

He had to hold her, take her, and damn the consequences.

Now she was lying beneath him, her long legs stretched down the length of his. She pulled his mouth down onto hers, her arms wrapped tightly around his neck and nipped at his tongue, his lips, as she kissed him. Grinding herself against his erection, it sent sharp spikes of desire coursing through him. Jesus, he was so hard. She was driving him crazy with her need. There was an urgency in Tara tonight that hadn't been there the other night when they'd kissed. It called to something equally urgent in Coop, compelling him to gather

her even closer in his arms, needing to feel her soft, warm body tight against his.

He wanted to see her naked. Forgetting everything else, he leant all his weight into his left arm, meaning to reach down and start undoing her shorts.

'Oww.' His grunt of pain was involuntary, and it was out before he could stop it. He'd forgotten all about his sore shoulder. He went back to trailing his mouth down Tara's neck, ignoring the pain, but she stiffened beneath him. Goddamnit! Why couldn't he have just kept quiet?

Instead of pulling away, as he expected, she said, 'Let me try something.' She braced her legs and then she started to twist, until he was the one lying on his back in the soft undergrowth, and Tara was on top. 'Better?'

'Mmm hmm,' he replied, a shiver of anticipation running through him. Tara had always been a take-charge kind of girl.

Were they really going to do this? Out here in the jungle? Coop knew Martin wouldn't come looking for them. Coop and Tara barely even registered on Martin's radar right now. He'd be wound up too tight worrying about the *mission* to worry about what they were up to. Graeme would know better than to come looking for them, his astute gaze missed nothing. And bumbling Bruce wouldn't have any inkling of what they might be doing. He sure as hell wouldn't come looking for them unless Martin told him too. He'd be too busy worrying about Tony, and how badly he'd stuffed up the mission, as well as his partner's chances of remaining in the terrorist unit after such a huge mistake. Truth be told, Coop should be worried about the mission too. But right now, nothing else in this whole wide world mattered as much as being here. With Tara.

This might be his one and only chance and he was going to grab it with both hands.

Tara sat up, and Coop grabbed her hips.

'It's all right, I'm not going anywhere,' she murmured. He relaxed his grip. In the low light it was hard to make out exactly what Tara was doing. He could vaguely see her outline against the trees and sky above. Was she … Holy mother of … She'd just taken off her shirt and bra and brought both Coop's hands up to cup her breasts. Full, round and ripe. He ran his thumbs over both her nipples and they puckered under the attention. A low moan escaped her, and she tipped her head back, twisting in ecstasy as he continued to skim over her nipples and around the soft flesh underneath each breast. Her moan ignited a burning fire within his veins.

Tara ran her hands over his chest, gliding down his abdomen and with her sure, steady fingers undid his belt buckle. Then she left him for a second and was tugging down his jeans, pulling them over his feet. She stood up and unzipped her own shorts and he could see her silhouetted against the grey sky above. God she was beautiful. More beautiful than he could've ever imagined.

'Have you got a ….' She didn't have to finish her question, he knew what she was asking.

'In my wallet. Back pocket of my jeans.' She twisted around and dug though his pocket, then her nimble fingers were back on his chest, her teeth tearing at the condom package.

Those nimble fingers ran down his belly, circling his erection, playing with him, touching him.

'Tara,' he growled. His demand drew forth a giggle, but it also stopped her erotic teasing and she gently sheathed him with the condom. Ever so slowly, she lowered herself back down, straddling him. The feel of her naked body pressed along the full length of him nearly sent him over the edge, and it was his turn to moan, deep and low in his throat. He reached up and pulled her mouth down to his lips. Her hips ground against his in an almost unconscious rhythm.

Tempting him. Arousing him even further, letting his cock slide against her taught stomach as she moved. Oh God, he needed her to stop doing that. It'd been a long time. A very long time, since he'd been with a woman. If she kept that up he wasn't sure how long he'd be able to take it.

'Tara ….'

'I want this as much as you do,' she said, gliding down his body until he could feel her centre resting on the very tip of his erection.

'It's been a long time. I'm not sure how long I can—'

'Shhh.' She placed a finger to his lips, but he could still feel her hovering above him, so wet and ready. He couldn't stand it any longer, pulling on her hips, he pushed inside her, revelling in the tight, burning heat that engulfed him. She cried out as he entered her. A raw sound that pierced through him. Then she started to slide up and down in slow, measured movements.

He watched her face as she moved. Her lips slightly parted, she panted out in little gasps with every upward thrust he made.

How could one woman be both so angelic and so ferocious all at the same time? It was the last coherent thought he had, as primal pleasure overtook every other sensation in his body. He raced towards that knife edge, unable to stop now, even if he wanted to. He could hear Tara panting above him, moving quicker and quicker as she too came close to climax.

He thrust, once, twice, then like a runaway train, he crashed over the brink and his body became rigid, sensation overwhelming him.

Tara responded to his climax with a loud gasp, then she clamped around him, oh so tight, as waves of pleasure charged through her.

'Coop!' She cried out his name as she collapsed on top of him.

* * *

It was the annoying high-pitched whine of a mosquito that finally roused Tara from her torpor. She was half-lying on top of Coop, as he lay sprawled in the tall grassy undergrowth. Swatting the mossie away, she went to sit up. Coop's arm tightened around her waist, holding her against him.

'Where are you going?' His voice was a rumble from deep within his chest. A very contented rumble. She stopped struggling to get up and snuggled back into him. At least the night was still pleasantly warm. If you were going to have sex outside, this was a damn good place to have it. The only problem was the amount of animal life the balmy night brought to life. Soon the place would be teeming with creepy crawlies.

'We're going to be eaten alive if we don't put some clothes on,' she said. Truth be told, she didn't ever want to move from this spot. Didn't want to go back to reality. She wanted to stay in this cocoon of their lovemaking afterglow forever. Breathe in Coop's essence. Listen to his strong, beating heart beneath her ear.

'I'll protect you,' he countered, rolling her over and covering every inch of her naked skin with his own. She giggled.

'Sorry that was a little … faster than I anticipated,' he said into her ear. 'I've not had too much practice lately.'

'Oh.' She tilted her head to the side so she could look into his face. 'I thought you and Jade …' She let the rest of her sentence trail off, confused.

'No, we haven't. We've only been on a few dates. It was Jade who started it back up. I didn't want to … I'm just not sure whether I want to.' Her heart did a few happy skips at the thought Coop hadn't in fact slept with Jade.

And now she'd jumped in with both feet and probably tangled things up even worse for him. Should she apologise?

How could she feel guilty about what they'd just done together? It'd been beautiful.

'And when I found out I was being sent to Byron. Well, you know. It's kind of ancient history now that ....'

His unsaid words hung between them. Tara was in Byron. And they had unfinished business. But what exactly had he been hoping to get from her? Answers? Probably. Closure? She'd left without much explanation, she owed him that much. So yeah, he deserved closure. But what else had he been hoping for. This? Had he been hoping for sex with Tara? Or was there more? Was he hinting he still had feelings for her?

Now wasn't the time or place to investigate that thorny issue.

Keeping her voice light, she said, 'Doesn't matter. Quick and dirty can be just as much fun as slow and sensuous.'

'Shall we try for the slow and extended version? Like, right now?' he said eagerly.

'And have Martin walk in and interrupt us?' They'd been gone a long time now. Definitely longer than tending to a few scratches should take. Her hand pressed against his chest, ready to push him away from her. 'I don't think so.'

'Stay. Just for a few more minutes.' The note of entreaty in his voice pulled unexpectedly at her heartstrings. So she snuggled back down into the grass, stretching out her long legs, their feet entwining together. Laying her head on his chest she went back to enjoying the sound of his heart, thudding gently in his ribcage. His arms curled protectively around her and she was lost in the peaceful bliss of their quiet moment together.

'Tell me about the dream.' His words were a quiet swish of breath against her ear. She drew in a long, deep sigh.

It'd only been a matter of time before he asked. But where to start?

'Sometimes, I dream about my brother.'

'Which one?'

'Kane, my younger brother. The one who died.' She'd told Coop the barest details about her brother back when they'd been partners. That Kane had only been a teenager when he died. It'd been one of the few things she wouldn't discuss openly with him. She never talked about Kane. Not to anyone. It was just too painful. And apart from that, she scorned the thought of anyone pitying her because she'd lost a brother. Pity made you weak, smaller in other people's eyes.

'Oh.' His simple reply was soft and full of compassion, and set her heartstrings dancing again. Perhaps she'd misjudged him. Perhaps, if she'd been brave enough to share her loss with him back then, it might not have been pity he offered, but some sorely needed comfort instead. Things might've been so different between them.

Time to regret her choices later. But at least she could let him into some of her secrets now, even if the past couldn't be repaired so easily.

'You've got a tattoo. Of his name.' He touched her back where the tattoo rested next to her backbone, his fingers soft and warm against her skin. 'I saw it on the beach the day you took me surfing.'

'Yeah, I got it just after I moved here to Byron.'

'Do you want to tell me how he died?' Again there was that soft compassion in his voice, letting her know it was okay, even if she chose not to tell him about it.

'He was shot by a gang of ignorant thugs in a drive-by gone wrong.' She couldn't keep the brittle edge out of her voice. Even after all those years, it still hurt like a knife thrust to her solar plexus to think about his senseless death. And how he'd lain on the sidewalk, his life ebbing out of him, and no one had done anything to help him. So senseless. 'Such a waste of a beautiful life.'

She hadn't realised she'd said that out loud until he replied, 'Oh, Tara.'

Out of nowhere, tears threatened. This wouldn't do, she shouldn't be crying. Not after what she and Coop had just done. Seconds ago she'd been feeling euphoric and now look at her, ready to blubber like a baby over something that'd happened a lifetime ago. Dragging her hand over Coop's chest, she used the solid thud of his heartbeat under her fingers to ground herself, bring her back from the precipice, and pull herself together.

'But it's not his death that worries me in my dreams. When he's in my dreams, they're usually nice, safe dreams. We just sit and talk, and he tells me things.'

'What kind of things?'

'We talk about him, and my parents. He tells me about myself. Stuff he thinks I need to hear. What happened in the past … And about what might happen in the future.'

'Okay,' he said slowly. 'That's a good thing, isn't it? At least you haven't forgotten him. And future predictions are ….' She waited for him to scoff at the thought. 'Well, who's to say what you're capable of in your dreams.' Ha, he'd neatly skirted the issue, but at least he hadn't dismissed her out of hand. 'But none of that sounds nightmarish. What was so bad about your dream the other night?'

He'd cut right to the chase. Taking a deep breath, she said, 'You were in it.'

'Yeah, I got that part.'

'You were … hurt.' Her voice became small as she remembered the vivid details of his tortured body.

'And you were worried about me?'

'Yes.'

'Hurt how?'

'I … I don't know,' she faltered. Now that wasn't the complete truth, but how was she supposed to tell him he'd been tortured and beaten by one of the terrorists. It sounded absurd even in her own head. There was no way she was going to say the words out loud. The probability of them even catching up to the group way out here in the jungle was pretty thin. Let alone that one of them might get their hands on an armed cop and abduct him. It was ridiculous.

'And me being hurt scared you?' he prodded.

'Yes.' Her voice was still barely a whisper.

'Why, Tara? Did I die? Are you worried your dream is a premonition?'

'God, no.' Of course Coop wasn't going to die. A small huff of impatience left her lips. How was she going to explain this to him without sounding completely insane? If she told him what Claire said, that Kane was her guardian angel, looking out for her, there was no doubt in her mind he *would* laugh out loud at her. And why wouldn't he, she'd never given this kind of mumbo jumbo a second thought back when she'd been his partner. Actually, she'd actively shunned the whole idea. Why would he ever accept she'd done a complete about face and become a believer now?

'I'm not going to die, Tara. Perhaps your subconscious is confusing your brother's death with me? I intend to stick around for a long, long time. Especially if you promise you'll do this,' he ran his hand seductively over her hip and down the length of her thigh, 'again soon.'

'I'm not confusing you with my brother,' she said, doing her best to ignore his hand. 'That wasn't it at all.' And she was sure that was the truth. But how did she explain the feeling of Kane trying to warn her of something imminent. How to explain the dark foreboding that'd seeped from the poster on the wall into her soul? She'd been going over and over the dream in her head today, trying to decipher its meaning. She couldn't tell him to stay away from the terrorists. It was his job to chase them. Her stupid dream wouldn't be enough to change that. Not even the fact she was scared enough to suggest it would stop him. And she couldn't blame him. If the tables had been turned, and he was the one trying to tell her not to do her job, she would've shrugged off his well-meant concern too.

But she still had to try. Try and warn him.

'Coop, you have to stay away—'

'Where the bloody hell are you two?' Bruce's voice broke through the jungle, stopping her mid-sentence.

* * *

His shoulder hurt like a bitch. Coop rolled over *again*, to find a more comfortable position in his tiny bivouac. Nope, that didn't work either. Now his bruised ribs were taking the brunt of his weight and that hurt just as much. He sat up. Maybe it was time to admit he needed those painkillers after all. Tara left them in the little alcove outside his tent, with a bottle of water. She recognised he'd need them sooner or later. God he hated it when she was right.

He unzipped the tent fly and reached out a hand, feeling around until the foil package crinkled under his fingertips. Sitting in the dark enclosed space of his bivouac he tipped his head back and swallowed the two little pills, chasing them down with a large gulp of water.

The sounds of the night crept into his tent as he sat and waited for the pills to take effect. There was a buzzing and rustling against the tent material above his head. Some kind of large—and probably extremely ugly—jungle insect trying to get inside. Most likely to suck his blood. He'd never encountered so many unfriendly, and overly large bugs in his life before. And the spiders. Ugh. An uncontrolled shiver ran over him at the thought of the big hairy monsters he'd seen so far. He was doing his damnedest to pretend they didn't scare the living bejesus out of him every time he came across one, but he could tell by Tara's suppressed giggles and

Graeme's amused glances, he wasn't doing a good enough job. Bloody hell. Jungle living took some getting used to.

Martin tossed and turned in his sleeping bag. His boss obviously wasn't sleeping either, worrying about what they were going to find tomorrow. If the group they'd spotted was the terrorist cell, then the likelihood they'd heard something from today's debacle was high.

So they could be packing up their camp this very second. Leaving no trace behind. Not even waiting for dawn. While Martin and his crew had to wait for daylight because they couldn't risk moving at night. Not in unknown territory, towards an unknown quarry. It would've been suicide.

Coop felt for Martin. Understood his fear the terrorists were moving out of range; escaping their carefully planned trap. Martin didn't like to lose. And he sure as hell wouldn't want to go back and tell his superior he'd lost the cell, not after he'd been so close. Coop could almost smell the desperation oozing from his tent walls.

But even as Coop listened to Martin's restless movements, his mind couldn't stay focussed on the ramifications of how badly they might've stuffed up today. It was already wandering onto more pleasurable topics.

The topic of him and Tara having sex, to be exact.

Before this afternoon, he would never have believed the wildest, most amazing woman he'd ever known, would've come to him so unfettered and willing. For so long, he'd believed her lost to him.

And then afterwards she'd surprised him again, by telling him about her brother, Kane. What a way to lose someone you loved. And she'd been so young, too. If only she'd told him about it earlier, when they'd still been partners. He might've been able to … He wasn't sure what he would've done. Perhaps nothing.

Tara didn't talk much about her mother, either. All he knew for sure was she'd just up and walked out one day, leaving Tara's father, Vincent, to raise his four kids alone. Coop had a suspicion Tara probably stepped in to fill her mother's shoes. There was an ache low down in his chest as he thought about a young, vulnerable, naïve Tara being abandoned by her mother. Then taking up the responsibilities of caring for herself and her younger brother. No wonder she grieved for her younger brother. She would've been almost like a mother to him. And no wonder Tara had become tough and resilient. She hadn't really had a choice.

Coop thought he remembered Tara telling him her mother had been a cop too, in her younger days. Something about the fact she always regretted giving up being in the force when she started a family. Perhaps this was why Tara put up such fortified walls around her heart. She'd been brought up to believe a woman couldn't have both a career in the police force and a family.

He was falling for a woman who was afraid to love him back.

The pills finally started to do their job, and Coop lay back down, willing himself to fall asleep. But his eyes weren't ready to close yet. Now he worried about tomorrow, his brain turning different scenarios over and over in his head, like a dog constantly digging up and then reburying an old bone. To be specific, he was worried about Tara. He recognised she had that reckless streak, which appeared at the most inopportune moments. He was worried if they did find the terrorists still camped down-stream, she'd want to be involved in whatever plan they devised.

His injuries, although not serious, might also slow him down.

Would he be strong enough to protect her? Tara would've punched him in his sore shoulder if she suspected he was entertaining that thought. She was so determined to look after herself. Such a tomboy. Albeit a beautiful tomboy. It probably stemmed from the fact she had two older brothers. They'd imbued her with a lot of their strength and masculine ways.

Tara was so lucky, to have two older brothers to look up to. Being an only child, it was something he'd often wished for himself. A brother to share in life's ups and downs. To have someone to tell his secrets to when he was younger. The simple pleasure of stomping in a muddy puddle. Equal disgust and fascination watching a spider drain the blood from a fly caught in its web. The sheer physical satisfaction of a good wrestle for possession of the football on the back lawn. And later, when he was a young adolescent, he'd hungered for a brother to share his burden. The family shame of his father's drunken rages. Then perhaps he wouldn't have had to sit alone in his room, trying to block the sound of his father beating his mother, using a pillow to cover his head.

Coop had been too scared to bring any friends home. Scared and ashamed they might find out what kind of monster his father was.

But at least he'd been able to protect his mother, in the end. Come to think of it, his mother had accused him of having a hero complex. Much like Tara was always accusing him of wanting to shield her from the harsher realities of life. But at least his mother said it with an exasperated, half-proud sigh. Unlike Tara who made it sound like he was demeaning her abilities somehow.

Coop sighed. Twisting around in his sleeping bag, he tried to rid himself of the spectre of his father's face, twisted in an alcoholic rage bearing down on him. Why was he dragging up the past now? It'd do him no good, and he needed to sleep.

But his father's face wouldn't leave him. Coop was transported back to that night, the day after he'd turned twelve. Listening to the sounds of his father's fist pounding again and again into flesh. The small whimpers of pain his mother couldn't smother through his father's snarls of rage. After so many nights of sitting in his room listening, but not doing anything, he never knew why this night was different. But something inside him finally snapped. Throwing his bedroom door open he'd run down the corridor and into the dark, dingy kitchen. There was his mother, on the floor, cowering in the corner between two kitchen cupboards. Travis loomed over her, spewing a string of swear words, his shoulder leant up against the fridge for support as he drunkenly waved a fist in front of her face. Maggie didn't look at him, her chin was tucked right down into her chest, her arms hugged her knees tight as she tried to make herself as small a target as possible. She looked like a wounded animal, terrified beyond reason, glued to the spot by fear as the predator toyed with his prey. Only the predator wasn't a vicious animal. It was his father.

Coop looked around and his eyes came to rest on the top drawer, left half open. Cutlery lay strewn all over the floor, glinting dully in the dim light. Amongst it all lay a large carving knife. Coop picked it up and held it in his small fist. It made him feel brave.

'Leave her alone,' he'd shouted at his father's back.

'What do you want, boy?' His father slurred, turning slowly around to face him. 'Get back to your room, *boy*.' Travis rasped the last word out, making it sound filthy and patronising, like Coop was worth less than his spit. Coop's hand tightened on the knife and he bared his teeth at his father. A grin split Travis' face, the glazed eyes brightening at the sight of his son standing there with a knife in his hand. Defying him.

'Leave her alone,' Coop said again, his voice small in the suddenly quiet kitchen.

'Well, well, boy. Think you can take your old man on now, do ya?' Spittle dripped from his father's mouth as he took a step towards Coop.

'No!' His mother's brittle voice cut the air. 'Travis, don't.' Coop didn't dare break his stare with his father, but out of the corner of his eye he saw his mother start to uncurl.

'Whatcha gonna do, boy? Stab me?' Derision dripped from his father's mouth. Coop didn't know exactly *what* he was going to do. All he knew was he wanted to stop his father, the monster, no matter what it took.

Then his father lunged at him. Coop was too shocked to move for a second. He tried to step out of the way. Too late.

'Give me that thing.' Cold fingers wrapped around his fist like steel bands as his father tried to wrench the knife away from him.

Terror squeezed his heart and he screamed, a wild guttural sound.

'No!'

He wrestled for ownership of the knife with his father, their grunts filling the small kitchen. Coop lost his footing, as Travis kicked out at his legs, and he fell. Father and son crashed to the linoleum floor. Travis landed like a ton of stone on top of him. All the air was knocked out of Coop's lungs and for endless seconds it felt like he was going to die.

'David.' His mum's scream penetrated his foggy brain and her ice-cold hands dragged at him, pulling him out from underneath his father.

They both scrambled backwards, as far away from Travis as they could get in the small kitchen, expecting him to rear up like a rabid dog and attack again. But he never moved.

Much later, after the police wrapped Coop in a blanket, and his mother sat on the edge of the couch, wild-eyed and dishevelled, they told him the knife had pierced directly through his heart. Travis was killed instantly.

Even though Coop was cleared of any wrongdoing, the judge deeming it self-defence, he'd never gotten over the fact he'd killed his own father. He'd been numb for months afterwards, stumbling through automatic day to day routines in a kind of grey half-life. Until finally his mum had come to him while he lay on his bed one night, not sleeping, and told him she didn't blame him. That she loved him with all her heart. That he'd been braver than she ever was. He'd freed her. Freed them both.

After that, life was better, a sense of relief slowly filled in the spots where only shadows haunted before. But it was a secret he lived with for the rest of his life.

Having to endure his father's evil treatment certainly shaped Coop's existence, and to some extent, his personality. It made him determined to help other people. Those who found themselves in similar situations. Driven to assist the vulnerable, the underprivileged, the people exhausted by a life of constantly being beaten down. That's why he worked at the homeless shelter, volunteered his time whenever he could. It gave him a sense of comfort, a balm for his bruised soul, a small feeling of release from the terrible guilt he still endured. Guilt at killing his own father. At not being able to stop the abuse years before.

Working at the shelter also led him to meet Alex Carmondy, the man who Coop quietly idolised. Alex did pro-bono work for the shelter, giving his time freely and easily. It was his compassion and dedication Coop held in awe. It proved there were still good people in this world. Coop would never have told anybody this, but Alex was more of a father figure than his real father had ever been. He wanted to be more like Alex, even going as far as completing a lawyers assistant certificate online, at night, so he could help Alex with his work at the shelter.

Alex tried to convince him he should go further, become an established lawyer. He knew Coop had the smarts, just hadn't had the right opportunities. He talked to Coop on many occasions, trying to convince him he'd make a great lawyer, all the hard work would pay off in the end. But Coop had chosen a different path, some might say the quicker path. To become a cop took less than eighteen months, not the six to seven years it took to become a practicing lawyer. He still thought about Alex, still ran into him at the shelter whenever he found the time to volunteer there. He felt in some way he'd let him down, but also knew he couldn't dwell on it. It'd achieve nothing in the end.

Tara was the only other person, besides his mother and his recruiting officer, he'd ever told about his father. And when he'd finally worked up the courage to tell Tara his sad tale, she'd looked him straight in the eye and retorted he was a good man, a very good man, and he was a stronger person because of what he'd survived. Her words struck a chord deep inside. And he'd worked even harder towards the worthy image she painted of him.

Coop moved, restless now at thoughts of his father and Alex Carmondy. He noticed the sharp edge of pain was subsiding, the drugs doing their job at last. He turned onto his uninjured side and pushed the disturbing images out of his head. Filling his mind instead with Tara. And a replay of this evening's naked tryst. The memories would probably also keep him awake, but at least they were powerfully pleasant ones.

CHAPTER NINE

The crack of a twig snapping made Tara flinch and turn instinctively towards the sound. It was Coop. *Idiot*, she wanted to yell at him. They weren't supposed to make any sound. No fast movements, no noises that might give them away.

She motioned for him to come and lie down next to her behind the fallen log. He joined her in the moist undergrowth, easing himself down quietly. She could tell his stealthy hunkering down was only partly due to him not wanting to make any noise. Coop was still in a lot of pain, it was obvious from his stilted movements, and the way his breathing became more laboured as he lay down. But she kept her misgivings to herself. Coop wouldn't thank her for turning into his nagging mother. Not today. Not out here.

They lay together, shoulder to shoulder, peering over the top of the log into the surrounding jungle. Waiting for Martin's return.

They'd found the terrorists camp. Well, what they *hoped* was the camp. And Martin had gone off to reconnoitre. It should really have been her doing the scouting; she knew how to move silently through the jungle, to avoid the hidden strangler roots and the large leaves of the stinging tree. But

Martin didn't trust anyone else. So Coop, Bruce, Graeme and herself were hunkered down. Waiting.

Coop stirred next to her and when she turned her head there was a gun filling her field of vision. Held out to her like an offering on Coop's open palm. What the … She raised her eyebrows at him but he pushed the gun towards her. She reached up and took it.

Not daring to break the silence with even a whisper, she frowned and pursed her lips at him.

'Take it,' he mouthed, closing her fingers around the butt. 'It's loaded. I brought it for you. Just in case.'

She nodded and reached down to tuck it into the waistband of her cargo shorts. She knew Coop was giving her this gun without Martin's knowledge.

It was a standard issue .38 pistol. Coop trusted her to handle the gun, even if she was only a civilian now. It was probably his spare, his back up. Which made her both angry and grateful all at the same time. He was worried about her. She gave a wry smile. Because she was just as worried about him.

They went back to staring into the jungle, side by side, until Tara couldn't stand it any longer and cast him a quick sideways glance. His rebellious curls were stringy and plastered against his forehead, wet with sweat from the jungle heat and humidity. The temperature had soared today, summer stamping its mark with absolute certainty. Combined with the arduous pace Martin set to get to the terrorist campsite, it'd left them all drowning in perspiration.

Her own cheeks would be pink with exertion, too. They'd broken camp well before dawn, dismantling their bivouac's as quietly and quickly as possible. Then Martin pushed them hard, letting Tara lead the way, but always right on her heels. The clammy morning air soon gave way to the steamy heat of a tropical summer day, and they'd all been dripping with sweat after the first hour. Tara made sure they drank enough water, aware of how easy it'd be for one of them to succumb to heat exhaustion under the relentless pace. She'd also been worried at how Coop would fare with his bruised ribs and cut shoulder. But in true Coop style, he gritted his teeth, hadn't said a word and kept up with them. He was probably stiffening up now they'd stopped. She opened her mouth to offer him some more painkillers, but shut it again just as quickly. She *wasn't* his mother.

Her stomach rumbled, and she remembered they hadn't even had time for a meal this morning. Martin had been so on edge, so anxious to get moving and they'd all caught his sense of urgency. Feverishly stuffing sleeping bags into their backpacks and bending the aluminium poles of their tents in their hurry to be away. Dinner last night had been fairly meagre fare as well. Vlad still had the little metho burner in his backpack, so they'd no way to heat the vacuum-sealed meals. Somehow cold, congealed chicken curry just wasn't nearly as appealing as the hot version. Tara had left most of her food on her plate, untouched.

They'd found the terrorist's camp in a little over two hours. Tara slowed their pace as they drew nearer to the clump of cabbage palms she'd spotted from the top of The Castle. At first she hadn't been sure anyone was even there. She'd made them all hunker down, silent and staring, behind the large spreading trunk of a Moreton Bay Fig. It'd taken a while, but once her ears became accustomed to the other jungle sounds, she was able to filter out the sounds that didn't belong. A low rumble of a male voice over the buzz of the cicadas. They all heard the distinctive clang of something metal being dropped on the ground. But that was the extent of the sounds and Tara was impressed at how good these guys were. It meant at least one of them was well versed in jungle warfare.

Martin expressed his surprise the terrorists were still here. Perhaps Tony's yelling hadn't carried as far as they thought. Even though he'd sounded like a baby elephant in a china shop back at the cliff, the thick jungle and humid air had probably muffled the sounds more than they imagined. Martin wasn't one to look a gift horse in the mouth, so he'd set off to reconnoitre. Now the four of them were waiting for him to come back and confirm these were no ordinary campers.

Her shoulder touched Coop's as she readjusted her position and she couldn't stop the surge of heat from the contact. It brought back memories of what they'd done last night. Had it only been last night? Tara knew her cheeks were turning even pinker at the memory. Had that really been her? Sitting astride Coop, letting passion make her inhibitions run wild? Throwing caution to the wind, not caring about the fact that Martin or Graeme could've come looking for them at any second. Making love in the middle of the jungle. His hands in her hair.

Unlike her outward appearance, Tara had always been on the conservative side when it came to sex. Never very self-assured or confident. Always making sure the light was turned off. Preferring to leave her t-shirt on to cover her nakedness. But last night, it was as if she'd given in to her animal instincts. Was making love with Coop going to be like that every time? Sensual and uninhibited, but also deeply intimate. And then Bruce had come to find them. She'd only just managed to get dressed in time, and she was sure there was suspicion in Bruce's brown eyes as they emerged from the undergrowth. He'd never said a word, however.

Wait. Had she just admitted there would be a next time with Coop? Just because she'd let her defences down once didn't mean he wasn't going to go back to his old life in Sydney, and she back to Alive and Kicking when this was all over. But things had changed between them. She'd changed. As much as she hated to admit it, the reasons she once had for not being with Coop had changed also. She was no longer a cop, no longer his partner, and after her revelation the other night, she knew she wasn't ever going back to being a cop.

Coop shuffled irritably next to her, trying to get into a more comfortable position, still careful not to make any noise. Tara wanted to ask how he was feeling, to check under the bandage on his shoulder. Make sure the cut was still clean and dry. The dressing would need changing soon. Worry gnawed at the edges of her conscience. A wound could quickly become infected in the jungle.

There was a sound right in front of her, the subtle rustle of leaves brushing against something. She tensed and touched Coop's arm. There was a flash of blue between the low shrubs off to their left and Tara made out the shape of a man, creeping stealthily. It was Martin, she could tell by the colour of his shirt. He came around from behind the large trunk of a tree and scanned the area. Tara was secretly pleased; she'd made sure they were well enough hidden so even Martin couldn't see them. Coop moved next to her and he was on his feet so that Martin could see him.

Martin gave the sign for them all to follow him and headed away from the terrorist camp. Graeme and Bruce stood up from where they'd been hunkered down behind a saltbush and wended their way after him.

'It's definitely them,' Martin confirmed in a whisper, once they'd all gathered under the spreading branches of another fig tree. The light of anticipation glowed in his eyes. 'I recognised at least two of them from the board.' Tara assumed *the board* was some kind of list of wanted terrorists, usually posted in every police department staff room around the country. Coop stood next to Tara, listening to his boss, face deadly serious. She had to resist the urge to reach out and take his hand. For some uncharacteristic reason she felt the need to hold his fingers in hers. A steadying presence, something to ground her in the face of this unsettling news. It was now all terribly real. No longer just a game of hide and seek. They'd found their quarry. A deadly quarry, who'd stop at nothing to gain their objective. An ice-cold shiver ran up her spine.

'How many?' asked Graeme in a low voice, passing Martin a bottle of water. It was the question on all their lips.

'Seven.'

'Fucking hey?' exclaimed Bruce in a low whistle. At last they now knew how many men they were hunting. There was always a sense of relief when it was confirmed, even if they were outnumbered.

'Looks like two of those are women,' Martin continued in hushed tones, taking a big gulp of water. 'They're both wearing niqabs.' Bruce gave another quiet whistle of amazement, echoing all their thoughts. Women jihadists. The idea always struck a different level of dread into Tara. But they could be just as lethal, and just as accurate as their male counterparts.

'They're all heavily armed. AK47s and other automatic rifles, from what I could see.'

'Yeah, and God knows what else those women have hidden under those bloody long dresses,' Bruce whispered with a dark smirk. Martin gave him a withering look.

'Our orders are to hold for now. We've done our job and found the bastards. Now it's up to the Feds to come down on them like a tonne of bricks. I'll need to radio this in.' Martin cast a quick, appraising look at Tara. 'Can you take me somewhere I can talk to my chief superintendent on the Sat Phone, where I won't be heard?'

'Sure.' She gave a nod of her head.

'After I radio this in, we're going to set up a perimeter around their campsite and watch them like hawks.' Martin's mouth twisted as if he'd tasted something bad. 'Much as I hate to do this, Cooper, do we have a spare earwig for Tara?'

'Yes, I've still got Tony's in my backpack. Why?'

'Because we're down a man, and I want all eyes on the prize to make sure they don't slip through our net. I want her watching as well.'

'Now hang on just a minute—'

'I know what you're going to say, Cooper, and while I agree we shouldn't involve a civilian in this, the stakes are just too high. Besides, you've already vouched for her, told me she can more than hold her own. You even said she used to be an excellent cop.' That stopped Coop in his tracks. He weighed up Martin's words. His blue eyes found her face, and he stared at her, as if trying to read her mind. In the dappled jungle light, his eyes were startlingly blue. Her stomach lurched at the thought of what Martin was asking her to do and sweat dampened the shirt at the back of her spine.

'This is nothing more than a stake-out, Coop,' she said. 'I can do this in my sleep.' She was daring him to argue. He still didn't speak, and they glared at each other for many more long seconds, the others momentarily forgotten. She knew without having to be told he was fighting an internal battle. One where he desperately wanted to protect her. But she didn't need protection. Why couldn't he understand that? Bruce gave an uneasy cough and their connection was broken. Closing his eyes for a second he turned away from her. His back was rigid, square shoulder blades outlined against the black fabric of his t-shirt.

'Fine,' he muttered. 'But she stays close to me. In my line of sight at all times.'

'That sounds fair to me,' Martin replied, already rummaging in his bag for the phone.

* * *

A dratted fly buzzed around Coop's ear, but he daren't swish it away. He'd hardly moved for the past two hours. If he didn't readjust his position soon, his muscles would start to cramp. His bruised side had been screaming from early this morning, as soon as they'd started the walk through the bush, and now the bump on the back of his head was throbbing along in time with the rising ache from his shoulder. He'd need to move soon, even if it was to reach into his pocket to grab some of those pain pills Tara had given him.

A couple more flies joined the first one and they buzzed angrily near his face until he was forced to lift a hand, ever so slowly and bat ineffectively at them.

It was only just past midday, and it was like sitting in a sauna. There wasn't a breath of air down here in the thick jungle underbrush and the sweat rolled freely down his face and back. Because it was so humid the sweat did nothing to cool him down.

Casting a glance to his left, he could just make out Tara, lying in the long grass about a hundred and fifty metres away. Was she being eaten alive by the resident jungle insects as well? If she was, she didn't show it. She looked as cool as a cucumber, never flinching or swatting at any of these annoying little bastards. How long were they going to have to endure this?

Martin said HQ was dispatching three units to back them up, but they wouldn't arrive until after sundown. There was supposedly a fire-trail higher up on the hill the other crews could use to get close to the campsite. It was a good thing the reinforcements would arrive under the cover of darkness, but it meant a terrible wait through the heat of the day for Martin and his team. He'd be scratching bug bites for weeks to come.

But that might be the least of his worries. If this thing went south for any reason, there was a good chance one of them might get hurt. Shot. Killed, even. The firepower they'd catalogued on the terrorists in the camp was disconcerting.

One of the men held a semi-automatic FN FAL rifle, the other a sawn-off shotgun. Both of them cradled the guns to their chests, as if they were babies. They never put them down, not even for a second. Martin told them he thought the two women were carrying Beretta pistols, tucked into a belt around the outside of their clothing. The other men looked to be carrying some form of semi-automatic rifles as well, it was hard to tell the exact make from this distance.

The scariest of them all was the big man dressed in black. He had the trademark long beard and dark eyebrows lowered over a heavyset forehead. But it was his eyes that made him really scary. They were coal black, and expressionless. As if there was no one living inside the body standing there guarding the camp. As if his soul had departed and left an empty husk of a man behind. Totally devoid of any human emotion. Scary also, was the fact he carried a fully-automatic AK-47. It was jet-black and longer than his arm, the curved chamber built to hold thirty bullets protruding out the bottom of the angular gun. A lightweight, but deadly assault rifle. Gas operated and magazine fed it was reliable and accurate, a favourite of most jihadist groups. If he started shooting, they'd all be killed in a matter of seconds in the hail of bullets that gun would produce.

No, he shouldn't think like that. Once the back-up arrived, he'd make damn sure Tara was safe, and well out of the way before he even thought about joining in the fray. At least he'd managed to get her to take his gun. Martin wouldn't like that he'd given away his backup, but there was no way he was going to leave Tara completely unprotected. He had no idea if Tara kept up her shooting skills since she'd quit. But she was a pro. She'd been the best marksman he'd ever seen. And firing a gun wasn't something easily forgotten.

Coop tried to talk to her as they were getting into position, under his breath, with earwig out so no one else could hear.

'You're only going to sit and watch, do you hear me? I gave you that gun for self-protection, nothing more. If anything starts up, you need to get the hell out of here.' Her gaze flickered, taking in everything going on around them. 'Tara, look at me.' It'd taken her a few seconds, but she eventually let her eyes slide over to meet his. 'Did you hear me?' he repeated. He leaned in and grabbed her upper arm, his fingers digging into her bicep, punctuating his request. She nodded her compliance. But he knew her better than that. There was a stubborn set to her alluring mouth. And her beautiful eyes were hard as glass, not soft and dark, filled with passion. Like they'd been last night.

'Tara.' His voice was quiet but full of warning.

She'd flashed him her teeth in a cheeky smile of defiance and mouthed to him, 'Of course I did.'

Then he'd kissed her in an act of self-preservation. The only thing he knew how to do right then.

Now she was lying over there, looking fresh and inviting. Those long legs sprawled out behind her, breasts pushed forwards as she lay on her elbows, dark eyes watchful and intense.

'Damn stubborn woman,' he muttered to himself.

'What did you say,' whispered Martin.

'Nothing, boss,' he replied, subconsciously kicking himself. Of course everyone could hear him through his comms set.

He went back to studying the area in front of him. The group in the campsite had been quiet. Only the murmur of low voices could be heard every now and then and the occasional muffled thud as something was moved around. They weren't close enough to see everything in the camp.

Coop only caught glances of bodies moving around through the tall blades of grass and shrubbery, but it was enough to glean what was going on.

Martin kept his team well back from the outer perimeter. The cell would've posted sentries to keep watch. Coop caught the outline of a man—dressed in army fatigues so he was hard to spot at first—leaning against a tree, one of the semi-automatics held loosely against his thigh, about two hundred meters further down the slope.

They'd done well keeping their camp small and inconspicuous. But once you got close it became obvious the group had been here for a while; a few weeks at very least. It was a tightly-run camp. Neat, tidy, squared away. Whoever was in charge of this group definitely had a military background. There were two large tents set up side by side, both in army camouflage green. And three smaller, two-man tents tucked in close by, also in camouflage colours. They'd even erected green camouflage netting over the camp, which'd make it almost impossible to spot from the air.

The campsite was set up at the bottom of a shallow valley, close to the running stream. This provided them with enough fresh water to stay out here indefinitely. Tara told them about the fire-trail on which their back-up was supposed to be arriving. It was about a fifteen-minute walk up the hill. She theorised perhaps they had some kind of vehicle stashed away up there, but they daren't send anyone up to confirm her theory. It was too risky. They couldn't take the slightest chance of spooking these guys.

A few other dark shapes set right at the back of the camp intrigued Coop. It looked like they'd covered something with a tarp. Was it where they stored their rubbish perhaps? Or a stash of food? Hand grenades? More guns? God forbid it was more weaponry. Their team were sorely outnumbered as it was. If these terrorists had hand-grenades, or tear gas, and had a chance to use them against his team … It wasn't worth thinking about. One step at a time, he reminded himself. Never let self-doubt infiltrate your mind. To second-guess yourself in high stress situations such as this, was tantamount to failure. Go with what you know and keep it simple. He drew in a deep breath and let it out again, slowly.

Suddenly he heard Tara in his ear. 'Heads up, Coop, I think something's going on.'

He glanced over to where she was lying and saw her motion to the east side of the camp. There was indeed a flurry of activity and voices, raised louder than they'd been all morning.

'Graeme, what's going on?' Coop asked quietly. There was no answer. These comms had a certain range, of around one kilometre, outside of which the reception became crackly and then faded to nothing. But they were all well within a one kilometre radius of each other, so Graeme should be able to hear him. The only other alternative was Graeme couldn't answer. Either because he was unconscious, or he didn't want to give himself away by speaking. Both scenarios weren't good.

'Bruce, can you see anything?' Coop asked.

'There's definitely something going on,' Bruce shot back. 'Looks like they're packing stuff into bags.' Martin spread his team out like five spokes around a wheel, roughly equidistant from each other, surrounding the camp. Bruce was almost on the opposite side of the camp to Coop, so he couldn't see him. Graeme was next to him, a couple of hundred metres to his right. He'd be the person closest to whatever was covered by the tarps.

'Graeme, answer us with a grunt, or anything to let us know you're alive.' That was Martin's anxious voice in his ear now. They all waited, silent and very much alert for what seemed like endless second after endless second.

'I'm okay.'

Coop released his breath. Thank God.

'I just had to move back out of hearing range,' he whispered. 'They've just uncovered three motorbikes.' There was silence, and Coop dared to move up to his knees to get a better view through the waving grass fronds. The guard was still there leaning against the tree, but he'd turned around to face back into the camp. So that's what'd been under those tarps. He could see the glint of metal now.

'It looks like at least some of them are about to move,' whispered Graeme.

'Shit.' That was Martin's expletive in their ear.

'Whaddya want us to do boss?' asked Bruce.

'Our orders are to hold them here until back-up arrives. Observe and report. But we can't let them get away. I've worked too long and hard on this one,' muttered Martin. Coop got into a crouch and pulled out his gun, ready for whatever Martin's next command might be, wincing as his bruises sent shafts of pain though his torso. Glancing over, he could see Tara doing the same, her movements fluid and practiced as if she'd never been away from the force.

He tried to catch her eye, wanting to motion for her to move back, fade into the undergrowth. Was she avoiding his gaze on purpose? She was on her knees and had the gun out and pointed down in front of her, relaxed but ready to move at the slightest provocation.

He was just about to say her name into his comms, when Graeme said, 'It looks like two of the men and one women are putting on backpacks. Sorry boss, I can't hear what they're saying. They might be speaking in Farsi. Bruce can you hear them?' One of Bruce's redeeming qualities was he could speak Farsi. It was one of the reasons he'd been asked to join the counter-terrorist unit in the first place.

'Nah,' Bruce replied. 'Let me see if I can get a bit closer, I might be able to—' he broke off. 'Shit, they're leaving. The three of them with backpacks are leaving the camp. Heading up the ridge on a small track. What do we do now, boss?' There was undisguised worry in Bruce's voice now.

'Fuck me,' growled Martin, and Coop could imagine him running a hand through his cropped hair in desperation. 'Graeme and Bruce, follow them up the track. We can't let them leave. See if you can take them from behind, preferably once they're out of hearing range.' Graeme and Bruce were dedicated cops and well trained in hand-to-hand. But two against three was a bit of a gamble, even if they did have the advantage of surprise. But then, Martin didn't really have any other choice. Neither, he nor Coop were close enough to be of any help, not without giving themselves away in their rush get around to the other side of the camp.

'Cooper, see if you can get around to the other side, to cover the gap Graeme's leaving. Tara, can you move further round as well? We need to make sure none of the rest of these bastards leave either.'

Coop was about to argue, when Tara said, 'Sure thing. *Boss*.' She let the last word drip innuendo, which wasn't lost on Coop. Tara knew what Martin thought about her. But when push came to shove, he wasn't above using her. Before he could do anything to stop her, she gave him a tiny wave, her face serious, and melted into the jungle.

Goddamn Tara and her stubborn streak. And goddamn Martin as well. But she was gone and if he didn't get his butt moving soon, Martin would be hollering in his ear. Muttering curses under his breath he moved off in the opposite direction, not quite able to stop himself taking one more glance over his shoulder as he went. But Tara Hunter was nowhere to be seen.

* * *

Her heart was going to beat right out of her ribcage. Adrenalin fizzed through her veins, and she had to concentrate on taking big, deep breaths so she didn't hyperventilate. She gave a tight smile. Damn, she'd missed this feeling.

Tara took another stealthy step and stopped behind the cover of a gangly cabbage palm. Swapping the .38 into her left hand, she wiped her right hand down the fabric of her shorts. Sweat was making her hands slippery.

She could see clearly into the camp and it looked like the remaining radicals were grouped together in the middle, talking quietly. Every now and then one looked up the ridge towards where their three companions had disappeared. Four left. And only three of them if anything went wrong. Tara automatically started running scenarios in her head, deciding what she'd do if one of them made a break for it, or God-forbid, started shooting at her. The cop training and instincts were still there, tucked into the back of her mind, ready to be unpacked at a moment's notice. It was good to know after two years, her mind picked up right where it'd left off.

Her little .38 wasn't going to be much of a match for any of those semi-automatic guns. Especially no match for that AK-47 the big, broad-shouldered guy was waving around. She'd have to be bloody accurate if she needed to take a shot. Two years ago that wouldn't have been a problem. Back then Tara earned herself one of the highest marksmanship scores out of the whole precinct. Maybe she should've kept her skills up at the local Byron firing range … It was too late to lament that right now. The gun was fully loaded and she had another four rounds of ammo in her pocket. That'd have to do.

A loud crack came from over her left shoulder. A gunshot. From the direction of the ridge. The group in the camp all swung their heads around at the same time and crouched down, like four lions sensing danger. Then came the unmistakeable report of a semi-automatic weapon discharging into the sudden deathly silence.

Shit. Shit. Shit.

Grunts and yells came to her through the comms set from either Graeme or Bruce. One of the four—the big one, with large muscled biceps and the AK-47—took off at a dead run straight up the hill towards the gunshots, while the other three scattered around the camp, finding better vantage spots. Tara got a quick look at him as he took off. He was dressed in black from head to toe, with a long dark beard covering much of his face.

'Graeme, there's one more coming your way,' Martin said in a deceptively calm voice. 'Cooper, and, Tara, hold your positions. Graeme, give me a sit rep. Do you need help?'

'Yes, sir. We got two of them, knocked them out cold. But the other one, the woman slipped through. She's holed up in a dead tree just above us.' Graeme's voice was steady and controlled. 'It's not life threatening, but I've taken a bullet. Bruce is gonna get that bitch in the tree, but you need to send someone after the other guy coming up the hill. I won't be much help.'

Oh God. Graeme was down. Shot. How could he sound so calm?

'Tara, get after that other guy. Stop him anyway you can,' yelled Martin. He'd dispensed with the stealth mode now, it was more than obvious they were here. 'Shoot him if you have to, before he gets to Bruce and Graeme. Stop him getting away.'

'On it,' she said, and her feet were moving before she even had time to register the fact. Martin obviously knew she had Coop's gun. How he knew, she didn't have time to think about right now. And Martin had no qualms about sending her after an armed assailant. So much for her being a *civilian*. When it suited him, he was prepared to put her in harm's way. His double standards would have to wait for another time. Right now she needed to help Graeme.

'Tara, be careful,' Coop yelled into ear. There was desperation in his voice, tinged with anger. He needed to stop worrying about her and think about his own predicament. She could tell he wanted to follow her into the underbrush.

'Coop, you bloody well hold your ground. I need you to cover the big bastard behind the tent.' Martin had obviously figured out the same thing. Tara put Coop out of her mind. *Concentrate on catching the crim.* It was hard work, crashing her way through the jungle. She was running as fast as the undergrowth would allow, but it kept snagging on her t-shirt and rising up from the ground to make her stumble and trip. Her skin was ripped by sharp fronds of the pandanus palms, but funnily enough she didn't feel the cuts. The adrenalin surged relentlessly through her body now, driving her on and she felt no pain. She must sound like a baby rhinoceros thundering through the bush, each step pounding heavy against the earth. Could he hear her following him?

A volley of shots echoed from below her, and a bullet exploded into the trunk of a tree ahead of her. One of those arseholes was shooting at her. They couldn't possibly see her through the thick foliage, so they must be taking wild pot-shots at all the noise she was making. All she could do was hope they were wide of their mark. One of her team returned fire, and the bullets stopped whizzing around her.

Finally she hit the little track the man in black had disappeared up, and running became much easier on the well-used trail. Would he hear her? He was still running towards Bruce and Graeme. But she was gaining on him. Her long legs did have their advantages sometimes. As well as her intimate knowledge of the jungle. This helped her avoid most of the dangling vines waiting to snag around her neck and arms, as well as keeping well away from the spiky tendrils of the salt bush. There were no more sounds—or bullets—from below, which must mean the others had settled into the *watch and wait* mode.

Thank God she kept fit after she quit the force, otherwise she'd never have been able to keep up with this guy. Even so, her breaths were coming as ragged gasps of air. The man ahead of her started to slow. She matched her steps to his.

Surely he knew someone was after him? Even if he hadn't heard her, he must suspect something. If he'd any kind of combat training at all, he'd be watching his back.

More shots echoed from below. Single shots, which meant either Coop or Martin was firing. She'd have to trust Martin and Coop to keep those other thee pinned down, guarding her back. She'd slowed right down now, but continued at a stealthy jog up the trail.

'Graeme, where are you?' she whispered into her comm.

'Keep coming up the hill, I've got the other bastard in my sights, but I can't see you yet.' She almost didn't catch his reply, his voice was so quiet and muffled. She kept jogging up the track, her antennae on high alert, ears searching like a bat for any sound from the terrorist ahead. She flinched at any flash of movement or shadow nearby.

There. A flicker of black between the branches. It was him, she was sure of it. The black form slipped behind a large tree trunk and disappeared. Using the tree to shield himself from anyone who might follow from behind. At least she had a bead on him now. Keeping low and out of sight, she crept towards the tree.

There was a single gunshot from above—Graeme and his Glock—and then a round of automatic blasts from the AK-47. Out of nowhere an echo of semi-automatic gunfire sounded from higher up on the ridge. It must be the woman Bruce had holed up in the tree, taking advantage of her comrade distracting them. Letting him know where she was. Tara heard both Bruce and Graeme return fire, and the jungle was filled with air-shattering sounds. She struggled with the intense urge to cover her ears. It was loud, bullets shattering the air like small explosions all around her. Memories started to crowd in around her. The jewellery heist. People screaming, random gunfire piercing the ballroom walls.

No.

No, she wouldn't succumb to this. Not now. She needed to help the others. That was her job. She pushed the memories back into the box where they belonged.

'Tara.' She heard Graeme's shout, even without the comm in her ear. 'You gotta—' The sound of more automatic gunfire rending the air cut through whatever he was about to say. The terrorist was shooting at Graeme. Tara didn't even know where Graeme was, or how well protected he was. Did he have cover, or was he lying out in the open? An easy target? She had to stop this terrorist.

Keeping her gun pointed ahead, she took great loping strides towards the tree where she'd last seen the man in black disappear. The sound of gunfire got louder and louder as she approached. Her ears began to ring, like the bullets were ricocheting around inside her skull. Suddenly a black-clad shoulder came into view. The guy had got sloppy, revealing his back to her by accident. She raised her gun. It was a hard shot to take. Practically impossible. But if she could just wing him it might be enough to get him off Graeme.

This was the first time she'd fired a gun since … Hadn't even held one until this morning. *Stop it.* No time for uncertainty. This was just like riding a bike. Nothing to it. *I can do this.*

Holding her breath she steadied, took a second to plant her feet wide, lock her arms straight and take a careful sight down the barrel. Crack! The bullet flew straight and true and found its mark. The man went down. Tara released her breath.

But in the next second, the man was back on his feet, swinging around and pointing his rifle straight at her.

Holy fuck!

She dived into the grass, scraping her elbows and knees as she hit the dark earth, nearly losing her hold on the .38 in her mad scramble to get underneath a nearby log. Bullets rained down on her. Instinct made her flinch and cover her head with her arms as dirt flew in all directions, thrown up in great clods by the zinging bullets. She could hear shells thudding into the wood of the dead tree above, close to her head. So close. What the hell was she doing out here? She was going to die. Coop was yelling something in her ear, but she couldn't hear him. Her ears were still ringing and his words were distant and far-removed, drowned out by the sounds of the world-destroying barrage. The night of the jewellery heist came howling back from her memories. Images of men waving weapons, yelling loud threats, screaming people running, a rifle pointed straight at her, Coop diving in front of the bullet as it sped towards her. Coop lying on the floor, bleeding. His ruby red blood pooling on the wooden parquet floor. Her hands pushing down on his wound, trying to stop him from bleeding to death. His eyes rolling back in his head as he groaned in agony, while carnage still raged around them. She'd thought he was going to die. And it was all her fault. If he hadn't been trying to protect her … And now she *was* going to die. Here in the jungle, in an avalanche of terrorist bullets. She made herself as small as possible, hugging her arms tight around herself, pulling her knees up and curling into the foetal position. How the hell had she even thought she was capable of this? Her hands were shaking. The barrel of the gun dangerously loose in her grip.

Then the bullets stopped. Tara forced her eyes open and listened for a moment. Nothing. No more shooting. She lifted her head to peer under the gap beneath the log and the ground. The man in black was cursing at his gun, scrabbling to fix it. It was jammed. One of his arms was practically useless. He was trying to unjam it one-handed. It wasn't an impossible task, but it definitely slowed him down. She'd hit him. That one in a million shot had paid off.

She should run while she had the chance.

The thought had her legs moving almost instinctively before she could stop herself. But no. Graeme was up there, relying on her. And so was Bruce. She wasn't some petrified woman who wanted nothing more than to hide under a log until it was all over. She wasn't a coward. The training she'd done in the force had taught her to handle situations like this. *Get up Tara*. And she did, lifting one leg and then the other, she got onto her knees and levelled the gun at the man in black, using the log to steady her hands. Hands that were now suddenly solid as a rock.

The man un-jammed his weapon and raised it awkwardly to his hip.

Tara squinted, narrowing her focus onto him. Him. Just him. Nothing else in this world mattered. After taking a long second to aim the gun, she squeezed the trigger. The recoil kicked in and it jerked her backwards a little. By the time she regained her footing and looked up, the man in black was gone.

CHAPTER TEN

'You got him, Hunter,' said Coop. They were back in the terrorist campsite, the body of the man Tara had shot covered by one of the tarps used to hide the motorbikes. Coop stood next to her, as close as he dared, without touching her. Just to let her know he was there if she needed him. If the others hadn't been around he would've gathered her into his arms. Actually he had done just that when she'd reappeared down the tiny track with Bruce and the two captives. He'd pulled her into a tight, fierce embrace, everyone else be damned. Needing the reassurance of her warm body held against his, to know she was truly okay. Her face was pale and her dark eyes had a vacant, glazed look to them. Streaks of mud covered her clothing and face where she must've hit the dirt when that bastard started firing at her. There was a bloody scrape on her knee and another on her elbow. Her long auburn hair was no longer in its neat, jaunty ponytail. Instead tangled strands of hair fell around her face. But her hands stayed steady. They didn't shake as she kept her gun—his gun—trained on the two terrorists they'd brought back down off the ridge.

Coop felt a righteous rage rise in his gut for the second time today. Actually, scratch that. His anger hadn't really abated since Martin sent Tara into battle. The gall of the man, risking the life of a civilian just to achieve his end goal. Coop had been ready to punch the guy straight in the mouth, and still would, given the slightest provocation.

'Straight through the heart. He probably never even knew what hit him. One minute alive, the next second dead. I can't believe it. You haven't lost a scrap of your accuracy.' Coop's words were tender despite their content. 'You could shoot the arse end off a fly at one hundred metres.' He gave her a wide grin of appreciation.

'Yeah,' she said, tone deadpan, not reacting to his gentle jibing. He knew shock when he saw it, and she was definitely suffering from a mild dose. Tara needed time to sit down and process everything that'd just happened. She'd just killed a man.

Coop thought back to her time in the force. Had she ever killed anyone before? Searching his mind he came up with at least one other time she'd been involved in a shooting. They'd only been partners for a few months, when they'd been sent to check out a lead in a *supposedly* empty drug house. The house had been cleared that morning by the TRG unit, but the boss hadn't counted on the two desperate drug dealers coming back to try and salvage the last of their stash of amphetamines. As he and Tara entered the building, the two guys made a dash for freedom. The first one ran down the corridor and leapt out the kitchen window. Coop gave chase, so he hadn't seen when the second guy, who'd been hiding in the linen closet, stepped out and confronted Tara. He'd tried to take her gun, they'd fallen down to the ground together, wrestling for ownership of the weapon. She'd shot him in self-defence. Back then she'd been brash and young and desperate to show just how good of a cop she was, so she'd hidden any trace of guilt or distress at having taken the life of another human being.

Today, Tara was a very different woman. He wanted to tell her he was proud of her. For both today and back then, but it wouldn't look good in front of the other cops.

She glanced up at him, and her eyes cleared a little. 'I'm okay, Coop. Worry about those people over there.' She pointed with her gun at the group of terrorists stretched out on the ground, bound hand and foot and gagged.

There were four of them left alive. Tara shot the one all dressed in black, the big burly one. Coop figured he was the leader of this cell. Bruce had taken out the woman who'd been holed up in the tree. When she saw her comrade go down with Tara's bullet through his heart, she came out of her hiding-hole screaming like a banshee and firing wildly. Bruce had no choice but to return fire. It was him or her. And he'd done so with frightening efficiency, according to Tara.

Coop shot the third one. All hell broke loose when the extremists in the campsite heard the woman from the tree screaming. Coop and Martin were lucky to get out unscathed. Lucky that one of the three left in the clearing was a woman. When she'd rushed out from behind one of the tents shooting with a fierce determination that belied her small stature, her long black abaya tangled in the jungle vines and she'd fallen flat on her face. That gave Coop enough time to race over and train his gun at her head. Keep her down until he'd secured her with zip ties.

Another one went for the motorbikes, hoping to make a break for it. He was short and stocky, with a swarthy face, and surprisingly, clean-shaven. His stature hadn't made him any less ferocious, and he continued firing his gun, while trying to kick-start the bike.

Martin was tied up keeping the third guy pinned down, but had yelled through his earwig, 'Don't let that fucker get away.' So with one knee in the middle of the woman's back to hold her down, Coop took careful aim, and fired as the man sped by on the motorbike. Amazingly his aim had been true today. The man and bike had come to a crashing halt, dirt flying, the smell of petrol heavy in the air. Coop had no other choice, the short man couldn't be allowed to get away and warn his buddies. This whole cell had to be kept contained. People's lives depended on it. Perhaps tens, or even hundreds of people's lives. Coop repeated that fact to himself every time his gaze happened to fall on the man's body, still hunched over his bike, eyes vacant. He needed to drag a tarp over and cover his body.

That left three men and one woman alive. They'd gagged them to stop them shouting, Allah Akbar, over and over again. Two of the men left alive were Caucasian, one of them blonde-haired and blue-eyed like himself. And young. Really young. So young his downy facial hair couldn't even be called a beard. Perhaps not eighteen yet. The guy he'd killed trying to get away on the motorbike was also very young. Coop was surprised, but not shocked. These were home-grown terrorists. Adolescent kids radicalised right here in their own backyard. Brainwashed. The other man was large and bald, with a myriad of tattoos sprouting up his neck. Some kind of bikie-terrorist connection perhaps? He wouldn't put it past some of the bikie gangs to be dipping their hands in as many illegal honeypots as they could. All of the men were ranting curses in Farsi before they were gagged, leaving Coop in no doubt as to their affiliation.

Bruce was speaking Farsi to one of the bound men on the ground.

The female sobbed gently into her gag. Coop ignored her and went to check on Graeme. He'd been shot in the lower leg, a through and through. Luckily the bullet had missed the major artery and Graeme, who was well versed in field first-aid, had staunched the bleeding. And managed to keep shooting at the fucker who'd come up the hill towards him.

'Still alive?' he asked as he hunkered down next to Graeme, who was sitting on the ground with his back against at tree.

'Yep, I'm fine,' the older man replied. 'Might need a few weeks off after this one though,' he said with a resolute grin.

'Hell of a way to get time off work,' agreed Coop. And didn't he know it. It'd taken months of rehab before he'd managed to get back to work, and even then he hadn't been one-hundred per cent for quite a few months more. A lot of damn good it'd done him too, taking that bullet to save Tara. She'd just up and run away anyway, leaving him to cope with all the pain and doctors and the self-doubt on his own. It would've been nice to have someone to lean on back then. But seeing her now, after what they'd shared last night, he couldn't keep condemning her. As he glanced over his shoulder he noticed her face seemed to have regained some colour, which was good.

'Martin's already radioed for a medi-vac helicopter. It shouldn't be too much longer. I'll be damned if I know where they're going to land.' Coop took a good look around. There didn't seem to be a piece of flat land for hundreds of kilometres in any direction.

Graeme laughed at him. 'They'll probably winch me up, or some such nonsense.'

'That'll be fun,' Coop replied. 'At least you're not afraid of heights. Not like Tony, anyway.'

'Yeah,' said Graeme, a tad too morosely, leading Coop to believe that perhaps he *was* afraid of heights. But then, he'd never show it. Coop thought back to their descent down the cliff, and the way Graeme had been cool and calm, taking it all in his stride. No one would've ever guessed. His admiration for the man went up another few notches.

Coop would be sorry to see Graeme go. He'd enjoyed working with the man. A father figure of sorts. And if anyone needed a father figure to look up to, it was probably him.

Casting another quick glance towards Tara, Coop reached out a hand, to show his appreciation to Graeme.

Taking it in his strong, steadfast grip, Graeme said, 'Nice working with you, Cooper.'

'Ditto,' Coop replied.'

'Make sure you look after her now, won't you.' Graeme tilted his head in Tara's direction, making it obvious Coop's subtle checking on Tara every five seconds hadn't gone unnoticed. 'She's a live-wire. You better not let her get away. You won't find another one like her again.' Graeme had just spoken more words than Coop could remember him saying over any of the previous weeks they'd worked together. He nodded his head at Graeme's sage words. He intended to follow the older man's advice. If Tara would let him.

'I'd better get back over there,' Coop said, indicating the group of trussed terrorists on the ground. 'Need to help with the interrogation.'

Graeme just nodded.

Martin was still talking into the Sat Phone as Coop walked back over to the campsite. The Inspector was updating HQ with the little information they'd so far gleaned, and organising for the extraction of both Graeme—to hospital— and the terrorists, to a secure location for interrogation. But he was also keeping an eagle eye on the four captured terrorists, his gun out and at the ready. He wasn't taking any chances. These guys weren't going anywhere. They were tied up tighter than pigs on a spit.

'Hey, Cooper, get your lazy arse over here and give me a hand with this one,' yelled Bruce. He lifted the sobbing woman off the ground and dragged her over to a pile of large metal cases so he could prop her up against one. She gave a few half-hearted kicks, but then her body went limp and her wails got louder. Her black abaya, the long coverall dress, was smeared with dirt and dust and was wrenched up around her knees.

The woman was also wearing a niqab head-covering, which only allowed her eyes to show. But as Coop got closer he could see dirty streaks where tears had left trails through the muck on her face. Bruce proceeded to remove her gag.

'Watcha doing?' Coop asked, suddenly on alert. Was this woman going to start screaming bloody murder again?

'I think she wants to talk,' Bruce grunted, helping her into a better position against the boxes, to make her more comfortable, which was almost impossible with her hands bound behind her back and her feet tied together. She had black army-issue ankle boots on; such incongruous footwear to be worn under a skirt. But then why was Coop surprised? She was as much a soldier as all the men in this camp.

She had extremely pretty eyes, hazel, with flecks of gold. Red-rimmed from crying, but quite striking. Not the eyes of a hardened killer. And a creamy complexion around her eyes, as if her face hadn't seen much of the the sun.

'Addar,' she sobbed. 'Oh, Addar.'

'Who's Addar?' asked Bruce roughly.

'He's dead.' Her wail grew louder and louder as she sobbed uncontrollably. If the woman hadn't been pointing a gun at him only a few minutes ago Coop might've felt more than an ounce of compassion. It was obvious her heart was breaking. But he felt nothing. Nothing but a sincere urge to shake her until she told him everything.

'Was he the one up on the hill?' Bruce asked, signalling with his chin to where the body of the bearded man in black lay.

'Yes. We are married. Oh Addar,' she wailed again. Her English seemed good. No need for an interpreter here.

The three men lying on the ground became agitated as the woman spoke, grunting and squirming. They didn't like the fact she was talking to them.

'Let's take her into the tent,' Coop suggested with a tilt of his head. She might be more pliable away from the pressure of the other men's gazes.

As Coop helped Bruce move the woman to the tent, he saw Tara rest her booted foot on the back of the closest man.

'Lie still,' she growled as he squirmed underneath her foot. God she was beautiful when she was acting all steely and grim.

'Tara, you right out here with Martin for a few minutes?' he asked. She nodded, but didn't lift her gaze from the man at her feet.

* * *

Tara looked at the man whose life she'd just snuffed out. Take away his long beard and his face was young, so very young. He was barely into his twenties. God, how did they become so radicalised, so violent at such a young age? She felt the nausea rise again and had to cover a sudden urge to gag.

She'd helped to carry him down off the ridge. It was the least she could do. She'd lifted the tarp to get a closer look. Dropping the covering she went over and sat on a log a little way from the camp, still thinking about his lifeless body.

The first extraction team had arrived a little over ten minutes ago, almost exactly one hour after the shoot-out. Which was pretty good considering they were stuck in the middle of nowhere. The extraction team had been on standby, awaiting Martin's call. The Tactical Response Team, or TRG, had rappelled down long, snaking ropes from two helicopters hovering above them. Now Coop, Martin and Bruce were being debriefed by a handful of burly men.

Another backup team was driving in to help clean up, but they wouldn't be here until after dark.

Tara rubbed her neck, easing the muscles in her shoulders. She was so tired. Today had been both physically and mentally exhausting. No, scratch that, gruelling, horrifying, enlightening, but most of all … terribly, terribly sad. Sad that these young people were filled with such hatred. And now they'd lost their lives because of that hatred.

Tara closed her eyes and rested her forehead on her arms. She could sleep for a week. At least it was over now. Yes, there were going to be hours of debriefing and analysing and talking. But at the end of it she'd be able to go back to her little cottage in Byron, stand under the shower for about two whole days to wash the dirt and grime and remorse from her body, and then collapse in her wonderful, welcoming bed.

The rest of the counter-terrorist unit would hang around for a few days to tidy up loose ends, and they'd all head back to Sydney, leaving her in peace. Leaving her to get back to a normal life.

And Coop would go with them. Back to Sydney. Back to his own life, and out of hers once more.

That was a good thing. She wanted her safe, secure, comfortable life back. The one without any complications, where she spent her time taking tourists climbing with Vlad and eating burgers at the pub for dinner.

So why was there a sudden ache in her chest at the thought of Coop leaving Byron? Leaving her. There was no way he would stay in Byron. Why would he, there was nothing here for him. His job, his life, was in Sydney.

Yes, she'd let her defences down long enough to have sex with him last night. She was no angel. She'd had other one-night stands before, and was happy to leave again the next morning. But this was different. It *had* meant something. Sex with Coop *had* meant something. More than something. It meant everything. She hadn't expected that searing thread of need, which wrapped tightly through her insides. Hadn't expected him to drive straight through her well-built walls, to the heart of who she was. To the heart of what she wanted. But what was she supposed to do? She certainly wasn't about to start blurting out that she was falling in love with him.

Coop had come here to make peace with her. To clear the air so things were no longer left hanging. He'd made it quite obvious how much she'd hurt him when she left Sydney. Which'd been unintentional, but necessary. She hadn't meant to hurt him, but she couldn't be with him, not back then. So she'd done the only thing in her power. Leave. As quickly as possible. Like ripping off a Band-Aid.

Last night had been as spectacular as it was unexpected. A taste of what things could've been like if they ever allowed themselves to be together. But it'd been an aberration, one that wouldn't happen again. He was going to leave. And she was going to stay.

'Hunter.' Coop's voice brought her back from her musings. Pulling that shield tightly shut over her heart, she took a deep breath and brought her head up.

'Yep.'

'Martin wants to see us both in the main tent. There's been some kind of development.' His sky blue eyes crinkled at the edges with worry as he walked towards her. 'It seems the woman who survived has chosen to cooperate.' He stopped in front of her, laying a hand on her shoulder. 'You okay?' That compassionate concern was back in his voice. The one that made her feel all gooey and vulnerable inside.

'I'm fine.' She stood up in a hurry, brushed his hand away and pushed past him. 'Let's go.'

* * *

Squashed between Bruce, who was driving, and Coop in the passenger seat, Tara wriggled her bum on the bench seat to get comfortable. But there was no room in the small truck's cab and she sighed and resigned herself to putting up with a numb bum. At least they were nearly to their destination and this interminable drive was almost over.

'How much longer?' asked Coop, as if reading her mind.

'We're already on the outskirts of Brisbane,' she replied, as the sign for Harrisville slipped past on the freeway. 'It's another half an hour, depending on the traffic. Once we hit the city traffic, it'll slow us down a lot.' Tara wished she was the one driving the truck, it would've been so much simpler, rather than constantly giving Bruce directions. But there was no way a woman could drive. Not on this particular mission. So she gritted her teeth and listened to Bruce grind the gears as he took the corners way too fast.

'That's good,' Coop replied grimly. Tara glanced over at him, taking in the serious line of his mouth, hard-edged eyes and deep frown that'd etched into his forehead over the past three hours. He wasn't happy with this plan. In fact he downright hated it. He'd argued with Martin, eyes flashing blue sparks, face tight with rage. But in the end it'd done no good. He'd only agreed to come along because Martin threatened to go in his stead if he refused. This was the best plan they could come up with in such a short space of time. The only way they were going to capture the other cell, and stop a potential terrorist bombing on Australian soil. They only had a small window of time to put the plan into action, and if they didn't act, they might never get another chance.

'You'd better put that … thing on soon. Now we're in the city we can't take the chance of being spotted,' said Bruce, looking at the black fabric draped in Tara's lap. Glancing down, she took in the niqab, removed from the woman terrorist, Nazima, back in the jungle. But she was loath to touch it. In her mind it represented repression and radicalisation all rolled in to one. Bruce was right. If she wanted to pass as a Muslim woman, she'd have to adopt the traditional dress. Sooner rather than later.

'Do you need a hand?' Coop asked, the scowl on his face clearing a little as he turned to her.

'Sure,' she replied as he reached up a fatigue-clad arm to help her adjust it over her head. She almost hadn't recognised Coop when he came out of the tent earlier wearing an army fatigue jacket—borrowed from one of the TRG blokes—long black pants and a black cap pulled down over his eyes to hide his blonde hair. They'd rubbed dirt into his face, and together with the fact he hadn't shaved over the past few days, combined to make him look ragged and unkempt. As if he *had* actually spent the past few weeks camping in the bush.

Bruce was dressed all in dark clothes, long pants and long sleeves, the same as the man Coop had shot trying to get away on the motorbike. Martin decided Bruce was most similar in stature and complexion to him, muscular and clean-shaven. Bruce hadn't complained in the slightest about his new outfit, which surprised Tara. She'd been sure he never wore anything else but designer jeans and tight white t-shirts. Perhaps the man was actually capable of playing at a professional cop when the need arose. She'd also seen the aftermath of his cold calculating shot to the head of the woman radical. He hadn't even given the woman a second glance after he'd checked to see if she was dead. This Bruce was clinical and exacting. All the oafish, immature behaviour stripped away to finally reveal why he'd been appointed to work in the counter-terrorism unit.

Tara was sure she looked equally unrecognisable in the long black robes and now head-covering which hid everything but her eyes. Not an inch of skin was showing. She reached down and turned the air-conditioning up to full blast.

'Fuck, this thing's hot,' she growled. How the hell did Muslim women wear these things? Especially in the heat and humidity of the tropics.

'Tell me about it,' growled Coop. He was probably almost as hot in his get-up as she was. Almost.

The woman, Nazima, had revealed the next part of the terrorists' plan. Once Bruce got her talking, it was like a fountain they couldn't turn off. After the woman told her whole terrible tale, Tara felt a certain kind of begrudging empathy for her. At first they'd all assumed Nazima's near hysteria was because she was completely heartbroken by the death of her husband. As they listened to her, however, a much more sinister story unfolded. Nazima was only sixteen years old. When she was fourteen, she'd been forced into an arranged marriage with Addar. He was twenty when they were joined. Even though she was born right here, in Australia, even attended school in Sydney, her own father believed in strict Shari'a law. Her life had never really been her own. But with Addar it'd turned into never-ending day after wretched day. Her father had given her to Addar, so she might do what he couldn't. Help fight the war against the enemy. And so the principals of Islam would finally be upheld. That they might all be allowed to live under Islamic law.

For the past two and a half years Nazima had been living a life of fear and subservience. Addar ruled his wife with an iron fist, and beat her for even the smallest infraction. Perhaps his challow rice wasn't quite to the right temperature, or she forgot to put his shoes all together in a neat line under the bed. She'd never wanted to partake in all this animosity and violence, but she had no other choice. She went along with whatever her husband wanted her to do, blinded by a fog of indoctrination and terror.

Until Addar and two others in their cell had been shot dead right in front of her. Losing Addar brought into sharp reality that she was finally free. Nazima had been terrified she was going to die next. She wanted to live. She'd also realised what she'd been about to do. What might happen to scores, or even thousands of women if the terrorist cell were allowed to go ahead with their plan. Which was to bomb a popular, tourist spot in Brisbane, filled with families all making the most of the beautiful weather forecast for tomorrow's public holiday. Brisbane's Southbank. Mothers would lose children, wives lose their husbands, sisters lose brothers. All in the name of what? Nazima suddenly understood, it was in the name of hatred, not in the name of her God.

She'd told them the plan in great detail. The two men and the other woman were on their way out of the camp when Martin's team stopped them. They were on their way to meet up with another cell in Brisbane. They were to drive a small white, nondescript truck, cleverly hidden in the bush at the top of the ridge, into Brisbane and meet up with four members of this other cell.

The most interesting part of the whole plan, and the thing Coop, Bruce and Tara were now staking their lives on, was that neither of the two groups had ever met before. They didn't even have descriptions of what the others looked like. All they had was a time and place to meet.

'How could your intel have been so wrong?' Tara voiced the question she'd been pondering for most of the trip into Brisbane.

'Whaddya mean?' Bruce asked, never taking his eyes off the road.

'You thought they were after some big target in Sydney. But it was never about Sydney. Nazima said they'd been planning on hitting Brisbane all along, for months now. How could your intel guys have read the chatter so wrong?'

Bruce just shrugged. But Tara couldn't shrug it off so easily. They must've spent hundreds of man hours and millions of dollars chasing a supposed bombing in Sydney that was never going to happen.

'It really doesn't matter now, Tara. We need to concentrate on what's ahead of us, not the what-ifs,' Coop interjected. 'Let's go over our plan one more time,' he suggested.

'I'm going to drive the truck around the back of the warehouse and park it in the fourth bay down from the delivery door,' recited Bruce.

'Good,' replied Coop. 'Then what?'

A flutter of nerves shivered through Tara's stomach as she listened to Bruce continue to outline their plan. She really, really, really hoped it all went as it was supposed to. If there was the slightest hiccup, or if the people in the other cell even caught a whiff of suspicion they weren't who they said they were, they might all end up dead.

A crystal clear image from her dream the other night flashed into Tara's mind. Coop tied up and bleeding in a basement. The flutter of nerves became a full blown rush of fear.

No.

It was only a dream. That wasn't going to happen. She couldn't, wouldn't, let that dream interfere with the reality of their mission today. It was only a dream.

* * *

'Holy Fuck,' whispered Coop under his breath. 'There's six of them, not four.' Nazima either hadn't told them the truth, or she hadn't actually known the truth. Either way, they now had to deal with a whole crap load of terrorists.

They put an awful lot of faith in what Nazima told them. Not only were they staking their own lives on her intel, but possibly the lives of hundreds of civilians as well.

If they'd done what Coop had been urging them to do, which was just not make contact at all, it would've left the other cell high and dry. With no means of contacting the group in the bush camp, they wouldn't have known what'd befallen them. In Coop's mind they would've had no choice but to melt back into society and their daily lives, the bombing plan foiled. But Martin argued—and was probably right, goddamn the man to hell and back—if they left the other cell unaccounted for, then they would have the chance to re-group and carry out a bombing at a later date. Or they may go ahead with a smaller version of the plan. They had to capture the second cell if possible.

'We gotta stick to the plan,' muttered Bruce back to him. Tara sat motionless beside him. Her thigh was rigid, moulded from steel, where it rested up against his. She tensed every muscle, ready for whatever was to come. He could tell by her stillness she was assessing the situation, targeting escape routes, weighing up each and every man standing in the group before them. Exactly the same as he was.

The five men and one woman arranged themselves around the truck in a semicircle. The parking lot also held two other vehicles; both small white trucks, identical to the one they were driving. The men were of varying sizes and heights, most with dark hair and three of them with impressive beards. No guns were on show, but Coop wasn't dumb enough to believe at least some of them weren't carrying. They all had a decidedly dangerous look, as well as an air of expectant fervour.

Bruce drove the white truck down the small alley between two large warehouses and parked it in the designated carpark. Right in between the other two trucks. What were the other trucks for? This was an industrial area, set a few blocks back from Southbank. The carpark was completely enclosed by a number of old, and possibly unused, warehouse-type buildings. Hidden from the road and from all prying eyes. As soon as he'd shut down the engine, the other group materialised, exiting one of the larger buildings through a heavy metal door.

The really fucked up thing about this mission was that Martin decided it was too risky to wear any earwigs, or carry any phones. If the other terrorists did a thorough body search they'd find them easily. And both cells were supposed to have gone completely dark. Which meant no technology of any kind. No phones, or computers. Nothing that could link them to the outside world. Just another piece of the puzzle making their job harder.

He couldn't believe Tara agreed to come on this mission. And he couldn't believe Martin had practically blackmailed her into saying yes. But the plan wouldn't have worked is she hadn't agreed. A woman was supposed to be one of the three people delivering the truck. If there was no woman in the truck, their chance of surviving long enough to take down the other terrorists became almost non-existent. And she'd been the only woman available to go in the truck with them.

She'd impressed Martin with the way she'd handled herself in the shoot-out. Enough so he knew she'd be more than capable of carrying out the mission of pretending to be a female extremist ready to bomb a whole city full of people.

'Follow my lead,' Bruce said, taking his hands off the steering wheel and holding them up in front to show he was unarmed. 'Remember, no names,' he added out of the side of his mouth, just before one of the men came forward and opened the truck door. He motioned for Bruce to get out. Nazima told them that anonymity between the cells was key, and they shouldn't ask for the others names, or tell them theirs. Another man came forward to do the same thing on Coop's side of the truck. Coop fumbled for Tara's hand, finding her skin beneath the folds of the dress, and squeezed once, hard. He didn't look at her. Then he too, lifted his hands into view to show they were empty and exited the truck.

The guy who opened the door for Coop motioned for Tara to get down as well, and then Coop felt hands running over his body as he was patted down from behind. They were checking to see if he was carrying a concealed weapon. Coop got a good look at the man as came around the front and ran his hands down his torso and up and under his arms. He was tall, at least a head taller than Coop, with crooked teeth, an evil sneer and bad body odour. He wore dark nondescript clothing, like the rest of them. The unofficial uniform of a terrorist. Blend in.

Once he was satisfied Coop was clean he motioned for him to stand next to Bruce and then shouted something unintelligible. A woman wearing one of those full body outfits, where only the eyes were visible through an opening in the niqab headgear, appeared beside Tall Guy and started to pat down Tara. Of course, they wouldn't allow a man to do such an intimate act.

Once the woman nodded her approval, Tall Guy became suddenly animated. A large smile split his lips, showing his crooked teeth to their best advantage. Then he started speaking. Oh Shit. He was speaking in Farsi. Neither Coop nor Tara understood much Farsi.

Bruce nodded and said something back to him, his face serious.

'English is better,' Bruce continued, motioning towards Coop. They were taking a gamble. The guy Coop was supposed to be impersonating could actually speak Farsi, but hopefully Tall Guy didn't know this.

'Sure, sure,' he replied. He seemed almost genial now that the pleasantries were over. 'Show us what you have in the back, why don't you.' Coop noted the man's thick accent, but couldn't place it. His English was good, but not great. Bruce grunted at Tara and pushed her towards the back of the truck. She did a great job at acting obedient, keeping her eyes averted from Bruce and the rest of the men, shuffling forward to do his bidding.

Fumbling with the lock, it took Tara a minute or two to get it open, and Coop had to quell the urge to offer her a hand. Was it really Tara underneath all that black fabric? If he hadn't known any better he would've sworn not. He kept reminding himself the strong, independent, wilful woman was still there. The dress hid all sign of her slender curves, long legs, and acres of smooth flesh. There was something about the dress, this abaya, that seemed to suck all the individuality and vivacity straight out of her.

Coop clenched his fists by his side as his anger started to rise again. How dare Martin put this on Tara. How dare he put her in such an outfit and then throw her into the middle of the scariest scenario imaginable. Goddamnit, he was definitely going to punch Martin in the face next time he saw him.

He needed to use this time she was giving them to size up the rest of the terrorist cell, use any information he could garner to his advantage. But he couldn't drag his gaze away from Tara, as if she might disappear in a puff of black smoke if he dared to look away.

She got the lock undone and swung the back door of the truck open. Most of the other group leaned forward to peer into the dark depths. Then their eyes filled with a zealous light as they took in what sat in the back.

Three crates of plastic explosives.

CHAPTER ELEVEN

What had that tall man just said? Tara's Farsi was less than basic, but had he just mentioned the words, *Allah yakun aintihari*? If he had it changed everything. She recognised the word's *God* and *suicide bomber*.

Tara showed no outward sign anything was amiss, keeping her face tightly schooled, eyes averted from the tall man—probably the leader of this cell. The doors shut with a click on the truck and its terrible cargo.

'You'll take this one,' said the leader, pointing at one of the other trucks parked a few paces away. Whoa, another change to the plan. First there were two more men than they were expecting, and now they were taking a different truck back?

'Our orders were to drop off the cargo and then take the truck. Get rid of it,' said Bruce in a matter of fact way.

'We have our orders too,' replied the leader. 'And we're not stupid enough to leave the cargo here. We'll move it to a more secure location. In the other truck.' He pointed to the second truck. Another location well away from this one, so the three of them couldn't give it away. Smart. But bad for Martin's plan. Really bad. It'd make it harder to trace the explosives. There was a GPS tracking device hidden beneath the truck. They couldn't risk any tracking devices in the explosives, however. If the other cell opened them to check on their authenticity, they may well have spotted a tracking device, and their game would've been up. If the explosives were moved to another truck, it'd make it impossible to find them again.

Who were the two extra people in the cell? Were they suicide bombers? If so, then Martin's plan was unravelling faster than any of them could've anticipated. If the bombers took some of the explosives and disappeared into the night, they might not found them in time. Even if Martin managed to stop the three original bombs going off—which was looking less likely with every passing second—the other two bombers might still go ahead with their plan anyway.

Their weapons had been stashed in two secure places in the truck; one in the cab, and two in the back, along with two phones. Would they have time to retrieve them? They had to warn Martin. He needed to send in his other team in. Right now.

'What's going to happen to our truck?' Bruce asked. He made it sound like he didn't really care.

'We will ... dispose of it.' The leader gave a half-smile and a wink, and Tara knew exactly what he meant. They were probably going to torch it. Drive it down some deserted embankment somewhere and set it alight.

'Thank you, brothers and sister, you have done your part well. We are the true believers, and may we yet triumph. Now it is our turn to finish the job. Wish us well,' said the tall man, ushering them towards the other truck. It didn't look like they were going to have a chance to get their guns or their phones. Shit.

'*As-salamu alaykum*,' replied Bruce, and Coop echoed his words. Words that meant go in peace. How bloody ironic. She spoke them in a quiet voice as well, though the words threatened to stick in her throat.

Climbing into the second truck, her entire body was numb. The only thing they'd achieved was to deliver the explosives straight into the terrorists' arms. Now they were walking away with nothing. Allowing the terrorists to get away. They had to do something to stop this. But what?

Bruce put the truck into gear and drove out of the carpark.

'Holy shit,' Coop exclaimed as soon as they were out of the alley and back on the main road. 'Did they just say what I thought they said?'

'Yep,' Bruce replied grimly. 'Those other two are suicide bombers.'

'Fuck,' said Tara. Bruce had confirmed her worst fears. Her stomach churned at the news.

'This changes everything,' Coop said.

'Yep,' Bruce replied again, brows drawn down so far they almost touched together, forming one furry line across his forehead.

'We gotta get back in there and find out what they're up to.'

'What?' Tara wasn't' sure she'd heard right.

'I agree,' said Bruce.

'No.' Neither man looked at her and she wanted to yell the word again.

'Tara can take the truck back to the rendezvous spot and tell them what's going on. Then Martin can send backup.'

'No!' This time she did yell the word. 'You can't do this.'

'Do you think they bugged this truck?' Coop ignored her outburst.

'Did you catch the rego of the other truck?' Bruce asked her, keeping his concentration firmly on merging with the traffic.

'Yes, I did,' replied Tara loudly. 'That's one of the first things I memorised. But what difference—'

'Good, make sure you give it to Martin as soon as you get there. They might be able to track it.'

'As long as they don't change the plates,' chimed in Coop darkly.

This time she emitted a low growl, now completely pissed off at both men. She had to squash the childish urge to stamp her feet like a little girl. They weren't listening, and it sounded like they were forming some kind of lame-brained, half-baked idea to go back and follow the terrorists. Without her.

'We need you to drive the truck, Tara.' Finally Coop shot her a glance, mouth hard, but eyes earnest. 'Keep up the pretence that we're leaving. Then we need you to get word to Martin and the rest of the team ASAP.' Coop's voice was gentle, but his words hit her like bullets.

'No. I can't let you ….' He took her hand and held it tight. 'What do you think you're going to achieve?' she asked dully. 'You don't have any weapons, or even a phone.'

'We're creative, we'll come up with something. The trackers we've got hidden in our clothes will make sure you know where we are. You can come and find us. We'll make sure we stay out of sight. But we can't let these fuckers get away.'

'There's a set of traffic lights coming up,' Bruce chimed in. 'This is as good a place as any. There's lots of people waiting to cross the road, we should blend in with them pretty well.'

'Bruce and I are going to get out at the lights, and you're going to take over and drive the truck to meet Martin. Okay?' Coop took off his army jacket off, revealing a plain black t-shirt underneath. He also took the black cap off his head and shook his golden curls free. A small part of Tara's numb mind registered he was changing his appearance.

'I'll see you real soon. Okay?' His blue eyes locked onto hers and he grabbed both of her hands in his, holding them warm against his chest.

'Coop, I …' She couldn't get the words out. How did she say what she needed to, especially in front of Bruce? Gasping like a fish out of water, she stared into his beautiful blue eyes. *Don't do this. I have to tell you something before you go. I think I love you.* She stared into his eyes. His finger stroked the back of her hand. Then he leaned in and kissed her, hard and passionately on the lips, ignoring Bruce's shout of 'What the fuck?' Coop's lips funnelled all his heat and wanting and desire through into her own.

'I know,' he replied, his gorgeous trademark grin lighting up his face.

And just like that, he was gone.

Scooting quickly over into the driver's seat, she put the truck into gear, tearing her headgear off at the same time. Peering through the windscreen, she could just make out Coop's broad shoulders vanishing between the throng of people, his bright hair the last thing to fade down the street.

The lights turned green and she gunned the truck. Lucky she was used to driving her old jeep. At least it meant she could handle the gearshift in the truck with relative ease.

Her mind whirled, processing everything that'd just happened in the past two minutes. Driving through the chaotic Brisbane traffic forced her mind to take over the practicalities of driving in peak hour, while plotting the best route to get to Martin's rendezvous spot. It was only ten minutes away. Should she wait till she got there, or should she find the nearest pay phone and warn them straight away?

Oh God, Coop. What had he done? He was putting himself in mortal danger, and she wasn't there to help. Her dream played around the edges of her mind, filling her with foreboding. Something bad was going to happen, she just knew it. She wanted Coop back here, sitting next to her, telling his bad jokes and giving her that devil-may-care grin.

Why hadn't she told him how she felt about him back at the campsite? They'd had time. Coop was giving her shit about wearing the ill-fitting terrorist dress, about how *becoming* she looked in it. And he'd touched her arm, and looked deep into her eyes. She'd wanted to say something then. But she hadn't, she'd let the moment slide by, like she'd done so many times before. Because she was a stubborn woman, who couldn't ask for help if her life depended on it. Because he was going back to Sydney. And because she didn't want to admit she loved him, even to herself. She'd still been telling herself that things could never work out between them. His life was in Sydney and hers was in Byron.

It was clear she had problems with commitment. She'd known since her very first boyfriend. Their fledgling relationship hadn't made it past the third date. And she'd poisoned every relationship after that in the same fashion. It probably had something to do with her mother's desperate dissatisfaction with her own life.

But after her time spent with Claire the spiritualist, in the safe environment where she could talk about her brother, she'd finally come to terms with the fact she blamed her mother for Kane's death. And come to the realisation that somewhere deep down in her ugly subconscious, she'd made the decision to never let herself be that vulnerable again. If she never had a family of her own, then she'd never be able to let them down. Easy in theory. But things were never black and white in real life. Things changed.

She did actually want a family one day. She wanted to have babies. Watch them grow into good men and women. And she wanted to do it all with David Cooper.

Goddamn the man! Why did he have to do this to her now, when she was finally ready to tell him how she felt?

Well, she wasn't going to let him get away that easy. Because she wasn't going to take the truck back. Searching the streets, she looked for a parking spot and a public phone. Which was going to be harder than it sounded in this Friday afternoon peak hour traffic.

She finally spotted a loading zone and pulled in, not caring if the truck was going to get a parking fine. Pulling the black dress hurriedly over her head, she slammed Coop's discarded hat onto her head, jumped out of the truck and sprinted off down the street.

* * *

Coop let out a sigh of relief. They hadn't moved the explosives. Not yet at least. The two other trucks were still sitting exactly where they'd left them. Coop signed to Bruce he was going around the corner, to see if they'd posted a guard on the trucks. Silently, he prayed they hadn't. They might be able to retrieve one of the hidden guns or phones, or both. Bruce melted around the flank of the building on the opposite side of the alley.

Crouching behind a stack of wooden pallets, Coop peered through the gaps in the wood. Fuck. There was a guard. He hoped Bruce was staying out of sight. Now what? Had they taken the explosives into the warehouse or moved them into the second truck already? The only way to find out for sure was to get in to the building.

There was a window almost directly above his head. But he couldn't take the chance the guard might spot him when he climbed on top of the pallets. What else? He cast his eyes around the enclosed parking lot, checking out any other potential entries into the maze of dark grey buildings.

That's when he saw Bruce, a grim smile on his face, point at a flimsy corrugated iron door leading into what looked to be an abandoned warehouse. The iron was bent up at the corner, leaving a gap large enough for a man to crawl through. The windows were all broken and smashed along that side. Graffiti smothered most of the brick and iron walls. The place looked derelict and forgotten.

Bruce was hidden from the guard's view by an old, rusty forklift right in front of the door. The guard wasn't paying a lot of attention anyway. He chose that particular moment to wander closer to the building on the other side of the carpark, reaching into his top pocket to withdraw a pack of cigarettes. The guard bent his head into his cupped hands to light the cigarette and Bruce squirmed through the hole in the tin.

Bruce was in. That was a good start. Now if only—

A door opened in the building nearest the guard and Tall Guy came out, his sharp eyes scanning the area. Tall Guy laid a hand on the other man's shoulder and spoke to him in low tones. Then, to Coop's surprise they both turned and went back inside. Yep, that'd work.

Waiting for a good thirty seconds, to make sure no one came back out, Coop did a mad sprint across the empty carpark.

He made it to the truck. His luck continued when he found the door to the front cab still unlocked. Coop reached a hand underneath the driver's seat, and hallelujah, the burn phone was still taped securely to the bottom of the seat. With fingers that fumbled in haste, Coop released the phone, turned it on, and slipped it into the back pocket of his jeans. Then he felt along the backrest of the bench seat until he found the small rip in the seat's fabric. Slipping his hand inside he felt around until he located the Glock taped to the metal frame. He tucked it into the waistband in the small of his back.

He needed to check if the explosives were still in either of the trucks. He slipped around the side and pulled the back door open a crack, and they were … Gone. Ghosting over to the second truck he opened the back door and … Goddamnit. They'd been moved. Probably inside somewhere. Which meant Coop needed to get inside and see if he could locate them. And find Bruce to let him know. If those extra two men were actually suicide bombers, then they'd need a small amount of he explosives for themselves. Lucky they hadn't put tracking devices in with the plastic C4 after all.

Nazima thought the explosives were possibly going to be packed into large duffle bags and left at three pre-ordained points around Southbank early on Monday morning. If that was the case, each bag would need a separate person standing nearby to detonate it. Nazima wasn't sure of the timing, but it'd most likely be around lunch time, when the tourist crowd was at its peak. With children teeming in the man-made pools and parents sitting on their blankets on the grass eating their cold chicken and chugging down a beer.

They might set their bombs off in a domino effect, at different, allotted times. If they positioned them correctly they could set one off, wait a few minutes until people in their terror and confusion to get away from the first bomb, ran to the other end of Southbank. Then detonate the second bomb and then a third somewhere further on. It was one way to make sure of maximum casualties. Coop felt physically sick. Nazima hadn't known for sure, but she didn't think this was supposed to be a suicide mission. More likely a carefully orchestrated plan, where the bombers watched the carnage from a safe location, then got the hell out of there. Exulting in how they'd struck such a huge blow to the infidels.

It would be the first ISIS bombing on Australian soil. And it was a devious plan. But the presence of the extra two, possibly suicide bombers, added an intricate level of pure menace to the plan. Suicide bombers were a moving target. They could be anywhere in the crowd, blending in and making it impossible to find them. They were also moving bombs, and could follow the biggest mass of terrified people. Wait until they'd congregated together like flocking sheep away from the first bomb, thinking they were safe, and then blow themselves up right in the middle of all the panicked people. It was such a cold, calculating way to create maximum carnage. Coop's insides turned to ice, his heart freezing in his chest. How could people do this to each other? It was unthinkable, unexplainable and unforgivable.

They needed to find out who the destined suicide bombers were. Identify them, take photos if possible, then follow them. Grab them before they got too far. It'd do them no good to track the crates of explosives if the two suicide bombers still got away.

Checking the coast was still clear, he sprinted back across the carpark and dived through the hole in the tin that Bruce had discovered.

It was dark inside. Coop stopped and crouched down to give his eyes time to adjust. It was an old machinery plant of some kind. Perhaps a cannery? There were long conveyer belts, with piles of empty tins scattered all over the floor. The equipment was rusted and covered in years of grime.

He didn't dare call out to Bruce, so he scanned the huge warehouse, listening for any sounds, rustles or movements. After a few minutes, he was sure no one else was in the warehouse. Bruce must've found a way into the warren of buildings. There was a door in the eastern wall, possibly leading to the adjoining property. To where Coop hoped the terrorists were hiding. Before he moved, he took the phone from his pocket and dialled Martin's number. Tara should've reached the rendezvous spot by now and conveyed their predicament already. But Coop needed to check in. Let them know what he and Bruce were up to.

'It's the Tramp,' Coop gave his code name, dispensing with any pleasantries.

'Go,' said Martin.

'There's been a change of plan,' Coop whispered. 'Lady should be there by now. Has she filled you in yet?' Lady was Tara's codename.

'Negative.'

There was barely restrained exasperation in his boss' voice. Why wasn't Tara there yet? Had she got caught in traffic? Tendrils of worry curled through his belly. Bloody woman. He really, really, really hoped she hadn't done something stupid. Tara was a big girl, she could take care of herself. But the alarm bells ringing in his head wouldn't stop clanging.

Doing his best to ignore the chill seeping through his chest he said, 'Rambo and I have done an about face. The package is going to be moved, and there are more people on this job than we anticipated.' Would Martin get just how fucked up this plan had gotten with those simple words?

'Copy that,' Martin replied coolly.

'Rambo has already gone in,' Coop continued, 'The plan is to assess only. I'll leave my phone on. Get ready to roll, but don't charge the gate yet.'

He left his phone on so they'd have an open line. Martin would get backup ready, but not send them in unless Coop gave the okay.

'Copy that,' Martin said again.

Coop slipped the phone into the front pocket of his pants, facing outwards. Where the hell was Tara?

Five sweaty minutes later, Coop squatted down behind a large piece of machinery. The warehouse was hot and airless. His t-shirt stuck to his back, soaked through with perspiration.

Voices came from below. He'd managed to get up onto a first floor landing that ran the length of the back wall in the second warehouse. He crept up a set of rusty metal stairs, hoping to get a better view of what was going on down below. There'd been no sign of Bruce yet, which was concerning, but not surprising. He *was* supposed to be staying out of sight.

The voices got louder. Coop took a chance and raised himself up so he could peer between the top of the piece of equipment and the bottom of the landing's handrail. The light was dim in here and dust hung heavy in the air. Rays from the setting sun slanted through the odd hole or crack in the metal wall, illuminating the open space below. He could make out the tops of three people's heads. There was Tall Guy and two other men from the group they'd met earlier today. They were looking at something on the floor at their feet.

'We should just kill him,' said one of the underlings in English.

Shit. The hairs on the back of Coop's neck rose up, and he got a sick feeling in the pit of his stomach.

'I knew they were trouble as soon as I saw them,' continued the same man. 'We gotta get rid of him. Now.'

Fuck. Coop levered himself a little higher to see who they were talking about. Please God, don't let it be Bruce. Let it be one of the other radicals, who'd somehow betrayed their trust. A thought niggled at him. Why were they speaking in English instead of Farsi? Perhaps they only used Farsi when they knew someone could overhear them? Most of these guys were born in Australia, after all.

'No.' That was Tall Guy speaking, Coop was sure of it. 'We need to see if he knows anything first.' The voice was assured and calm. Torturing a man for information was an everyday occurrence for him. 'Take him out to the truck. Put him in the back with the explosives. We've gotta move fast.'

Shit, shit, shit. Coop licked his suddenly dry lips. Rising up high enough so he could poke his head over the railing, he looked down at the ground.

Holy Mother of God. It *was* Bruce lying at their feet. Bound and trussed and not moving. Coop's grip on the handrail tightened, until the muscles in his forearms cramped with the strain. He had to do something. He couldn't let these bastards take Bruce. They'd torture him and then kill him for sure. He needed a diversion, something to keep them occupied until Martin's backup arrived. Coop's gaze flickered quickly around the large warehouse. Panic twisted through his gut when his mind came up a blank.

* * *

Tara's breath came in great heaves as she sucked air into her screaming lungs. It'd taken her longer than she hoped to find a public phone. They were few and far between these days, everyone had a mobile, and public pay phones were almost obsolete. But she'd finally found one and in short, sharp sentences, Tara relayed all she knew. In turn she'd found out Coop had already contacted Martin—which meant he'd at least been able to retrieve a phone—and he and Bruce had gone into the warehouse.

Martin had ordered her back to the safety of the rendezvous spot. But she'd told him in no uncertain terms she was a civilian, and he had no authority over her. Then she hung up on him.

She'd managed the eight blocks back to the warehouse at a dead run, grateful her job kept her fit and athletic. But the lactic acid was biting and she bent over, hands on knees to control her breathing.

Now she was here, she wasn't really sure what the next step in her plan was. She needed her gun and a phone. The most perilous part of getting into the carpark was going down the alley. It was framed between the two high walls of the warehouses and there was nowhere to hide. If someone came down that alley while she was going in, she'd be dead meat. All the external doors and windows at the front of the abandoned warehouses were locked up as tight as a gnat's arse. The alley was the only way in. She took off, hugging the left-hand side wall.

She heard voices and stopped just before she rounded the corner into the carpark. As if her heart rate hadn't been high enough, it skyrocketed at the thought the terrorists were about to come charging out of the carpark in their truck. *Don't be silly.* Panicking wasn't going to help her situation. Edging forward slowly, Tara peered around the edge of the wall.

Four of the terrorists they'd met this afternoon were milling around the two trucks on the far edge of the carpark. Three men and one woman. Two of the guys had guns on show, held in the crook of their arms. That wasn't a good sign. It meant they'd been spooked. There'd been no guns out when they'd met with them earlier. Something had changed.

The back of the second truck hung open. Tara could see something inside. But in the deepening twilight, it was hard to make out exactly what it was. Possibly the three crates of explosives? The dimensions were right. There was something else in there too. A lumpy, black shape ….

She needed a better view. And she got her opportunity as one of the other cell members clattered out the door and started yelling something. All four people turned towards him, and Tara had enough time to nip around the corner and hide behind a convenient pile of old wooden pallets.

With all these people hanging around, her plan of retrieving a gun or phone went out the window.

She found a gap between the wooden slats where she could get a good view of what was going on. Finally she could see properly into the back of the truck. Oh no. No. There was a body slumped in the back of the truck.

Was it Coop?

She almost leapt out from her hiding place. Every fibre of her being wanted to charge at them like a screaming banshee.

Her hands shook with the effort of keeping herself hidden. Her teeth dug into the soft flesh of her bottom lip in an endeavour to stop herself crying out.

Coop. Oh, God, Coop. The metal door of the warehouse banged open and Coop stumbled into the carpark. Followed closely by the tall man, the leader, and another slender man with dark ebony skin. Both men pointed their guns directly at Coop's back. His hands were bound and blood was streaked across his face. She stifled a gasp, covering her mouth with her hand.

'Get over to the truck,' the leader snarled. 'Move.' Coop took a few, faltering steps towards the truck, obviously groggy. Had they hit him over the head? There was blood running down his temple.

'Don't do this,' Coop said. His voice was strong, authoritative, despite his grogginess. Trying to bluff the others into believing he still held a modicum of control. 'You'll spend life in prison if you kill a cop.'

They knew he was a cop. This couldn't get any worse.

The ugly tall man, their leader, spat on the ground. 'Do you honestly think we care about that?'

Coop stumbled up to the back of the truck and peered in. Looking at Bruce. What should she do? Instinct screamed she do something. Anything but stay hidden behind these wooden pallets like some frightened field mouse. Anything to get Coop to safety.

How was she going to do that? She had no weapon. They'd only take her hostage as well if she revealed herself. Which wouldn't help Coop at all. And these people didn't treat woman hostages well. Bruce and Tony had drilled that into her as they'd sat around their campsites chatting in the dark.

At last her police training started to take over, logic replacing the screaming, messy part of her mind telling her to rush out there and take on six armed jihadists on her own.

Fuck, where was Martin and his team? They needed to get here now!

Then the leader struck Coop, cracking him across the head with the butt of his gun, sending Coop sprawling to the ground. Tara slammed her hand over her mouth to stop herself crying out.

'Load the *cop* in with his mate. Let's get outta here.' He snarled the word *cop* as if it hurt his mouth to even speak it.

Two men dumped Coop's motionless body into the back of the truck, slammed the doors and hopped in. Forcing herself to cower down behind the pallets, she watched helplessly from her hiding place as they drove both trucks down the alley.

They'd taken Coop. Tara wrapped her arms around her body, suddenly chilled to the marrow. A moan escaped before she could stop it. The sound hurt her throat, but it did bring a tiny amount of clarity back to her stunned, broken mind.

Coop wasn't dead.

She wasn't going to give in to torment. Not yet.

She was going to get him back.

CHAPTER TWELVE

Tara stared out the window, worrying at her bottom lip. Her gaze rested on the dark road lit by the flickering streetlight. All thoughts turned inwards.

They'd taken Coop.

What were they doing to him? A hundred different scenarios played out, over and over again in her mind, each one worse than the last. More gruesome. More bloody. The sad truth was, she knew what these arseholes were capable of. And it chilled her to the bone. Turned her into a babbling incoherent imbecile, with only one rational thought.

She had to get Coop back.

No matter what the cost, no matter how many men it took, no matter if they tipped off a hundred other terrorist cells in their attempt.

'What the hell are we waiting for,' she snarled at Martin. 'We know where he is. Why aren't we going in?'

'We are, Tara. Soon. Very soon,' said Martin, using a pacifying tone that was as irritating as it was unusual. 'If we go in half-cocked we could just as easily get them killed as rescue them. You know that.' Of course she knew that, but at this particular moment she didn't care. Martin went back to talking to one of the men huddled over a myriad of computer screens set up in this makeshift HQ in the middle of Brisbane.

Tara glared at his back, then stomped over, pushed him away from the screen and got right up in his face.

'Fuck it, you know the longer we wait the more chance …' She didn't dare say the words out loud. The longer those monsters had to torture Coop. Cut off one finger at a time, until there were none left to take. Cut off his whole hand. Drive nails in all over his body. Between his toes. Into his eyes. Oh yes, she knew what they were capable of. 'Give me a gun, I'll go in and get him myself.' Did she sound hysterical? Well she didn't give a crap anymore. This interminable waiting was wearing her nerves to dust. She was a woman used to action. They needed to do something. Now.

It was Tony who grabbed her by the arm and stopped her from surging out of the room. 'Sit down, Tara.'

Tony had come straight from the hospital as soon as he heard, his arm in fresh plaster, sticking out from his body at an odd angle. He was as worried about Bruce as she was about Coop.

'No, I'm not going to sit down.' She reefed her arm away from him. Didn't they understand? She couldn't sit down. If she stopped moving it meant she was giving them more precious time to do … whatever it was they were doing to Coop. She needed to keep on the move, to keep doing something. If she stopped, then she was admitting defeat. These horrible emotions that crowded around her, threatening to drown her, would finally overwhelm her. And she'd be lost. Would end up a broken puddle of tears on the floor. Couldn't they understand. Her heart was breaking. Little by little, piece by piece for every second they took organising Coop's rescue?

She knew in her heart what those fucking fanatics were doing to Coop. Kane had shown her in her dreams. But she didn't want to believe it was true. If only he'd shown her exactly where they were keeping Coop. She'd be on her way right now.

It was more than two hours since they'd snatched Coop and Bruce. Martin was sure he knew where they'd taken them, both tracking devices hidden in the men's clothes had remained in the same position for over an hour now. The two men were still within the city limits, in an old office building scheduled for demolition. Martin ordered the internal plans for the building to be pulled up online as well as accessing heat-sensing imagery and infrared on the building. He was doing everything according to the book, making sure no one else from his team was put in any more danger than necessary.

Ordinarily, Tara might've admired Martin for the way he kept his cool, calm demeanour. It was no wonder he was the head of the team. But right now she wanted to throttle the man. Shake him until he showed some kind of emotion.

'I suppose there's no point in me ordering you not to go?' Martin was speaking to her again.

'Just you try and stop me,' she replied.

Martin sighed. 'Yeah, thought so.' He glanced up at her and she noticed how drawn and haggard his square face was in the fluorescent light. Sudden realisation dawned. This situation was taking its toll on him as well, he was just better at hiding it than the rest of them. 'Tony, take her down to the truck and get her outfitted. I assume you do have a licence to use that thing?' Martin nodded to the Glock Tara had retrieved from inside the warehouse. It was Coop's.

'Damn sure I do.' Thank God, she'd kept her paperwork up to date on some slim, misguided chance she might one day go back to the force.

'Great.' Martin ran a hand through his hair and went back to staring at the monitors. 'The Sergeant will brief you on the mission when you get downstairs. Please don't do anything

… stupid. You're only supposed to be riding along, to observe. I'm going to be wearing my arse in a sling for the next six months anyway for involving a civilian. But if you get killed ….' He let her figure out the rest without turning around. 'I'll see you down there shortly.'

'Let's go,' Tony said with a hitch of his chin to indicate she precede him out the door. She could see it in Tony's eyes. He was desperate to go on this mission, too. Desperate to make up for the blunder that stopped him from completing the mission. From being by his partner's side. Despite his arm in a cast, he still wanted to go. She knew he blamed himself for the fact Bruce was being held captive. It was in his flat, level stare and the slump of his shoulders. They had to get Bruce back as well.

'How's Graeme?' she asked as she took the steps downwards two at a time.

'He'll live. He's going in for surgery early tomorrow morning. But I can tell you, he wasn't happy about not being here. He was going to discharge himself, until one of the doctors physically sat on him to keep him in bed.' That sounded like Graeme alright.

The Sergeant lectured the squad while Tara got dressed in dark blue overalls, heavy, standard-issue steel capped boots and a black beanie. She was issued a leg holster for her Glock and body armour to wear underneath the overalls. The whole getup was stifling in the balmy Brisbane night, but this was nothing compared to what the terrorists might be doing to Coop.

The Sergeant directed her to jump into the back of a dark van, heavy on the window tint. She took a seat next to an unknown TRG operative. Martin hopped in just as they were shutting the doors and they were off.

* * *

It was the incessant drip, drip, drip of water that finally woke Coop. His head sagged against his chest. Opening his eyes required too much effort, so he did a mental check of his body instead. Catalogued all his injuries. And there were plenty. There wasn't one inch of muscle, bone or sinew that wasn't screaming in agony. Nothing broken, as far as he could tell. Using his tongue, he gingerly played with his right front incisor. It wobbled, hanging by a thread. The bastards hadn't been gentle.

He was standing against a wall, arms tied up above his head, the rope so tight it cut painfully into his wrists. But the rope was also the only thing holding him up. Without it he probably wouldn't be able to stand on his own. His legs were jelly.

Lifting his head, he had a go at opening his eyes. He could see out of the left one, albeit everything was blurry and distorted. No matter how hard he tried, the right one wouldn't open. It was swollen shut, filled with blood. From when that little guy had kicked him in the head. Repeatedly.

Groggily he wondered where Bruce was. Despite his blurry vision, Coop was pretty sure Bruce wasn't in this room anywhere. Coop hadn't seen him since they'd thrown him out of the back of the truck.

Where the hell was he? Vision still blurry, he looked around. He was in some kind of large enclosed room. A basement perhaps? Black shadows made most of the room impossible to see. But where he was strung up against the wall it was dimly lit by a single weak ray of light from a tiny window up high. The light was from a streetlamp or spotlight on the outside of the building.

The floor was dusty grey cement, the walls whitewashed. There was a row of cement pillars running down the middle of the room, and a couple of large rusty relics of equipment set over in the far corner. What looked to be oversized bike chains were draped from the ceiling, suspended on large hooks. The only pieces of furniture in the room were a corroded steel table with two moth-eaten padded armchairs next to it. As if waiting for two old ladies to come and sit down with their cups of tea and have a conversation with him.

Coop gave a low chuckle. He was going mad, or at least delirious from all those kicks to the head.

There was a large puddle spreading outwards from the left hand wall. A strip of slimy wetness ran down the white paint indicating where the water was leaking in through a small hole high up near the ceiling. At least he knew where that incessant, annoying dripping sound was coming from.

The place reeked of dust and damp, disuse and abandonment. No one had been down here in years, possibly decades. Coop tried to envisage where this building might be in the city. It was no good, he'd only ever been to Brisbane once in his life. He didn't know it nearly well enough to figure out where in hell he was.

Hopefully Martin knew though. Coop was pinning his life on one tiny little tracking device attached to his pants. Which he wasn't wearing, but could see tossed into a pile near the rickety table. At least they'd left his boxer briefs on. Tall Guy ripped his clothes off him as soon as they'd got here, looking for a wire, or hidden weapons. Coop prayed they hadn't found the tracking device. Hiding in plain sight, it was disguised as one of the buttons on the back pocket of his jeans.

Without any high-tech equipment the terrorists looked for bugs the old fashioned way. If they'd had one of those new bug-sweepers, Coop would've been screwed.

They'd taken his phone and the gun.

Actually, he was surprised he was still alive. Thankful, extremely and eternally thankful. But surprised. It meant one of three things. The terrorists thought they could glean information from him. Or they were waiting until after they pulled off the bombing, so nothing interrupted their plan. Or they were going to use him as a hostage, leverage for evading the aftermath. There was a huge difference in the force's mind between two *missing* cops and two *dead* cops. The first would have the police quietly and discretely out looking for them. The second would mean the whole force mobilised, turning the entire city upside down until the killers were brought to justice.

Bruce. Where the hell was he? Did they have him tied up in some other basement nearby? Tall Guy was certainly smart enough to keep his two captives separate. It was basic interrogation one-oh-one. Divide and conquer. Never let them corroborate their story. And certainly never let them have a chance to work together to create an escape.

It was his own fault he was here. He couldn't even blame Bruce. When he'd seen the three terrorists surround Bruce, he'd done something completely stupid and rash and totally against protocol. He'd stood up and declared himself. Yelling that Bruce was one of them and why had they tied up one of their own. He'd tried to continue the façade they were indeed who they said they were, comrades in arms. But the story was weak and he knew as soon as Tall Guy asked him something in Farsi, his game was up. Coop had reached for his gun then, but all it took was for Tall Guy to lower his gun and point it directly at Bruce's head to stop Coop in his tracks. There was a dark red pool of blood spreading outwards from beneath Bruce's body. Which meant they'd probably shot him, Coop couldn't tell exactly where, though. Was he even breathing? When Coop asked to be allowed to look at Bruce, Tall Guy had hit him with the butt end of his rifle and everything went dark and woozy for a while.

God, he hoped they weren't torturing Bruce. So far they hadn't shown any inclination towards that kind of thing. Coop had been soundly beaten, kicked and punched until he could no longer drag air into his burning lungs. Until every inch of his body screamed in protest. He'd be covered in an artist's pallet of multi-hued bruises when he got out of this. *If* he got out of this. But no torture.

He wasn't dumb enough to think he wasn't in real danger here. Even if Martin and his team knew where they were, it'd be a delicate operation to get them out alive. If the terrorists thought they were compromised, they'd kill their hostages.

Coop knew without a doubt, Tara would want to be involved in his rescue. He was still none the wiser as to why she hadn't reported back to HQ. Please let her have followed orders and not have turned that bloody truck around.

Shit, what if the terrorists had her too, and he just didn't know it? His head snapped up painfully. No, he would've seen her. Though they'd knocked him unconscious before they loaded him into the truck. Fuck. He sucked in a deep breath, trying to calm his racing thoughts. Searching his memory, he tried to find any small clue that might point to them having Tara as well. But he came up with nothing. Which was only a little bit comforting.

He remembered the worry etched onto her face when he'd jumped out of the truck. He'd dragged Tara into this in the first place. His goddamned selfish, egotistical need to find out *why* she'd left him back in Sydney had driven him to pursue her. If he hadn't asked her on this mission, she'd still be safe back in Byron. Guilt ripped shreds off his insides.

Tara's beautiful, beguiling face. What he wouldn't give to see her smile again.

The metal hinges on the rusty door creaked as it swung inwards. The light switch flicked on, causing a bank of fluorescent lights running the length of the ceiling to flicker numerous times before they stayed on. Weak, lurid light fell over Coop, and he blinked, owl-like in the sudden brightness. His one eye cleared just in time to see Tall Guy walk in, followed by the little bastard who'd kicked him in the face. Coop made sure he got a good look at the smaller man, committing his face to memory. He was going to make sure this guy paid for what he'd done.

The small man had a long face, made even longer by his military style short-cropped black hair. Even through the dark stubble covering his face, Coop could tell he was young, early twenties. But his dark eyes were dead, flat, holding no emotion. He walked through the door behind Tall Guy and his lip curled in an ugly sneer, showing open contempt for Coop.

The hair on the back of Coop's neck rose up and a sudden liquid hatred poured though his veins. God he wanted to hurt that man. No, he wanted to kill him. Kill them all.

'Ah, you're awake.' Tall Guy's tone was deceptively light. Coop switched his attention to the leader. 'You've caused us much trouble, you and your friend.' Coop didn't answer, but as the man came closer he could clearly smell him. This guy seriously needed to up his game when it came to personal hygiene.

'Yeah, well, you stink,' Coop replied, wincing inwardly at his lame retort. It was the best he could come up with, given the circumstances.

The smaller man put a black backpack onto the dilapidated table. He started to pull things out and place them, one by one, on the table. They looked to be an assortment of tools, the sort you'd find in any backyard shed. There was a pair of pliers, a couple of chisels, a hammer, and a hacksaw. Coop couldn't stop the automatic flutter of fear in his stomach. But he'd be dammed if he showed anything but derision in the face of his captors.

'We need to know what you know,' Tall Guy said.

'Sorry, I'm not in a real talkative mood right now. Why don't you come back later, perhaps bring me a beer and a burger. Then I might wanna talk.' Stall for time. He needed to find a way to buy him and Bruce more time. Martin would be here. Sooner or later. Coop needed to believe that. But Tall Guy just smiled, showing his yellow, twisted teeth.

'I could recommend a great dentist, over on Smith Street.' Coop forced an impudent grin onto his face.

'Shut up, infidel.' The civilised façade on Tall Guy's face disappeared in the blink of an eye.

'Answer my questions, immediately, or I will *make* you answer them.' Tall Guy turned towards Small Guy and pointed at the items on the table.

Coop showed his teeth in a savage grin. 'Do your worst, arsehole.'

* * *

For big guys, weighed down with a mountain of gear, they could move with deceptive speed and grace. Tara followed behind, directing her focus on remaining as stealthy as the rest of the TRG team.

It was now close to midnight and pitch black in the alley outside the abandoned building. Spider webs of light filtered into the mouth of the alley from the main street where the street lamps were still on. But there was no lighting in here. No spotlights or alcove lights above the doorways. Which was the way Martin wanted it. Dressed in their dark coveralls, his team was invisible in the blackness of the night.

The two extremists guarding the outer doors had both been dispatched, quickly and quietly. Both of them were still alive, only one of them needed medical attention. They were currently being taken away in a paddy-wagon for interrogation.

They all had earwigs in, so she could hear Martin's whispered commands as if he was standing on her shoulder. Tara stood with three other TRG guys, slotted in at the end of the line. Waiting for Martin to give the go-ahead to enter the building. There were two teams of four. The other team was led by Martin.

The tracking devices said Coop and Bruce were in here somewhere. And the heat-sensing imagery showed at least eight warm bodies in the building. Eight cops for eight terrorists. That seemed like a pretty even match. Well, seven cops and one civilian. But just for tonight, she again counted herself as part of the force.

This was going to be a complicated mission. They needed to get as far into the building as possible before they were discovered. Which meant being quiet, efficient and deadly. The less time the terrorists were aware they were being raided, the less chance they had to kill Coop and Bruce.

Tara's team would split into two, she and her mate, Daniel, were to go in second, behind the lead pair. Then they'd head off down the corridor to the left, leaving the lead pair to go right. Their objective was a room at the end of the corridor where two persons were hopefully sleeping, according to the heat sensors. The other rooms seemed to be empty, but they'd also need to clear them on the way.

The building was large, covering nearly a quarter of a block, and was four stories high. Luckily the terrorists had confined themselves to one deserted corner on the ground floor.

Once they'd cleared the ground floor then they needed to get down to the basement. The plans Martin had managed to appropriate were old and completely out of date, but they showed the building had a basement. The only problem with this was the X-ray thermal imaging couldn't pierce the extra-thick walls and ceiling of the basement. There might be no one down there. Or there could be many. That was the biggest gamble they were taking tonight. Coop was down there somewhere. It was the only thing that mattered.

Of course Tara hadn't mentioned her dream to Martin, but she'd suggested the possibility that the terrorists were keeping Coop and Bruce in the basement was high. To her surprise, he'd agreed without hesitation.

She should've been nervous, butterflies tumbling in her stomach—she'd often had that giddy, pulsating feeling before a raid. But today her sole focus was on finding Coop alive and bringing him out of there. There was no time for nerves or second-guessing herself today.

The image of Coop from her dream popped into her head. An unwanted spectre.

She heard the whispered command she'd been waiting for. 'Go, go, go.' And she went, the training from years ago driving her forward.

The corridor was in darkness, but the night-vision goggles let her see the details, even if it was a sickly green washed out version of reality. Daniel's broad, stocky form blocked most of her view down the corridor, but she followed his lead. In the dim light he could've been a vague monster from some childhood nightmare. With all the gear he was wearing, his bulky form was reminiscent of some sort of Frankenstein. And when he turned in profile, the night-vision goggles morphed his head into a lumpish, inhuman shape. When Daniel went to the right and silently turned the door handle to the first room, she waited. Then when he indicated the room was clear, she moved past him to the next room on the left and did the same thing.

A rush of adrenaline coursed through her as she opened the door. There wasn't supposed to be anyone in there, but … Nope, it was indeed empty. Just some kind of old storeroom with papers strewn all over the floor and piles of boxes in the corner. Moving onto the next room, she worked on keeping her breathing quiet and even. A hard thing to do when her heart was going a million miles an hour. *Hang on Coop, we're coming.*

She shifted the weight of the Glock with the added silencer in her hands and waited for the next signal from Daniel. They continued down the hallway, opening a total of five doors. Tara found herself sweating with anxiety, as well as from the cumbersome outfit and heavy equipment.

At last they stood outside the final door. Hopefully this would go smoothly, and no one in this room had time to raise the alarm. Daniel slid the door open and they both glided in like wraiths. There were two people asleep on the floor in separate corners. It was so quiet she could hear their peaceful breathing, as they slept on, completely unaware.

In unison they both approached their victim. Taking the Glock in one hand, Tara landed knees first on the person's chest, using her free hand to cover their mouth, and the other to ram the tip of the Glock up against their forehead. Leaving them in no uncertain terms if they moved or screamed they would die. And Tara was quite willing to shoot. Whatever it took to get Coop back alive.

The man opened his eyes wide. Groggy disorientation turned to instant fear, but he didn't speak or move. Over on the other side of the room, there were faint sounds of a struggle and then a popping sound. The other terrorist hadn't been so compliant. He'd paid with his life.

Daniel came over to help her bind and gag her captive.

The first part of their plan had gone without a hitch. Daniel reported in, using low undertones to let Martin know their sit rep. Martin and his partner had to penetrate deeper into the building so they hadn't achieved their goal yet. Martin ordered them to hold position, which irked Tara no end. She was itching to find the stairs that led to the basement.

They waited for minutes on end, standing in the darkened room, listening to the sound of each other breathing.

Suddenly there was the sound of gunshots, followed by muffled shouts, both of which cut off abruptly.

Shit. They'd been discovered. Tara heard Martin's voice in her ear, urgently requesting information as to what'd happened. It must've been one of the other two-man teams who'd encountered a problem.

Tara couldn't wait any longer. She had to act now, with or without permission. Opening the door slowly, she ignored Daniel's gruff voice telling her to hold. She looked back at him and gave one quick shake of her head, then slipped out the door, not caring if he followed. Daniel gave a muffled curse but followed her out. She could hear him talking, low and urgent into his comms, letting Martin know of the change in plan

The corridor was empty and dark. Tara headed for the set of stairs at the other end which would take her downwards, hopefully towards Coop. Just a few steps away from the entrance to the stairs there was movement from further down the dark corridor and she stopped, motioning for Daniel to come forward.

Then all hell broke loose. At the other end of the corridor two terrorists came flying around the corner, intent on getting down those very same stairs.

Daniel shouted for them to stop where they were, they were surrounded by the police. The men never hesitated, they just lifted their weapons as they ran. Tara opened fire. She wasn't taking any chances with these guys. Daniel could try and get them to surrender if he wanted, but all she wanted was to get down those stairs.

The two terrorists both dove for cover into an open doorway, sending a few wild bullets whizzing down the corridor as they went.

'Go,' shouted Daniel, shoving her bodily towards the stair cavity. They both ducked into the opening.

'I'm going down.'

'No, we need to stay together,' he growled at her.

'Sorry. You can hold those two off,' she said, tilting her head back down the hall. 'No one else is coming from the other end,' she continued, pointing back to where they'd just come.

'What if more come in from the same direction,' he asked. He had a point. He might be able to hold off two men with guns, but what if four or five others arrived? It was improbable, Martin and the other teams were dealing with the other terrorists as they spoke. But not impossible. Daniel continued without letting her speak. 'It's not me I'm worried about,' he said. 'You don't know how many men are down there. You could make things worse by barging in.' He was right, but it was a chance she was prepared to take, so she just shrugged her reply. The plans for the building had shown two sets of stairs going down into the basement. If she didn't get down there now, more terrorists could be making their way down the back stairs. Going to kill their hostages.

'What's going on?' Tara heard Martin's voice inside her earpiece. 'Give me a sit rep, Corporal.'

Daniel stared at her for as long as he dared, before returning his gaze back towards the hallway, and answering Martin. 'There are two of them down here, both armed. We've got 'em pinned down. How did they get past Dave and Paul?'

Tara could hear Martin giving the details of how the others had escaped. Dave was injured, but Martin wasn't sure how badly. Martin told them to hang tight. He and his partner were on their way.

As they both listened, Daniel turned back towards her, and mouthed the words, 'Be careful.' He was letting her go. She gave a grim smile and headed downwards, into the dark.

There were only two flights of stairs, with a small landing in between. They were made of concrete and a musty, damp smell emanated the further down she went. What if there was someone waiting to jump her at the bottom? She stopped to listen, but couldn't hear anything over the sporadic gunfire above.

Turning the corner of the landing, she descended the last few steps, quiet as a mouse. At the bottom was a large metal door. She tried the handle. It was closed but not locked. A tiny slither of light was visible underneath the door. She lifted the night-vision goggles onto her forehead. The last thing she needed was to be blinded by too much light and lose precious seconds not able to see.

Resting her fingers on the handle, she forced her breathing to come back to normal, while she put her ear against the cold metal, listening for movement on the other side. It was hard to discern over the shouts and occasional shots coming from above, but there were definitely voices on the other side. She reloaded her gun.

Opening the door a crack, Tara peered inside the dim basement. All she could see was the shadowy far corner, but the voices were louder now.

'It sounds like your buddies are here,' a voice sneered. 'It won't be long now. When they come through that door, I will execute you in front of their eyes, the same way I killed your friend. And then I'll take as many of them with me as I can, before I go to paradise.' Tara's breath caught in her throat.

'Fayaad, they're coming, let me in.' There was a voice, muffled and vague, calling from outside the basement somewhere.

The man, Fayaad, said something in Farsi, and another, smaller, terrorist stepped into view. Tara opened the door a crack wider. Now she could see all the way into the basement. Down the other end, the tall one, the man she remembered as the leader, had turned his back and was striding towards a second door in the opposite corner. The small one hovered beside a table and some chairs. Was hr going to let the other radicals in? How many were behind that door? Whatever happened, she had to try and stop any more men entering the basement.

Then her gaze fell onto a dark shape over by the wall. She couldn't tell for sure, but it could be … a body. A dead body?

No.

The thought was the merest whisper in her head.

It was Coop. Just as she'd seen him in her dream.

She opened the door wide in time to see one more man stumble into the room. They were speaking in low agitated tones, gesturing back up the stairwell behind them. The clatter of booted feet descending sounded loud. More terrorists? Or some of her own? At this particular moment it didn't really matter. She was going in, whether it was against three or four or even five men, it was no longer relevant. Because Coop was in there. Arms tied above his head, he was strung up against the whitewashed wall. Unmoving. Head hanging low on his chest, golden hair falling lank and tattered over his face. Tara's heart stopped beating. And she knew it would never start again.

Unless …

As if by some miraculous, divine intervention, as if he sensed she was there, he lifted his head and stared straight at her. Sky blue eyes locked onto hers, and she drew in a deep breath.

He was alive.

One of the three terrorists spotted her, and started yelling, and shooting.

Tara ducked for cover behind the first of a row of three concrete pillars that ran the length of the basement. Clouds of cement dust flew around her as bullets rammed into the walls, the floor and the pillar shielding her.

Then she fired back, and made sure every bullet counted. The three terrorists were still out in open, either not having the time to find cover, or not caring. They fired wildly with their automatic weapons, screaming something in Farsi, the room filling with deafening sound and heat and noise. But she took aim and fired again and again, making them dodge and jump and flinch. Then she hit one of them. He went down with two bullets to the chest.

There was a commotion in the stairwell. Whoever was coming down those stairs would be in the room in seconds. The commotion distracted both radicals for a split second, but that was all the time she needed to dash forwards to the second pillar, closer now to both the terrorists and to Coop.

Coop yelled something, but she couldn't hear what he was saying in the room alight with the racket of shrieking and shooting.

She saw, rather than heard Fayaad gesture to the other remaining man to go and protect the door, while he kept Tara pinned down with a hail of bullets. But that was all she needed. When the other man turned towards the open doorway, she took him down with a bullet through the neck.

That just left Fayaad.

She came out from behind the pillar and stood, gaze locked with his. His eyes were dark and fathomless, full of heat and hate. He raised his gun and took aim at her, taking his time. But she was quicker, sending off a shot hitting him in the thigh. Fayaad went down onto his knees, but didn't drop all the way to the ground.

Tara cursed at her gun. She was out of bullets. How long to re-load?

Fayaad swung his head in a ponderous arc, first taking in Tara, and then Coop, who was still shouting from where he was tethered to the wall.

'Coop,' she screamed.

Then she saw a light of understanding descend into Fayaad's eyes, and in that split second everything became crystal clear, time slowed to a standstill and she could see everything as if it were being played in some old-fashioned sepia movie. He was going to kill Coop. So she did the only thing possible. She sprinted across the room. Out of the corner of her eye, she saw two TRG officers emerge from the darkened doorway, guns raised. But they were too late. She would protect Coop, no matter what it took. With her life if she had to.

Fayaad turned and fired at Coop.

CHAPTER THIRTEEN

'Let me up,' Coop roared, ripping the oxygen mask from his face. He pushed the paramedic away from him and went to stand up. And found he couldn't. He fell back on the ambulance trolley with a thump. There was no strength left; his body was letting him down. God, no. Please give him the power to keep going for ten more minutes, that's all he was asking. Ten minutes. To find Tara.

No one would tell him where she was.

Every inch of him hurt like hell. He must look an absolute mess. Like some kind of zombie come to life. Covered in scratches, cuts and bruises, eye swollen shut, blood around his mouth and dripping from his nose. But he didn't care.

Confusion reigned in the streets around the old abandoned building. There were police cars, ambulances, uniformed officers, plain clothes police, flashing blue and red lights, sirens blaring, men shouting orders, makeshift spotlights turning night into day. Even a large fire engine and the whole fire brigade was milling around in the street.

But no sign of Tara.

Fumbling at his arm he managed to rip off the tape holding the drip in place and pulled the needle out before the ambulance officer could stop him. Mustering all his energy, he braced his arms on the edge of the bed and forced his legs to take his weight. Finally, he was standing. But all it took was for the paramedic to lay a heavy hand on his shoulder and his backside landed with a thump again on the trolley.

'I can't let you leave, sir. You're in no fit state to be walking around.' The ambo's tone was deep, but also unexpectedly gentle.

'I have to find her. Let me up, or God help me …' He kept his hard gaze locked on the man's face. The paramedic was only doing his job, but his health wasn't important right now. He needed to find Tara. To see her with his own eyes. To make sure she wasn't dead.

She'd thrown herself in front of those bullets. To protect him. He'd seen her get hit. More than once. Her body jerked like a puppet on a string under the impact, but she'd kept coming. She'd grabbed him around the neck, shielding him from the terrorist's bullets, burying her face in his shoulder. But he couldn't grab her back, his arms were still tied above his head.

Things had been chaotic then. Gunshots continued to ring out as TRG officers in dark blue uniforms flooded into the basement. There'd been lots of yelling. Someone had pulled Tara away from him, ignoring his pleas, so they could cut him down. The last he'd seen, Tara was lying on the floor. Then they'd taken him away.

Coop gritted his teeth and made a fist with his right hand. He was seriously considering punching the ambo when Martin's face appeared around the edge of the ambulance door.

'Cooper?'

'Jesus Christ, Martin. Where the hell have you been?' Coop barked. 'You gotta get me out of here. I need to find Tara.'

Martin's normally featureless face took on a serious frown. 'Now just settle down there, mate. Tara's gonna be fine. But you need to stay here.'

'No, I have to see her. Now.' Coop's voice took on an edge of hysteria that surprised even him.

'Believe me, Cooper, Tara will be fine. She's with another ambo team, they're getting her set to go to hospital.'

'But I saw her get shot,' Coop said.

'Yes, and she's going to have some nasty bruises and perhaps a broken rib or two. Nothing that won't heal.'

What was Martin talking about? Tara had taken two bullets to the torso. She wasn't going to be fine. If she even lived she'd need many surgeries and months of rehab, and ....

Martin must've seen the look of horror on his face. 'She was wearing body armour. Do you really think I'd send her in unprotected?'

All of the air left Coop's lungs in a sudden rush of relief. Of course she was wearing a vest. And the vest had saved her life.

'I still need to see her.'

'Alright, I'll see what I can arrange. But don't you bloody well move. You hear me. And by the way, you look like death warmed up.' Coop was okay with that, as long as he could see Tara again. Touch her again.

It was the longest two minutes of his life. The paramedic put the drip back in his arm, grumbling and muttering about *crazy cops*. Then Tara was there, standing beside the ambulance, being supported on one side by Martin.

'Coop.' Her voice was weak and shaky. 'I'm okay.'

Something dark and heavy and tight that'd been sitting right in the middle of his chest released at the sight of her.

She climbed up into the ambulance and the paramedic shuffled up a few paces to give her room. She winced as she sat and her face was pale and drawn. Raising a smile—which was hard work with his mangled teeth—he reached out a hand towards her and she took it, her fingers cool against his. *I love you Tara Hunter*. He so desperately wanted to say those words. Had wanted to say them for so long now. But he wouldn't embarrass her in front of Martin and the ambo. He'd waited this long, he could wait just a little while longer. It was enough just to stare into those beautiful mahogany eyes of hers, and know she was alive.

'But you're not.' Her eyes suddenly filled with tears.

'What?'

'You're not okay. Jesus, Coop, look at you.'

'Oh, baby, believe me, I'm fine. I'm going to be fine. Thanks to you.' Was that all she was worrying about? 'I've had worse than this,' he said, giving a nonchalant shrug. Well that part probably wasn't true, but he was entitled to stretch the truth a little today. Pulling her fingers up to his mouth, he tried to lay a gentle kiss against her knuckles, but it came out more like a warped wet slobber because of his busted lips and broken teeth.

'I can't believe you risked your life for me,' he said.

'I didn't. Not really.'

'Yes, you did.' Then it hit him. He'd done exactly the same thing two years ago. Only she'd reversed the stakes. Did she realise the enormity of her act?

'It's okay, Tara, I won't run away.' Confusion swirled in the brown depths of her gaze. But the confusion slowly morphed into comprehension. Guilt flashed across her face. Then regret. And finally, determination.

'I'm not going to run again either,' she said, her voice suddenly husky. 'I love you, David Cooper.'

Martin cleared his throat uncomfortably from outside the ambulance, but Tara never broke eye contact with Coop.

'And that's a good thing, Tara Hunter. A very good thing. Because I love you too.'

'Okay, time to get these two love-birds to the hospital,' Martin interrupted, nodding his head to the paramedic. 'We can do all this soppy stuff later. Much later.' Martin turned away from the ambulance, but Coop didn't miss the half-smile on his face.

Staring into the depths of her gorgeous brown eyes, he was finally able to lay back and let the ambo do his worst. She said she loved him.

Nothing else mattered.

* * *

These hospital beds definitely weren't made for two people. Despite that fact, Tara was nestled against Coop's shoulder, her long legs stretched out, her feet off the end as she lay next to him, trying her best not to touch his poor, battered body.

Coop sat propped up on pillows, his chin resting on top of her head. It was the wee hours of the night, and a hushed blanket of calm hovered over the dim hospital corridors. Only the quiet ticking of the clock above the door and the muffled beeping of medical monitors from a room next door broke the silence.

After spending all day and most of the evening being prodded and poked by doctors and given the third degree by Martin, Tara had finally been left to sleep. But of course she couldn't. So she'd snuck down the hallway and crept into Coop's private room. She needed to feel his comforting warmth surround her.

'Nurse Debbie is gonna tell you off if she comes in and finds you here,' said Coop, humour lightening his voice.

'I can handle nurse Debbie.'

'Aint that the truth. Even though nurse Debbie can be just as scary as any terrorist I've ever come across.'

She tried to contain her smile. 'Don't make me laugh. It hurts.' She had three fractured ribs, where the bullets had shattered against the Kevlar vest. But the vest had done its job and she was still alive.

'You sure did kick some arse today, girl,' he said quietly. 'I don't think I'll ever get tired of replaying the image of you busting through that door when you did.'

'Hmm.' She didn't really want to talk about her role right now. She'd already talked and talked and talked, till she was almost hoarse, to every nurse, cop, lawyer and even the Chief of Police. All who wanted to debrief her. She just wanted to enjoy the luxury of feeling Coop's chest hairs flutter beneath her fingers, hear his heartbeat, strong and unfailing, beneath her ear. Small indulgences she'd thought she may never get again.

'Poor Bruce,' she said, voicing the thought that'd been haunting her all day. 'His poor wife.' Tears, which'd been close to the surface all day, threatened again. Martin had confirmed her worst fears once they'd reached the hospital.

'Yeah, I know.' His voice broke slightly, and she tightened her grip on his hand. Shame would be weighing heavy on him tonight. In fact it might never completely leave him. She'd seen it before. Cops who'd lost partners, or friends in the force. Some of them never recovered from the sadness and guilt. But she'd be there to help Coop get over this one. This time she wasn't going anywhere. Like she'd already told him, this time she was going to stay. If he'd have her.

'That could easily have been you.' The ache in her chest was so fierce she could scarcely breathe.

'Yeah, I know.'

'I know I shouldn't say this, but I'm so glad it wasn't.' It was awful to say the words out loud, but he deserved to know how she felt. Bruce's death would be a terrible pall that'd hang over them, probably for the rest of their lives. But if it'd been Coop lying on that cold concrete floor....

She wouldn't have been able to survive that.

'I think he was already dead by the time they unloaded us at that second building,' said Coop, his voice quiet and faraway. 'Or soon afterwards.' Bruce had died from blood loss due to a neck wound.

'At least they didn't torture him.' That was the only small —very small—glimmer of light in this otherwise dark and terrible deed. Coop just shrugged by way of an answer.

'Tony told me the funeral's going to be on Friday, down in Sydney. I don't care what the doctors say, I want to go.' Tara recognised that belligerent tone. He'd walk out of here, against doctor's orders, if that's what it took. They'd told him he might need to spend at least the next week in hospital. They were monitoring him for internal bleeding, and bruised kidneys. And he'd need more dental surgery. Then there were the three deep cuts on the left-hand side of his chest, where they'd attacked him with some kind of blunt, garden variety chisel. Tortured him. Tara raised her head in a silent salute to whoever was watching over Coop that day, allowing her and the TRG to arrive in the nick of time. God only knew what else that bastard might've had in store for Coop if they hadn't.

'I'll take you down to Sydney,' she replied. 'We both owe him that much.'

'Thanks.'

Earlier in the day, Martin had filled them in on exactly what'd unfolded during and after the rescue. His face was forbidding and haggard, lined with the sorrow everyone was feeling at Bruce's loss. Tony had been there as well, his face even more ashen and grief-stricken than Martin's. It'd been a harrowing day for Tony. He'd been the one to break the news to Bruce's family and Tara's heart went out to him. He was leaving as soon as Martin finished the debrief, to go back and stand by Bruce's widow's side, help her through the next few days. Graeme was also been wheeled in, still in his hospital bed, and still on pain meds from his surgery early this morning, to hear what needed to be said.

Just as Martin started to speak, Vlad sauntered into the room. Tara had never been gladder to see him in all her life. She stood up from her chair in the corner and let him take her into one of his big bear hugs, first warning him to be careful of her ribs.

'We got them all,' Martin said, standing next to Coop's bedside. 'And we found the vests they were going to use, too. Thank Christ they hadn't armed them yet.'

There were murmurs of appreciation and grim relief.

'I don't want to think about what might've happened if even one of those bombs had gone off in their designated target area. We saved tens, perhaps hundreds of lives today.'

Martin went on to tell them how the raid had gone down. They'd taken four of the eight terrorists alive. Fayaad, the leader was shot dead when the TRG stormed the basement. After Tara shot him in the leg. Now came the long and arduous task of finding out what the remaining four terrorists knew. Months of following tenuous leads, tracking down other individuals or groups associated with this cell. Trying to stop this happening again. It was a never-ending job. When one cell was neutralised, another always rose to take their place.

Before he'd left, Martin told Coop there'd be a lot more questions to come. About his and Bruce's decision to go back into the terrorist compound. Tara guessed there'd probably be an inquest. But she knew without a doubt Coop would be cleared of any wrongdoing. Especially in the part he played in Bruce's death.

After Martin's debrief, Tara grabbed Vlad by the arm and led him back to her private room. She wanted to make sure he was okay with this whole ugly mess. It was great to see his face again, so familiar, reminding her so much of home. Home suddenly took on a brand new meaning. Now she knew Byron was where she wanted to be. It was such a relief to finally know where she belonged.

'Wow, when you told me you used to work as an undercover cop, I never in my wildest dreams imagined you'd be such a badass,' Vlad said as soon as she'd closed the door. She made her slow way over to the chair in the corner and sat down gingerly. These broken ribs and the bruises covering her back and side would take a couple of weeks to heal. She was going to need some time off work. She was damn lucky she didn't have any internal bleeding, or hadn't ruptured her spleen. Or so the doctors told her.

'I didn't do anything you wouldn't have done in the same circumstances,' she replied. 'How's Brad? And Sarah?'

'Brad's great, although very unhappy with how this all panned out. I think the NSW police force is going to be hearing from our boss.' Vlad gave his trademark Nordic grin, making Tara want to give him another hug. But there was no way she was getting out of the chair again. So she gave him an affectionate smile instead. 'Sarah, well ... she's kinda mad at me right now.' He looked a little crestfallen. 'She doesn't like that I won't tell her where we've been or what we've been up to.'

'A valid reaction,' Tara said. 'She'll come round, Vlad, don't worry.'

'Yeah, you're probably right. We might be moving in together.' He said the words as if it pained him to say them aloud.

'That's great, Vlad. That's really great.' His gaze lifted at her happy words. 'You guys are so cute together, you're really good for each other.' A wide grin grew at the corners of his mouth. But just as quickly the lines between his eyes creased up into a small frown.

'I know it's early days and everything, but are you coming back to work sometime?' Vlad suddenly found the linoleum floor highly interesting.

'Of course I am. I'd miss working with you way too much.' She was rewarded by another of his toothy smiles. He came over and knelt beside her chair, resting his long-fingered hand on her knee.

'I'm glad to hear that. I thought after all this,' he gestured into the air, 'you might want to go back to being a cop.'

'Not on your life.'

Vlad left then, promising to come back and visit her tomorrow, and this time he was going to bring Brad and Sarah.

Tara adjusted her leg slightly to find a more comfortable position in the squashed bed. Coop's breathing had become deep and regular. He'd fallen asleep. The doctors put him on some pretty strong painkillers, so she wasn't surprised. Tara let her eyes close as well. All she wanted right now was to stay here, by Coop's side. Forever. Nurse Debbie be damned.

CHAPTER FOURTEEN

Tara stood in the outdoor shower, letting the warm water run down her body, between her shoulder blades and cascade over her breasts. As she soaped her skin, she listened to the Catbird sound its strange, strangled meowing call. Such a familiar sound to her now, and she welcomed the bird's call, eyes searching through the foliage until she spotted it. There, high up on a branch in the ficus tree, its olive speckled body blended well with the greenery of the leaves. Pity Coop wasn't here to see it. He was still freaked out by the Catbird's bizarre sound; said it reminded him of a baby crying.

Today had been one of the best morning's surfing they'd had so far. Coop was getting much better, his balance improving every day. And being a boy, he was more likely to try out the challenging moves, cut backs and swivels. Choosing the bigger waves, he hared down the face with arms outstretched, whooping and yelling. God he was funny. God she loved him.

In a change from their normal routine, however, Coop had refused to come home and have a shower with her. He had some errand or other to run in town. Instead they'd agreed to meet at the lighthouse for a picnic lunch in a few hours' time. Coop was going to bring them some sandwiches from the local bakery.

In a rare occurrence, they both had the day off in the middle of the week. No tourists were booked in for an Alive and Kicking experience today. Vlad said he would go in and clean up the warehouse, but there was no need for her to go in as well. Coop only worked four days a week, and he'd rearranged his days with his boss, so they could spend this day together.

Tara was glad to have this bit of time to herself. She'd been meaning to pop in and see Claire for a while. Her visits to Claire had become less frequent now Kane no longer haunted her dreams. But she still liked to drop in for a chat every now and then.

She'd seen Kane only once since they'd captured the terrorists. It'd been on the second night after the shooting. Coop was still recovering in hospital. They'd discharged Tara, as there was nothing much they could do to help her broken ribs heal. Time and lots of it was the remedy. But she couldn't force herself to leave the hospital, not while Coop still lay there in pain. She kept a vigil by his bedside. Despite her valiant efforts, fatigue got the best of her and she'd fallen asleep in the chair. And that's when Kane snuck back into her dreams.

At first she hadn't known he was there, her mind was lost in dark corridors with doors leading off into shadowy rooms, the threat of being found by vague, distant men made her whimper in her sleep. But then the dark foreboding dream lifted, lightened. Thoughts of love and laughter came instead. And those thoughts tightened something within her—a shivery anticipation. He was coming, and so she reached out her hands to welcome him.

There he was, slouching along beside her down the corridor, black beanie drawn down over his head, that green jumper almost swallowing him up. They were in their old family home, back in LA.

'I love you, Tara,' he said.

'I love you too, bro.'

'You're all good now, huh?'

'Yeah, everything's good now. Thanks for your—' When she turned to look at him again, he was standing with his arm around their mother, Francisca.

'I love her too,' he said and tilted his head in Francisca's direction. Waves of different emotions washed over Tara as she stared at her younger brother with her mother. Francisca never looked Tara's way. She just gazed at Kane. Her love for her son glowed in her face. The sight shocked Tara to the core. Kane was trying to tell her he didn't blame his mum for what happened to him. But all Tara could feel towards her mother was ... Anger? Yes, there was still anger, but was that also regret? Watching the truth of how much love showed in her mother's eyes. Perhaps it'd been harder for her mother to leave than she first thought.

Tara woke with a start from the dream, sucking in a loud gasp of air. But instead of a loss, she was left with a residual peace. She still hoped Kane would come back to her. But so far he'd stayed away.

Claire confirmed Kane had achieved his goal of protecting her and now he'd gone on to other things. As usual, Tara took whatever Claire said with a grain of salt. She still loved to go and sit with the spiritual woman in her warm sheltering home and talk about life. And love. Coop was a little perplexed at their friendship, not really understanding what Tara got from it. But still happy for her to spend her time with the woman.

After that dream, Tara found her antagonism towards her mother soften. So much so, she'd actually picked up the phone and called her a couple of weeks ago. Their conversation was stilted and short. But it was a beginning; one Tara may even explore further. Soon. But not today.

Tara wandered through the lounge room, wrapped in a towel and went up to the photo of Kane, still in its place on her bookshelf. Trailing a finger over the photo she smiled at him and stood in the quiet for many minutes with her brother. It was the subtle splashing sound as drops of water slid from her legs onto the wooden floor that finally brought her back to reality.

She strode into the middle of her bedroom, wondering what to wear today. As her eyes roamed over the room she noticed all of the small changes having a man in the house had made. Gone was the pile of books she'd always kept on the spare bedside table. Now it was covered with all of Coop's paraphernalia. A broken watch he'd been meaning to get fixed for months, a pair of reading glasses—it still freaked her out he wore glasses, it made him look so civilised. A pile of surfing magazines and a digital radio alarm clock. Small changes in the overall scheme of things, but massive in the scheme of her life. And now his clothes took up half her closet as well. They might need to invest in a bigger one, to stop it bursting at the seams. She walked up and ran her hand over a row of his shirts hanging next to her dresses, breathing in the scent that was Coop.

It was still hard to fathom Coop had moved in nearly a year ago, straight from leaving the Brisbane hospital. Actually, now she thought about it, the anniversary of Bruce's death was coming up in two weeks' time. Back then, it'd seemed the obvious choice. Coop needed someone to look after him. He couldn't go home alone, so she'd told him he was moving in with her.

A hot flash of guilt spiked through her at the thought of Coop when she'd first brought him home. Not because of the state he'd been in a year ago, but because it made her sorely aware of how much he must've struggled on his own two years before that, when he'd been shot. And she'd left him. It still twisted her heart whenever she remembered. Part of her asking him to come to stay with her had been a form of atonement. But if Coop thought her only reason for looking after him was to redress her previous sins he would've flatly refused to come. They both understood it was much more than that. A bond, a connection had formed between them. One that couldn't be broken.

So he stayed.

Along with his ugly dog, Monty. There was no way Coop would leave his beloved dog behind, so she'd been more than happy to welcome him in. The first day they'd brought Monty home he'd settled in so quickly it'd surprised even Coop. The dog gave the back yard a perfunctory sniff, lifted his leg in at least four places, then trotted inside, leapt up onto the couch and lay down. He gave a little snort, lowered his snout onto his paws and emitted a contented sigh. From that moment on the couch became his favourite spot.

Tara liked having Coop living with her. At first she'd been the one running around caring for him, while his poor battered body healed. But very quickly their partnership became fifty-fifty. She'd rub bio-oil on his scars and bring him his favourite donuts from the bakery in town. He'd make her a cup of tea in bed every morning, no matter how early her start was. For the first time in her life, she had someone to really share things with. Someone she could rely on. When she came back from an extra stressful day, filled with cantankerous tourists, he'd sit behind her on the couch and rub her shoulders until the stress dissipated.

Coop quit his job at the NSW police force without a moment's hesitation. He'd told her it'd been one the of the easiest decisions of his life. The day after Bruce's funeral, he'd gone in to see Martin, to hand in his resignation. Martin tried to argue with him, telling him he needed time to think about it. That it was a knee-jerk reaction from Bruce's death.

Residual guilt about Bruce getting killed. And Coop had agreed with Martin. Part of why he was resigning was for those reasons. But there was more to it than that. Tara being the biggest one.

At first Tara was adamant Coop not give up his career in the police force just to be with her. There was no way in hell she wanted to be responsible for someone giving up their dream job. But Coop laughed at her, that hearty chuckle he kept for those special times when Tara was making an absolute fool of herself.

'I'm not doing this for you, girl. I'm doing this for me. It's time for a change. I'm tired of this never-ending merry go-round of chasing bad guys. Let someone else do it from now on. Besides, I have other plans I want to explore.'

I'd been a month or so later she found out what he meant, when he came home with a six pack of beer and a smile as wide as a Cheshire cat on his face.

'Would you believe it,' he said, popping the top off a stubbie of beer and handing it to her, then helping himself to one. 'I've managed to con someone into giving me a job.' Tara had been equal parts surprised and delighted. She clinked her bottle with his in congratulations and they'd gone out onto the veranda to watch the sunset.

'I'm going to be working in the family shelter in town. As the lawyer's assistant. It doesn't pay much, but I'm happy with that. I'm going to go back and try and finish my law degree, part-time.' She remembered Coop telling her how much he'd loved working with Alex Carmondy, the lawyer at the homeless shelter back in Sydney. Alex was the one who'd prompted Coop to get his lawyers assistant certificate and then tried to convince him to go that one step further to become a fully-fledged lawyer. Coop had chosen a different route, and become a cop instead. He wanted to help the underprivileged, those without a voice of their own. Now he was going back to finish what he'd started. Going back to find another way to help the people who mattered to him. Perhaps this was even a better way.

Tara shook her head, chasing away the reminiscences. If she didn't get her butt moving soon she wouldn't have time to see Claire before she had to meet up with Coop.

What to wear? Running her fingers over the clothes hanging in her closet, she stopped at a pretty pink dress, made of floaty material that fell in soft waves down from a halter neck line. Nah, it was too dressy for an informal little picnic with just the two of them. But her fingers wouldn't leave the fabric, and she knew she was going to put it on. Coop would love it, and what was the harm in looking nice for the man she loved.

* * *

Coop embraced the Byron Bay fashion with a vengeance. He loved the loose flowing linen shirts and easy-wear flip-flops and board shorts. But today was a little different, so he'd swapped his surf gear for a white button-up shirt and some cream cargo shorts.

Wending his way up the last few metres of the trail, he emerged from the relative cool of the jungle path into the bright, open air at the top of the headland. The basket was heavier than it looked, and the fifteen-minute walk up the trail brought him out in a sweat. Monty broke from the jungle path and charged ahead of him, frolicking on the expanse of green grass. Coop couldn't stop the smile forming on his face at the dog's antics. Monty stopped to glance back, making sure Coop was still coming. His tongue lolled out the side of his mouth, bottom teeth protruding, one ear flopped down over his head while the other one stood up. Yep, his dog was still as ugly as ever. But he loved the mutt even more for all his physical deformities.

The fresh sea breeze touched him with its salty tendrils, cooling him after his walk up the hill. You could drive up to the lighthouse, but parking was often non-existent, and Coop liked to take the meandering walking track up instead, providing spectacular views out over the ocean. Today, he even spotted a pod of dolphins frolicking a few hundred metres out.

The stark white of the Byron Bay lighthouse rose up above him. His gaze travelled up the height of the walls to rest on the black nest at the top. As lighthouses went, this was a fairly squat version, but it didn't need to be tall. The headland was more than tall enough to do the job. There was hardly anyone here today, the open knoll was empty, except for a group of four tourists clustered at the base of the lighthouse, reading the information plaque telling them this was the eastern most point in Australia. The area surrounding the lighthouse was all bitumen, but there was a small grassy hillside, sliding away from the front of the lighthouse, where you could sit and gaze out at the panorama.

Even better, Tara wasn't here yet, which gave him time to set up. He chose a spot in the shade of the large lighthouse, and plonked the heavy wicker basket on the lush grass. Monty came up to give the basket a quick sniff, then galloped off following the trail of something. Coop cast his gaze out over the vista of the open ocean. There was a sprightly breeze tickling the low swell, but it'd pick up by mid-afternoon, becoming a brisk north-east wind. Which would be great for the surf. Perhaps he might be able to convince Tara to go down for a sunset surf afterwards. The bright mid-day sun hit the ocean, sending up diamonds of sparkling dancing light-spots. A perfect day.

It was surprising how easily he'd picked up reading the weather patterns here. Knowing when the southerlies were going to bring in booming swells with waves too huge to surf, or when the fresh westerly was going to make the small, happy waves that the children loved to paddle in. Watching the ocean change her moods with the ups and downs in weather had become one of his personal fascinations.

Something—he wasn't sure what—made him turn away from the vista of the ocean, towards the dark mouth where the path emerged from the trees.

And there was Tara, standing at the edge of the sunlight, her face alight with a smile. She was so beautiful. Tall and elegant, wearing a fresh, frothy pink concoction that made her legs look impossibly long and tanned. His heart flipped over in his chest so quickly it was almost painful; a physical manifestation of his love for her. He was in love with her. Deeply, inescapably, utterly. It'd been that way from the very first time he'd set eyes on her, over five years ago.

When he'd thought he'd lost her, when she'd bolted from Sydney, the pain had been so raw and unmanageable, he thought his heart would never be whole again. But all that pain, anguish, railing at the world and how unfair it all was, he'd go through it again in a heartbeat if he knew Tara would be waiting for him on the other side.

Monty loped up to Tara, romped a couple of happy circles around her until she bent down and gave him a pat, smoothing down his ears and speaking softly to him. Then he was off again, tail up, nose down, headed towards the top of the hill and another intriguing smell.

'Wow, you've gone overboard today.' She shot a look of interest at the overflowing basket of food. 'Which is good, because I'm starving.' She wrapped her slim arms around his neck, taking his mouth in a delicious, long kiss. He loved that her height allowed him access to her lips without having to crane his neck downwards. Pulling her in close, he deepened the kiss, luxuriating in the feel of her lithe body tight up against his. Her legs resting against his thighs, her breasts pressed against his chest.

'That's good you're hungry.' He broke their kiss with a reluctant grimace, but kept her hand tucked into his. 'So am I.' He led her over to where the basket sat on the grass. 'I even brought something to sit on.' He pulled a red and black chequered blanket out of the basket with a flourish.

'Oh, right.' He could see the tiny lines between her eyes forming. Which meant she was suspicious already. Shit, of course she would be. They hardly ever sat on a blanket. The grass was usually good enough. Quick, he better get on with it, before she started asking questions.

'Yeah, I went all out today.' He gave her one of his wolfish grins, hoping to distract her. 'Look, I've got oysters, your favourite.'

'Mmm.' She snagged one from the plate before he even had time to uncover it completely. 'Yummy, and so fresh too. I love them when they're all salty and tangy, straight from the ocean.'

'I've got all of your favourites,' he replied, continuing to spread out more food. 'Mangoes and fresh figs. They're in season you know. Chilli, lots and lots of chilli in that Thai noodle thing you like, from the Thai place over in Bay Lane.' He took a white cardboard box out of the basket. 'And your favourite chocolates too.' Opening the box, he revealed dark, rich organic chocolate. It was made right here in Byron, and he'd never tasted anything better in his life.

He was rambling, but he couldn't stop as he continued to pile the food on the blanket.

'I even got us one of those organic red wines.'

'Wow. That's … a lot of food.' Her eyes widened as she took it all in. 'Thank you,' she said through a mouth full of chopped mango pieces. 'This is so sweet. Where did you … Hey, wait a minute. These foods are all ….' She fixed him with a stare, half sceptical and half playful. 'Are you trying to get me to have sex with you, David Cooper. Because these foods are all aphrodisiacs.' She picked up a chocolate and waved it in his face, before taking a large, seductive bite. 'You know you don't have to resort to this, you can just ask. I'm more than happy to oblige.'

'Oh, I know that, babe.' The sex was still wild and wonderful and rewarding. Actually, he couldn't wait to try out all these foods, to see if there *was* any truth to the myths behind them.

'So what's going on then, Coop?' She'd stopped eating now and focussed her full attention on him. All of a sudden there were butterflies in his stomach. Goddamnit, he shouldn't be nervous about this. He loved her, with all his being. And she loved him back. He just needed to say it.

'There's something I'd like to ask you, Tara.' Now he had her full attention, and it wasn't just because he'd used her first name. He hadn't rehearsed this, because he didn't want it to sound artificial. But now he almost wished he had.

'You know my track record with fathers in general isn't the best.' She was smart enough to understand he was referring to the fact he'd watched his father physically abuse his mother for years, until he'd killed him in self-defence. Concern filled her eyes.

'Of course I do—' she started to say, but he put a finger to her lips.

'Just let me get this out first, hey?' Taking both of her hands in his, he stared into her beautiful brown eyes. And was rewarded by seeing the unconditional love shining there. It gave him added courage to continue.

'I know that doesn't recommend me well for fatherhood and all it entails.'

She sat very still, letting him talk.

'For so long, I thought I never wanted to have kids of my own. There was no way I was going to bring a child into this warped, broken world, full of gun-toting drug lords and greedy arseholes who'd stop at nothing to get what they wanted. Certainly not when one of those dysfunctional miscreants was me.' He smiled at her, but she didn't smile back. 'Being constantly bombarded by the seedy underside of society, I didn't hold much hope for the human race. The risk of things going wrong if I had a child was just too high. The risk of me turning out like my father was too great.' At these words he could see Tara balk, and it looked like she was about to say something. 'But you've changed all that, Tara. You've changed me, and shown me this world is not such a bad place after all.' She smiled, one of her gorgeous, wide mouth full of white teeth smiles that lit up his heart.

Coop drew in a deep breath. 'What I'm trying to say, in my round about way, is I want to have kids with you, Tara.'

'Okay.' The frown was still deeply etched into her lovely forehead. 'So you're *not* asking me to marry you then?' There was real confusion on her face now and he had to hold back a laugh.

'God no. You'd hate that.' It was true, she was too much of a free spirit. The two times Coop had broached the subject—the second time only recently, when they'd been at Vlad and Sarah's wedding—he'd commented on how happy they looked and she'd given him a dark look and said, 'Please do me one favour in this life, Coop. Don't ever ask me to marry you. Because my answer will disappoint. And if you don't then we may have a chance to be happy for a long, long time.' And he was okay with that. As long as he could have Tara in his life, he would take her just the way she was. With all his heart and soul and passion.

'But I do want to grow old with you, Tara. Spend the rest of eternity with you. Forever. And I want us to have a whole crowd of tiny ninja assassins to keep us busy. With your courage and strength, integrity and honesty and my dashing good looks, we just can't fail.'

She opened her mouth, but no words came out, she just stared at him with those wide, brown eyes.

Nervous that she might actually turn him down, even though he'd thought he knew her better than that, he said, 'So what do you say, Tara Hunter, will you have kids with me? We could start right now if you like.' He waved a hand at the enormous pile of food in front of them. Still she didn't speak. Shit. Had he blown it all after all?

* * *

Tara was lost for words. A feeling, intense and earthy, starting right at the pit of her stomach, rose up through her body, turning the air in her lungs to fizzing bubbles of rapture.

Of course she'd imagined having children with Coop. She'd been hesitant to bring up the subject though, as she thought he'd struggle with the concept. And she'd been right about him thinking of himself as damaged goods when it came to the fatherhood department. And of course she had her own mother as the worst example of what not to do when you had children. But David Cooper had managed to surprise her again, with his easy acceptance of what life had thrown at him. Perhaps it was time she did the same thing. Perhaps it was time to accept that she wasn't her mother.

Byron Bay was the perfect place to bring up children.

Monty took that particular moment to come up and shove his wet nose against the back of her bare arm. She laughed at his intrusion. Then, as if he knew something momentous was going on, he sat on the grass next to them, looking up with expectant brown eyes.

'I was thinking we'd go for two to start with. Kids, that is.' Coop ignored his dog and searched her eyes for an answer.

'But we could definitely have four or five, a whole tribe if you want.'

'Yes, David, I will have children with you.'

'Really?' The pure joy in his face made her eyes start to prickle. Please let her not cry like some teenage schoolgirl full of hormones.

'Yes.' An enormous lightness filled her chest, as if her lungs had taken in too much air and were about to explode. Happy. She was deliriously happy. This man made her happy. He leaned across and took her mouth in his. And they kissed and kissed and kissed, his lips funnelling all the joy and goodness and desire into her heart.

Finally, Coop broke their kiss and started to fumble in the pocket of his pants for something, never breaking eye contact with her as he did so. She sat on the rug in the shade of the lighthouse, drinking him in. His scruffy, blond surfer hair hung down in his eyes. And those eyes, reflecting the brilliant blue of the ocean. She'd never get tired of looking at that wonderful face, so expressive, so familiar.

'I've got something for you,' he said and brought out a small black velvet box. 'This is not an engagement ring, or a friendship ring, or an ownership ring, or anything like that,' he qualified quickly. 'So you don't have to wear it if you don't want to.' He opened the box and held it out to her, suddenly shy. Which was odd for Coop. 'It's a family ring,' he concluded.

She took the small box and held it up to her face so she could look closely at the ring nestled inside. It was a plain gold band, wide and smooth. In the top of the band a large ruby was imbedded, the rich russet colour of a fine red wine, set next to an equally large diamond. Both of the gems sent shards of light sparking off in the sunlight. Next to the ruby, two smaller pink stones ran down the side of the ring.

Running a finger lightly over the stones, she asked, 'What are the pink ones?'

'They're pink diamonds,' he replied. 'The ruby is for you, with all your fire and heart and determination. The diamond is me, of course, and it needs no explanation. And the pink ones are our kids. A combination of both of us.'

This time the tears came and she couldn't stop them. 'Oh God, Coop.'

'Hey, babe.' He gathered her into his arms. 'Those are happy tears, right?'

'Yes. Yes, of course they are,' she replied, unable to stop the stream of tears falling now. This was so unlike her, she never cried. Well at least she hadn't before Coop came into her life. But now everything seemed to have more weight to it, more gravitas. Sunset hues were more gaudy. Surfing the big waves with him around was more exhilarating. And when he took her hand as they strolled down the street, it felt as if he was surrounding her heart with his fingers.

'Summer, the girl from that little jewellery shop in the main street helped me design it. I put two stones in there because I thought it was a good start, but we can always add more to the ring when we have more kids, or at least that's what Summer told—'

'I love you so much.'

'I love you too. Forever, together,' he said, his heart in his eyes.

She smiled and tried to wipe away the tears. 'Put it on for me.' She held out the box to him. He slipped the ring over her finger and it fitted perfectly, sitting warm and snug against her skin.

'Vlad's gonna notice I have this on the moment I walk in to work tomorrow,' she said with a grin. 'He keeps asking me when we're going to get married. He definitely won't understand this.' She laughed. 'This is strange, even by Byron Bay standards.'

Ever since Vlad and Sarah had been married, in a beautiful civil service up in the hinterland of Byron Bay, Vlad had been dropping small hints to her, saying things like, 'Married life is good for your heart,' and 'It's so nice to know I've found my soul mate, I feel like a different person now,' until Tara had become really good at ignoring him.

'Well, you'll just have to tell him straight, that we're not the marrying kind,' Coop said, pulling her up with him as he stood. Slipping her shoes off, she stood on the grass barefoot, snuggling in under his shoulder. They stared out over the ocean, watching the seagulls call and wheel overhead. Totally complete and so fulfilled, so utterly in love. Right now her heart was soaring up there with those birds, high and free. And it was because of this man. Now she understood, when you found the right person, nothing was impossible. He'd unbound her from the fears that held her back. Their life together was going to be full of laughter and joy. And kids. With a solid, tangible love that would bind them forever.

'Kiss me,' she said.

And he did.

Connect with the Author

I really hope you enjoyed reading Chasing Bullets. For more action romance info, upcoming release dates, and access to free books join the exclusive Suzanne Cass reader club. As an added bonus, you'll get a copy of my FREE STORY.

Solar Flare

http://www.suzannecass.com/contact/

Or you can stay in touch via my website
www.suzannecass.com

Or

Also by Suzanne Cass
NEW

Stormcloud Station Series
(A Stargazer Spinoff Series)
Small Town Romantic Suspense

Clear Skies
Starlit Skies
Crystal Skies

Stargazer Ranch Romance Series
Small Town Romantic Suspense
Combustion: Prequel Novella
Wildfire
Firelight
Snowbound: A Christmas Novella
Snowfall
Cloudburst

Island Bound Series
Mystery Romance (on an Island)
Books can be read as stand-alone
Bound by Truth
Bound by Silence
Bound by the Stars

Colors of the Earth Series
Small Town Romantic Suspense
Books can be read as stand-alone
Shadows in the Dust
Shadows in Deep Blue
Shadows of Red Earth

Romantic Suspense
Single Title
Island Redemption

Glass Clouds
Chasing Bullets

Love in the Mountains Novella Series
Small Town Short Romance
Novellas can be read as stand-alone
Rain on a Tin Roof
Lost and Found
Rescue his Heart

Please Leave a Review

The greatest gift you could ever give an author is to leave a review. You will be helping other people to discover this book and making a difference to me as an Independently Published Author. If you liked this book and want other people to read it too, please leave a review.

About the Author

Suzanne Cass is an Australian author who writes rural romance and romantic suspense abounding with passion and danger.

Her debut novel, Island Redemption, won the Romance Writers of Australia Emerald Award in 2016. Suzanne was also a finalist in the 2019 Romance Writers of Australia RUBY award.

She had always had a fascination with the tough resilience of people who live in our amazing red-dirt outback country. When not writing about the characters that inhabit her head, Suzanne can be found roaming the Perth beaches with her border collie, or encouraging from the sidelines as her two sons play sport.

Stay in touch via my website

www.suzannecass.com

Acknowledgements

The journey towards writing and publishing is never achieved alone, and the path towards my second novel, as always, took a village to help me along the way.

To my husband, Gary, for spending so many lonely nights on the couch while I huddled over my computer, writing. You have supported me through all this and believed in me when so many others doubted.

Thanks to all my wonderful friends and family who read my first drafts of this novel and helped shape it into the book it is today. And to my many author friends who've imparted their invaluable knowledge to guide me when I got stuck, thank you so much, you are all so gorgeous and generous.

Byron Bay itself is such a beautiful Australian setting, I see it almost as another character in the book. I love visiting Byron and the laid back, easy lifestyle keeps me going back time and time again, as do the sublime beaches and lush tropical hinterland

To Rachel, thanks again for all your patience in pointing out the many mistakes in my early drafts and your unfailing belief in me.

And to my readers, thank you for coming along on this journey with me. You are my reason for writing.